The Land of Laughs ◯

Books by Jonathan Carroll

The Land of Laughs

Jonathan Carroll

ORB

A Tom Doherty Associates Book
New York

THE LAND OF LAUGHS

First published in Great Britain by Hamlyn Paperbacks, 1982.

An Orb Edition
Published by Tom Doherty Associates, LLC
175 Fifth Avenue
New York, NY 10010

www.tor.com

Design by Heidi M. G. Eriksen

Library of Congress Cataloging-in-Publication Data

Carroll, Jonathan.
    The land of laughs / Jonathan Carroll.—1st Orb ed.
        p. cm.
"A Tom Doherty Associates book."
ISBN 0-312-87311-5 (alk. paper)
    1. Children's stories—Authorship—Fiction. 2. Biography as a literary form—Fiction. 3. Biographers—Fiction. 4. Missouri—Fiction. I. Title.

PS3553.A7646 L3 2001
813'.54—dc21   00-047839

First Orb Edition: February 2001

Printed in the United States of America

0   9   8   7   6   5   4   3   2   1

For June, who is the best of all New Faces,
and for Beverly—The Queen of All

Be regular and orderly in your life like a
bourgeois, so that you may be violent and
original in your work.

—Flaubert

Part One

1

"Look, Thomas, I know you've probably been asked this question a million times before, but what was it really like to be Stephen Abbey's—"

"—Son?" Ah, the eternal question. I recently told my mother that my name isn't Thomas Abbey, but rather Stephen Abbey's Son. This time I sighed and pushed what was left of my cheesecake around the plate. "It's very hard to say. I just remember him as being very friendly, very loving. Maybe he was just stoned all the time."

Her eyes lit up at that. I could almost hear the sharp little wheels clickety-clicking in her head. So he *was* an addict! And it came straight from his kid's mouth. She tried to cover her delight by being understanding and giving me a way out if I wanted it.

"I guess, like everyone else, I've always read a lot about him. But you never know if those articles are true or not, you know?"

I didn't feel like talking about it anymore. "Most of the stories about him are probably pretty true. The ones I've heard about or read are." Luckily the waitress was passing, so I was able to make a big thing out of getting the bill, looking it over, paying it— anything to stop the conversation.

When we got outside, December was still there and the cold air smelled chemical, like a refinery or a tenth-grade chemistry class deep into the secrets of stink. She slipped her arm through mine. I looked at her and smiled. She was pretty—short red hair, green eyes that were always wide with a kind of happy astonishment, a nice body. So I couldn't help smiling then too, and for the first time that night I was glad she was there with me.

The walk from the restaurant to the school was just a little under two miles, but she insisted on our hiking it both ways. Over would build up our appetites, back would work off what we'd eaten. When I asked her if she chopped her own wood, she didn't even crack a smile. My sense of humor has often been lost on people.

By the time we got back to the school we were pretty chummy. She hadn't asked any more questions about my old man and had spent most of the time telling me a funny story about her gay uncle in Florida.

We got back to Founder's Hall, a masterpiece of neo-Nazi architecture, and I saw that I had stopped us on the school crest laid into the floor. Her arm tightened in mine when she noticed this, and I thought I might as well ask then as anytime.

"Would you like to see my masks?"

She giggled a giggle that sounded like water draining from a sink. Then she shook her finger at me in a no-no-naughty-boy! way.

"You don't mean your etchings, do you?"

I had hoped that she might be half-human, but this dirty little Betty Boop routine popped that balloon. Why couldn't a woman be marvelous for once? Not winky, not liberated, not vacuous . . .

"No, really, you see, I have this mask collection, and—"

She squeezed me again and cut off the circulation in my upper arm.

"I'm just kidding, Thomas. I'd love to see it."

Like all tight-fisted New England prep schools, the apartments that they gave their teachers, especially single teachers, were awful. Mine had a tiny hallway, a study that was painted yellow once but forgot, a bedroom, and a kitchen so old and fragile that I never once thought of cooking there because I had to pay all of the repair costs.

But I had sprung for a gallon of some top-of-the-line house paint so that at least the wall that the collection was on would have a little dignity.

The only outside door to the place opened onto the hallway,

so coming in with her was okay. I was nervous, but I was dying to see how she'd react. She was cuddling and cooing the whole time, but then we went around the corner into my bed-living room.

"Oh, my *God!* Wha . . . ? Where did you get . . . ?" Her voice trailed off into little puffs of smoke as she went up to take a closer look. "Where did you get, uh, him?"

"In Austria. Isn't it a great one?" Rudy the Farmer was brown and tan and beautifully carved in an almost offhand way that added to his rough, piggy-fat, drunken face. He gleamed too, because I had been experimenting that morning with a new kind of linseed oil that hadn't dried yet.

"But it's . . . it's almost real. He's shining!"

At that point my hopes went up up up. Was she awed? If so, I'd forgive her. Not many people had been awed by the masks. They got many points from me when they were.

I didn't mind when she reached out to touch some of them as she moved on. I even liked her choice of which ones to touch. The Water Buffalo, Pierrot, the *Krampus*.

"I started buying them when I was in college. When my father died, he left me some money, so I took a trip to Europe." I went over to the Marquesa and touched her pink-peach chin softly. "This one, the Marquesa, I saw in a little side-street store in Madrid. She was the first one I bought."

My Marquesa with her tortoiseshell combs, her too-white and too-big teeth that had been smiling at me for almost eight years. The Marquesa.

"And what's that one?"

"That's a death mask of John Keats."

"A death mask?"

"Yes. Sometimes when famous people die, they'll make a mold of their faces before they bury them. Then they cast copies . . ." I stopped talking when she looked at me as if I were Charles Manson.

"But they're just so *creepy!* How can you sleep in here with them? Don't they scare you?"

"No more than you do, my dear."

That was that. Five minutes later she was gone and I was putting some of the linseed oil on another mask.

2

My father used to say whenever he finished making a movie that he'd never do it again as long as he lived. But like most of the other things he said, it was bullshit, because after a few weeks of rest and a fat deal cooked up for him by his agent, he'd go back under the lights for a forty-third triumphant return.

After four years of teaching I was saying the same thing. I had had my fill of grading papers, faculty meetings, and coaching ninth-grade intramural basketball. There was enough money from my inheritance to do what I wanted, but to be honest, I had no real idea of what to do instead. Correction: I had a very specific idea, but it was a pipe dream. I wasn't a writer, I didn't know the first thing about doing research, and I hadn't even read all the things that he'd written—not that there were that many of them.

My dream was to write a biography of Marshall France, the very mysterious, very wonderful author of the greatest children's books in the world. Books like *The Land of Laughs* and *The Pool of Stars* that had helped me to keep my sanity on and off throughout my thirty years.

That was the one wonderful thing that my father did for me. On my ninth birthday—momentous day!—he gave me a little red car with a real engine in it that I instantly hated, a baseball that was signed "From Your Daddy's Number One Fan, Mickey Mantle," and as an afterthought I'm sure, the Shaver-Lambert edition of *The Land of Laughs* with the Van Walt illustrations. I still have it.

I sat in the car because I knew that was what my father wanted me to do and read the book from cover to cover for the first time. When I refused to put it down after a year, my mother threatened to call Dr. Kintner, my hundred-dollar-a-minute analyst, and tell him that I wasn't "cooperating." As always in those days, I ignored her and turned the page.

"The Land of Laughs was lit by eyes that saw the lights that no one's seen."

I expected everyone in the world to know that line. I sang it constantly to myself in that low intimate voice that children use to talk-sing to themselves when they're alone and happy.

Since I never had any need for pink bunnies or stuffed doggies to ward off night spooks or kid gobblers, my mother finally allowed me to carry the book around with me. I think she was hurt because I never asked her to read it to me. But by then I was so selfish about *The Land of Laughs* that I didn't even want to share it with someone else's voice.

I secretly wrote France a letter, the only fan letter I've ever written, and was ecstatic when he wrote back.

> Dear Thomas,
> The eyes that light The Land of Laughs
> See you and wink their thanks.
> > Your friend,
> > Marshall France

I had the letter framed when I was in prep school and still looked at it when I needed a shot of peace of mind. The handwriting was a kind of spidery italic with the Y's and the G's dropping far below the line, and many of the letters of the words weren't connected. The envelope was postmarked Galen, Missouri, which is where France lived for most of his life.

I knew little things like that about him. I couldn't resist some amateur sleuthing. He died of a heart attack at forty-four, was married, and had a daughter named Anna. He hated publicity, and after the success of his book *The Green Dog's Sorrow*, he pretty much disappeared from the face of the earth. A magazine did an article on him that had a picture of his house in Galen. It was one of those great old Victorian monsters that had been plopped down on an average little street in the middle of Middle America. Whenever I saw houses like that, I remembered my father's movie where the guy came home from the war, only to be killed by cancer at the end. Since most of the action seemed to take place in the living room and on the front porch, my father called the movie *Cancer*

House. It made a fortune and he was nominated for another Oscar.

In February, the month when suicide always looks good to me, I taught a class in Poe that helped me to decide at least to apply for a leave of absence for the following fall before something dangerous happened to my brain. A normal lunkhead named Davis Bell was supposed to give a report to the class on "The Fall of the House of Usher." He got up in front of us and said this. I quote. " 'The Fall of the House of Usher,' by Edgar Allan Poe, who was an alcoholic and married his younger cousin." *I* had told them all that several days before in hopes of stimulating their curiosity. To continue. ". . . married his younger cousin. This house, or I mean this story, is about this house of ushers . . ."

"Who fall?" I prompted him, at the risk of giving the plot away to his classmates, who hadn't read the story either.

"Yeah, who fall."

Time to leave.

Grantham gave me the news that my application had been approved. As always, smelling of coffee and farts, he hung his arm across my shoulder, and pushing me toward the door, asked what I was going to do with my "little vacation."

"I was thinking of writing a book." I didn't look at him because I was afraid his expression would be the same I'd have if someone like me had just said that he was going to write a book.

"That's great, Tom! A biography of your dad, maybe?" He put a finger to his lips and looked dramatically from side to side as if the walls were listening. "Don't worry about me. I won't tell a soul, I promise. Those things are very *in* these days, you know. What it was really like on the inside, and all that. Don't forget, though, that I'll want an autographed copy when it comes out."

It was really time to leave.

The rest of the winter trimester passed quickly, and Easter break came almost too soon. Over the holiday I was tempted to back out of the whole thing several times, because leaping into the unknown with a project I didn't even know how to begin, much less complete, was not at all inspiring. But they'd hired my replacement,

I'd bought a new little station wagon for the trip out to Galen, and the students certainly weren't pulling on my coattails to stay. So I thought that no matter what happened, getting away from the likes of Davis Bell and Farts Grantham would do me good.

Then some strange things happened.

I was browsing through a rare-book store one afternoon when I saw on the sales desk the Alexa edition of France's *Peach Shadows* with the original Van Walt illustrations. The book had been out of print for years for some reason, and I hadn't read it.

I staggered over to the desk and, after wiping my hands on my pants, picked it up reverently. I noticed a troll who looked as if he had been dipped in talcum powder watching me from the corner of the store.

"Isn't that a superb copy? Someone walked right in out of the blue and plunked it down on the desk." He had a Southern accent and reminded me of some character who lives with his dead mama in a rotting mansion and sleeps under a mosquito net.

"It's great. How much is it?"

"Oh, well, you see, it's already sold. It's a rare one. Do you know why it's not around anymore? Because Marshall France didn't like it and refused to let them reprint after a certain time. Now, he was a strangey, that Mr. France."

"Could you tell me who bought it?"

"No, I've never seen her before, but you're in luck, because she said she'd be in to pick it up"—he looked at his wristwatch, which I noticed was a gold Cartier—"around now, eleven or so, she said."

She. I had to have that book, and she was going to sell it to me, no matter what the cost. I asked him if I could look at it until she came, and he said that he didn't see why not.

As with everything Marshall France had written, I fell into the book and left the world for a while. The words! "The plates hated the silver, who in turn hated the glasses. They sang cruel songs at each other. Ping. Clank. Tink. This kind of meanness three times a day." The way all of the characters were so completely new, but once you'd met them you wondered how you'd ever gotten along without them in your life. Like the last pieces in a jigsaw puzzle that go right in the middle.

I finished and quickly went back to passages that I'd particularly liked. There were a lot of them, so when I heard the bell over the front door ring and someone come in, I tried to ignore whoever it was. If it was she, it could end up that she wouldn't sell it and I wouldn't have another chance to see the book again, so I wanted to eat as much of it as I could before the big showdown.

For a couple of years I collected fountain pens. Once when I was at a flea market in France I was walking around and saw a man in front of me pick up a pen from a seller's table and look at it. I saw immediately from the white six-pointed star on its cap that it was a Montblanc. An old Montblanc. I stopped in my tracks and started a chant inside of me: PUT IT DOWN, DON'T BUY IT! But it did no good—the guy kept looking more and more intently at it. Then I wanted him to die right there on the spot so that I could pull it out of his lax hand and buy it myself. His back was still to me, but my loathing was so intense that it must have pierced him somehow, because all of a sudden he put the pen down, looked fearfully over his shoulder at me, and scurried away.

The first thing that I saw when I looked up from the France book was a nice denim-skirted fanny. It had to be her. PUT IT DOWN, DON'T BUY IT! I tried to cut my look straight through the denim and skin underneath all the way to her soul, wherever it was. GO AWAY, LADY! I WHAMMY YOU TO GO AWAY AND LEAVE THIS BOOK HERE HERE HERE!

"The gentleman over there is looking at it. I didn't think that you'd mind."

I suddenly had this wild romantic hope that she would be lovely and smiling. Lovely and smiling because she had the world's best taste in books. But she was neither. The smile was only partly there—a little confusion and beginning anger mixed together—and her face was pretty/plain. A clean, healthy face that was raised on a farm or out in the country someplace, but never in the sun that much. Straight brown hair but for a small upward flip when it reached her shoulders, as if it were afraid to touch them. A sprinkle of light, light freckles, straight nose, wide-set eyes. More plain than pretty the more you looked at her, but the word "healthy" kept going through my mind.

"I wish you hadn't."

I didn't know which one of us she was talking to. But then she marched over and pulled it out of my hand like my mother catching me with a dirty magazine. She brushed the light-green cover twice, and only then did she look directly at me. She had thin, rust-colored eyebrows that curved up at the ends, so that even when she was frowning she didn't look too mad.

The dealer came dancing up and whisked my beloved out of her hands with a "May I?" and moved back behind the desk, where he started wrapping it in beige tissue paper. "I've been right here on this corner for twelve years, and sometimes I've had quite a few Frances, but usually it's a drought with him, just an absolute desert drought. Certainly *Land of Laughs* in the first edition is easy enough to find, because he was so popular by then, but *The Green Dog's Sorrow* in a first or any edition is as hard to find as the Hydra's teeth. Say, listen, I think I have a *Land of* in the back of the store if either of you'd be interested." He looked at us, eyes atwinkle, but I already had a first that I'd paid a fortune for in New York, and my opponent was digging around for something in her handbag, so he shrugged off the No Sale and went back to wrapping. "That'll be thirty-five dollars, Ms. Gardner."

Thirty-five! I would have paid . . . "Uh, Ms. Gardner? Uh, would you be willing to sell the book to me for a hundred? I mean, I can pay you right now for it, cash."

The guy was standing behind her when he heard my price, and I saw his lips move up and down like two snakes in pain.

"A hundred dollars? You'd pay a hundred dollars for this?"

It was the only France book that I didn't have, much less in the first edition, but somehow the tone of her voice made me feel dirty-rich. But only for a moment, only for a moment. When it came to Marshall France, I'd be dirty all day, so long as I could have the book. "Yes. Will you sell it?"

"I'm really not one to interfere, Ms. Gardner, but one hundred dollars is quite an extraordinary price even for this France."

If she was tempted and if the book meant as much to her as it did to me, then she was feeling pain. I almost felt sorry for her in a way. Finally she looked at me as if I'd done something nasty to her. I knew she was going to say yes to my offer and disappoint herself.

"There's a color Xerox machine in town. I want to have it copied first, then I'll . . . then I'll sell it to you. You can come over and pick it up tomorrow night. I live at 189 Broadway, the second floor. Come at . . . I don't know . . . Come at eight."

She paid for it and left without saying anything more to either of us. When she was gone, the man read the little slip that had been in the book and told me that her name was Saxony Gardner and that besides Marshall France books she'd told him to keep an eye out for any old books on puppets.

She lived in a section of town where you rolled your windows up in the car as soon as you drove into it. Her apartment was in a house that must have once been pretty snazzy—lots of gingerbread and a big comfortable porch that wrapped around the whole front of the place. But now all that it looked out on was the singed skeleton of a Corvair that had been stripped of everything but the rearview mirror. An old black guy wearing a hooded gray sweatshirt was sitting in a rocking chair on the porch, and because it was dark, it took me a moment to see that he had a black cat on his lap.

"Howdy doody, partner."

"Hi. Does Saxony Gardner live here?"

Instead of answering my question, he brought the cat up to his face and crooned, "Cat-cat-cat" to it, or at it, or something. I don't like animals too much.

"Uh, I'm sorry, but could you *tell* me if—"

"Yes. Here I am." The screen door swung open and there she was. She walked over to the old man and touched him on the top of his head with her thumb. "It's time for bed, Uncle Leonard."

He smiled and handed her the cat. She watched him go and

then vaguely motioned me to his chair with a wave of her hand.

"Everyone calls him Uncle. He's a nice man. He and his wife live on the first floor, and I have the second." She had something under her arm, which after a while she took out and shoved at me. "Here's the book. I never would have sold it to you if I didn't need the money. You probably don't care about that, but I just wanted to tell you. I sort of hate you and am grateful to you at the same time." She began to smile, but then she stopped and ran her hand through her hair. It was a funny trait that was hard to get used to at first—she rarely did more than one thing at a time. If she smiled at you, then her hands were still. If she wanted to brush the hair away from her face, she stopped smiling until she'd brushed.

After I had the book I noticed that it had been neatly rewrapped in a piece of paper that must have been a copy of some old hand-written sheet music. It was a nice touch, but all I wanted to do was tear it off and begin reading the book again. I knew that'd be rude, but I was thinking about how I'd do it when I got home. Grind some beans in the Moulinex, make a fresh pot of coffee, then settle in the big chair by the window with the good reading light . . .

"I know it's none of my business, but why on earth would you pay a hundred dollars for that book?"

How do you explain an obsession? "Why would you pay thirty-five? From everything you've said so far, you can't afford *that*."

She pushed off the post she'd been leaning on and stuck her chin out, tough-guy style. "How do you know what I can afford and what I can't? I don't have to sell it to you, you know. I haven't taken your money yet or anything."

I got up from Leonard's tired chair and dug into my pocket for the fresh hundred-dollar bill I always carry hidden in a secret com-partment of my wallet. I didn't need her, and vice versa, and be-sides, it was getting cold and I wanted to be out of that neighborhood before the jungle war drums and tribal dancing began on the hood of the Corvair. "I've, uh, really got to go. So here's the money, and I'm very sorry if I was rude to you."

"You were. Would you like a cup of tea?"

I kept flashing the snappy new bill at her, but she wouldn't take it. I shrugged again and said okay to the tea, and she led me into the House of Usher.

A three-watt brown-yellow bug light burned in the hall outside what I took to be Uncle Leonard's door. I had expected the place to smell like low tide, but it didn't. In fact it smelled sweet and exotic; I was sure it was some kind of incense. There was a staircase just past the light. It turned out to be so steep that I thought it might lead to the base camp on El Capitan, but I finally made it up in time to see her going through a door, saying something over her shoulder that I didn't catch.

What she probably said was watch your head, because the first thing I did when I walked through her door was wrap myself in a thousand-stringed spiderweb, which gave me a minor heart attack. It turned out to be puppet strings, or I should say one of the puppets' strings, because they were hanging all around the room in elaborately different macabre poses that reminded me of any number of dreams I'd had.

"Just please don't call them puppets. They're all marionettes. What kind of tea would you like, apple or chamomile?"

The nice smell came from her apartment, and it was incense. I saw several sticks burning in a little earthenware bowl full of fine white sand on her coffee table. There were also a couple of strange, brightly colored rocks on it and what I assumed to be the head of one of the marionettes. I had it in my hand and was checking it out when she came back into the room with the tea and a loaf of banana bread she'd baked.

"Do you know anything about them? That one's a copy of the evil spirit Natt from the Burmese Marionette Theater."

"Is that what you do for a living?" I swept the room with my hand and almost dropped Natt on the banana bread.

"Yes, or I did until I got sick. Do you take honey or sugar in your tea?" She didn't say "sick" like I was supposed to ask what kind of sick, or was she feeling better now?

After I drank what had to be the foulest cup of hot liquid I've ever consumed—apple or chamomile?—she took me on a guided tour of the room. She talked about Ivo Puhonny and Tony Sarg, Wajang figures and Bunraku, as if we were all best friends. But I liked the excitement in her voice and the incredible similarity between some of the puppet faces and my masks.

When we were sitting down again and I liked her about a hundred times more than at first, she said she had something to show me that I'd like. She went into another room and came back with a framed photograph. I had seen only one picture of France before, so I didn't recognize this one until I saw his signature in the lower-left-hand corner.

"Holy Christ! Where'd you get this?"

She took it back and looked at it carefully. When she spoke again her voice was slow and quiet. "When I was little I was playing with some kids near a pile of burning leaves. Somehow I tripped and fell into it, and the burns on my legs were so bad that I had to be in the hospital for a year. My mother brought me his books and I read them until the covers came off. Marshall France books, and books on puppets and marionettes."

I wondered then for the first time if France really appealed only to weirdos like us: puppet-obsessed little girls in hospitals and analyzed-since-five boys whose fathers' shadows were stronger than the kids'.

"But where did you get this? I've seen only one picture of him, and that was when he was young, the one without his beard."

"You mean the one in *Time* magazine?" She looked at hers again. "You know when I asked you why you'd be willing to spend so much money for *Peach Shadows*? Well, do you know how much I spent for this thing? Fifty dollars. I'm one to talk, huh?"

She looked at me and swallowed so hard that I heard the *grumph* in her throat. "Do you love his books as much as I do? I mean . . . having to give this to you actually makes me almost sick to my stomach. I've been searching for a copy for years." She touched her forehead and then ran her fingertips down the side of her pale face. "Maybe you should take it now and just go."

I shot up off the couch and put the money on the table. Before I left, I wrote my name and address on a slip of paper. I handed it to her and jokingly said that she could come and visit the book whenever she wanted. Fateful decision.

3

About a week later I stayed up one night to get some reading done. For once it was nice to be in my mouse-hole apartment because one of those winter storms was blowing outside that go back and forth between mean, hard rain and wet snow. But I've always liked the changes in Connecticut weather after having lived in California, where every day is the sunny same.

Around ten o'clock the doorbell rang and I got up, thinking some clown had probably torn a sink off the wall in the boys' bathroom or thrown his roommate out the window. Living in the dormitory of a boarding school is maybe the third or fourth circle of hell. I opened the door with a halfhearted snarl ready on my lips.

She was wearing a black poncho that hooded her head and then went all the way down to her knees. She reminded me of an Inquisition priest, except that her robe was rubber.

"I came to visit. Do you mind? I brought some things to show you."

"Great, great, come on in. I was wondering why *Peach Shadows* was so excited today."

She was in the midst of pulling the hood off her head when I said that. She stopped and smiled up at me. It was the first time I realized how short she was. Against the black, rain-shiny poncho, her face glowed wet white. A kind of strange pink-white, but nice and sort of babylike at the same time. I hung up the dripping coat and pointed her toward the living room. At the last moment I remembered her puppets and that she hadn't seen my masks yet. I thought about the last woman who'd come to see them.

Saxony took a couple of steps into the room and stopped. I was behind her, so I didn't get to see the first expression on her face.

I wish I had. After several seconds she moved toward them. I stood in the doorway wondering what she would say, wondering which ones she'd want to touch or take down off the wall.

None of them. She spent a long time looking, and at one point reached out to touch the red Mexican devil with the great blue snake winding down his nose and into his mouth, but her hand stopped halfway and fell to her side.

Still with her back to me, she said, "I know who you are."

I leveled one of my best smirks at her lower back. "You know who I am? You mean you know who my father is. It's no big secret. Turn on the television any night to *The Late Show*."

She turned around and slid her hands into the little patch pockets of the same blue denim dress she'd worn in the bookstore that day. "Your father? No, I mean you. I know who you are. I called the school the other day and asked about you. I told them I was from a newspaper and was doing a story about your family. Then I went to an old *Who's Who* and some other books and looked up things about you and your family." She two-fingered a little square of paper out of her pocket and unfolded it. "You're thirty and you had a brother, Max, and a sister, Nicolle, who were both older than you. They were killed in the same plane crash with your father. Your mother lives in Litchfield, Connecticut."

I was stunned both by the facts and by her chutzpah in so calmly admitting what she'd been doing.

"The school secretary said that you went to Franklin and Marshall College and graduated in 1971. You've taught here for four years, and one of the kids in your American literature class that I talked to said that you're 'all right' quote-unquote as a teacher." She folded the paper up again and slid it back into her pocket.

"So what's with the investigation? Am I under suspicion?"

She kept her hand in her pocket. "I like to know about people."

"Yeah? And?"

"And nothing. When you were willing to pay all that money for a book on Marshall France, I wanted to know more about you, that's all."

"I'm not used to people getting up dossiers on me, you know."

"Why are you quitting your job?"

"I'm not quitting. It's called a leave of absence, J. Edgar. What's it to you, anyway?"

"Look at what I brought to show you." She reached behind her and pulled something out from beneath her gray pullover sweater. Her voice was very excited as she handed it to me. "I knew it existed but I never thought I'd be lucky enough to find a copy. I think only a thousand of them were printed. I found it at the Gotham in New York. I had been hunting for it all over for years."

It was a small, very thin book printed on beautifully thick, rough-textured paper. From the illustration on the cover (a Van Walt, as always), I knew that it was something by France, but I had no idea what. It was titled *The Night Races into Anna,* and what first surprised me was that unlike all of his other books, the only illustration was the one on the cover. A simple black-and-white pen-and-ink of a little girl in farmer's overalls walking toward a railroad station at sunset.

"I've never even heard of this. What . . . when was it done?"

"You didn't? Really? You've never . . . ?" She gently pulled it out of my greedy hands and brushed her fingers across the cover, as if reading braille. "It was the novel he was working on when he died. Isn't that incredible? A novel by Marshall France! He even supposedly finished it, but his daughter, Anna, won't release it. This"—her voice was angry, and she stabbed her finger accusingly at it—"is the only part anyone's ever seen. It's not a children's book. You almost can't believe that he wrote it, because it's so different from his other things. It's so eerie and sad."

I slid it back out of her hand and opened it gently.

"It's only the first chapter, you see, but even so, it's really long—almost forty pages."

"Do you, uh, do you mind if I sort of look at it alone for a minute?"

She smiled nicely and nodded. When I looked up again, she was coming into the room with a tray loaded down with cups, my brass tea kettle puffing steam, and all of the English muffins I'd planned to eat the next two mornings for breakfast.

She put the tray on the floor. "Do you mind about these? I haven't eaten anything all day, and I'm starved. I saw them in there. . . ."

I closed the book and sat back in my chair. I watched her devour my muffins. I couldn't help smiling. Then without knowing how or why, I blurted out my plan about the France biography.

I knew that if I talked to anyone before I began this book it should be her, but when I finished I was embarrassed by all of my enthusiasm. I got up and walked to the mask wall and pretended to straighten the Marquesa.

She didn't say anything and she didn't say anything, and finally I turned from the wall and looked at her. But her eyes slid away from mine, and for the first time since we met, she spoke without looking at me. "Could I help you? I could do your research for you. I did it for one of my professors in college, but this would be so much better, because it'd be looking into *his* life. *Marshall France's.* I'd do it really cheaply. Really. Minimum wage—what is it now, two dollars an hour?"

Uh-oh. A very nice girl, as my mother used to say when she introduced me to another of her "finds," but I didn't need or want anybody helping me on this, even if she knew a lot more about France than I did. If I was really going to go through with it, then I didn't want to have to worry about someone else, especially a woman who struck me as potentially bossy or selfish or, worst of all, moody. Yes, she had her good points, but it was just the wrong place at the wrong time. Sooo, I hmmm'd and haaa'd and nibbled around the edges, and it wasn't long before she got the point, thank God.

"You're basically saying no."

"I . . . basically . . . You're right."

She looked at the floor and crossed her arms over her chest. "I see."

She stayed there for a minute, then turned on her heel, and picking up the France book, made for the front door.

"Hey, look, you don't have to go." I had this terrible picture in my mind of her slipping that book back up under her sweater.

The thought of that woolen bulge broke my heart.

Her arms were spread high to let the still-wet poncho slide down onto them. For a moment she looked like a rubber Bela Lugosi. In fact, she kept her arms up like that when she spoke.

"I think you're making a really big mistake if you're serious about doing this book. I truly think that I could help you."

"I know what . . . uh, I . . ."

"I mean, I could really *help* you. I don't see at all . . . Oh, forget it." She opened the door and closed it very quietly behind her.

A couple of days later I came back to my place after a class and found a note stuck to the door. The writing was in thick Magic Marker, and I didn't recognize it at all.

I'M GOING TO DO THIS ANYWAY. IT HAS NOTHING TO DO WITH YOU. CALL ME WHEN YOU GET IN—I'VE FOUND SOME GOOD STUFF. SAXONY GARDNER.

All I needed was for one of my goody students to read that note and instantly interpret "stuff" as "dope" and start to spread the word about old Mr. Abbey's behind-the-closed-door follies. I didn't even know Saxony's telephone number and I wasn't about to look it up. But she called me that night and sounded angry the whole time we talked.

"I know you don't want me in on this, Thomas, but you should have called anyway. I was in the library a long time getting all of this for you."

"Really? Well, I really appreciate that. I mean, I do!"

"Then you'd better get a pencil and paper for this, because there's quite a lot."

"Go ahead. I have one here." Whatever her reasons for doing it, I had no intention of turning off Radio Free Information.

"Okay. First of all, his name wasn't really France—it was Frank. He was born Martin Emil Frank in Rattenberg, Austria, in 1922. Rattenberg is a little town about forty miles from Innsbruck, in the mountains. His father's name was David, his mother's name was Hannah, with an H."

"Wait a minute. Go ahead."

"He had an older brother, Isaac, who died at Dachau in 1944."

"They were Jewish?"

"There's no question about it. France arrived in America in 1938 and moved to Galen, Missouri, sometime after that."

"Why Galen? Did you find out?"

"No, but I'm still looking. I like this stuff. It's fun working in the library and trying to pull out things on someone you love."

After she hung up I stood there holding the receiver and then scratched my head with it. I didn't know whether I felt good or bad about the fact that she'd call again when she found out more.

According to her (a couple of days later), France went to Galen because his Uncle Otto owned a little printing business out there. But before he went west, our man lived in New York for a year and a half. For some reason she couldn't discover what he did there. She got a little nutty about it, and her calls got angrier and angrier.

"I can't find it. Ooo, it drives me crazy!"

"Take it easy, Sax. The way you've been digging around, you will."

"Oh, don't patronize me, Thomas. You sound just like your father in that movie I saw last night. Old James Vandenberg, good-hearted farmer."

My eyes narrowed and I tightened my grip on the phone. "Look, Saxony, you don't have to be insulting."

"I'm not . . . I'm sorry." She hung up. I called her right back but she didn't answer. I wondered if she'd called from some little phone booth out in the middle of nowhere. That thought made me feel so sorry for her that I went down to a florist and bought her a Japanese bonsai tree. I made sure that she wasn't home before I left it in front of her apartment door.

I thought that it was time I did something for a change instead of letting her do all the chasing around, so when the school had a long weekend at the end of April, I decided to go down to New York to talk to France's publisher about doing the biography. I didn't tell her that I was going until the night before I left, and then she was the one who called, all aglow.

"Thomas? I found it! I found out what he did in New York when he lived there!"

"Great! What?"

"Are you ready for this? He worked for an Italian undertaker named Lucente. He was his assistant or something. It didn't say what he did for him, though."

"That's pleasant. But do you remember that scene in *Land of Laughs* when the Moon Jester and Lady Oil die? He'd have to know something about death to have written that part."

4

I always have the same feeling when I go to New York. There was a bad joke about a man who married a beautiful woman and couldn't wait for the wedding night to get to her. But then when the time came, she pulled a blond wig off her bald head, unscrewed her wooden leg, and took the false teeth out that made her smile so alluring. She turned to him coyly and said, "I'm ready now, darling." That's me and New York. Whenever I come into the place—be it in a plane, train, or car—I can't wait to get there. The Big Apple! Shows! Museums! Bookstores! The Most Beautiful Women in the World! It's all there and has been waiting for me all this time. I zoom out of the train and there's *Grand Central Station* or *Port Authority* or *Kennedy Airport*—the heart of it all. And my heart's doing a conga: Look at the speed! The women! I love it! Everything! But that's where the trouble begins, because everything includes the bum wobbling into a corner to vomit and an obnoxious fourteen-year-old Puerto Rican kid on transparent rocket-ship high heels asking (threatening) me for a dollar. On and on and on. There's no need to elaborate on it, but I never seem to get it through my head about the place because every time I come, I half-expect to see Frank Sinatra come dancing by me in a sailor suit, singing "New York, New York." And in fact a man who looked vaguely like Sinatra did dance by me once in Grand Central. Danced right by and started to pee on the wall.

So now I've got it down to a science. I get off the train in high spirits. Then until the first terrible thing happens I'm great and loving every minute of the place. As soon as the terrible arrives, I let all of my hate and disappointment come flying out of me, and then I go on about my business.

This time it was a cabdriver. I flagged him down when I got out of the station and gave him the Fifth Avenue address of the publisher.

"Parade on Fift' tudday."

"Yes? So?" His license card said that his name was Franklin Tuto. I wondered how he pronounced it.

I saw his eyes in the rearview mirror sizing me up. "So I gotta go down Park."

"Oh, that's all right. Excuse me, but do you pronounce your last name Toot-o or Tut-o?"

His eyes were in the mirror instantly, drawing a bead on me before he answered this dangerous question.

"What's it to you, hey?"

"Nothing. I was just interested." Fool that I am, I thought I'd try to be funny. "I thought you might be related to the Egyptian Tuts."

"Like hell you did. You were checking me out, weren't you?" He grabbed hold of the bill of his checkered golf cap and pulled it around and down farther onto his head.

"No, no, you see, I saw your name there on the card—"

"You're another inspector! God *damn* you guys! I got the friggin' renewal already, so what the hell else do you want from me, blood?" He pulled over to the curb and told me that he didn't want me in his fucking cab—that I could fucking suspend him if I wanted, but that he was sick of "us guys." So we all got out of his cab, waved good-bye to Franklin Tuto as he screeched away, and sighing, hailed another.

The pilot of this one was named Kodel Sweet. I'm a great one for reading the names of cabdrivers. Scenery usually bores me. He had on one of those funky black velvet hats that look like something fell out of the sky onto his head and decided to stay. For better or worse he didn't say anything the whole trip except "Check it out" when I again gave the address of the publisher. But then when I was getting out of the car he said, "Have a nice day," and it sounded like he meant it.

The building was one of those all-glass Brave New World things like a huge swimming pool turned up on end without the water flowing out. The only time I've ever liked architecture like that is when it's one of those brilliantly sunny days in the spring or fall and the million windows reflect light everywhere.

I was surprised to find that a number of the floors of the building were offices of this publisher. Floors and floors of people working on books. I liked that idea. I liked the fact that Kodel Sweet had told me to have a nice day. There was a nice smell in the elevator, of some woman's sexy perfume. . . . New York's okay.

As I went up in the elevator, I felt a funny jump in my stomach to think that in a few minutes I'd be talking to someone who actually knew Marshall France. I've been plagued all my life with people asking me what my father was like, and I've always hated it, but now I had fifty zillion questions that I wanted to ask about France. As I came up with a zillion more, the elevator doors slid open and I walked out in search of David Louis's office.

Louis was no Maxwell Perkins, but he had a big enough reputation so that you'd hear about him now and then. When I reread the articles on France, they said that Louis had been one of the few people France was in contact with when he was alive. He had also edited all of the France books and had been made executor of the writer's will. I knew nothing about will executors (when my father died I went into total hibernation and didn't come out again until the battleground was cleared of rubble and bodies), but I assumed that Louis had to mean something to France to be made final overseer of his possessions.

"Help you?"

The secretary had on—I swear to God—a gold lamé T-shirt with gold sequin letters spelling out "Virginia Woolf" across her nice chest. There was a copy of *The Super Secs* facedown on her desk.

"I have an appointment with Mr. Louis."

"Are you Mr. Abbey?"

"Yes." I looked away because all of a sudden she had that "Aren't you . . . ?" glint in her eye, and I wasn't in the mood for her questions.

"One minute and I'll see . . ." She picked up the receiver and dialed an extension.

On one wall of the waiting room was a display case of the books the house had recently published. I started looking at the fiction, but what caught my eye was a gigantic coffee-table book, *The World of Puppets*. It cost twenty-five dollars but seemed so thick through the glass window that it had to have every photograph ever taken of a wooden head or string. I decided to buy it for Saxony for all the work she'd been doing. I knew that the gesture would mean something more to her than I probably wanted it to, but the hell with that. She deserved it.

"Mr. Abbey?"

I turned, and there was Louis. He was short and squat, probably around sixty, sixty-one years old, well groomed. He had on this very dapper tan suit with wide lapels, and a sea-blue herringbone shirt with a maroon ascot tucked down into the neck instead of a tie. Silver metal-frame glasses that made him look like a French movie director. Semi-bald, he gave me a semi-dead-fish handshake.

He led me into his office, and just before he closed the door, I heard his secretary snap her gum. The place was wall-to-wall books, and sneaking a glance at some of the titles, I realized how important he must be if he edited even half of these people.

He smiled apologetically and stuck his hands into his pants pockets. "Do you mind if I join you on the couch? Please, please sit down. I hurt my back playing racketball last week, and it hasn't been the same since."

Ted Lapidus suit, sequin secretary, racketball . . . Whether or not I approved of his style, he was my strongest link to Marshall France at the moment.

"You said that you wanted to talk about Marshall, Mr. Abbey." He was smiling a little wearily, I thought. He'd been over this territory before? "You know, it's interesting—ever since the colleges started teaching courses in children's literature, and people like George MacDonald and the Grimm Brothers have been established and made quote literary unquote, the interest in France's work has gone way up again. Not that the books haven't always sold. But now a number of schools have his things on their reading lists."

Next he'd be telling me that there were twelve people about to publish definitive biographies of France next month. I was afraid to ask the question but knew that I had to.

"Then why hasn't a biography of him ever been written if the time is so ripe?"

Louis turned his head slowly so that he was looking at me face-on. Until then he'd been gazing straight ahead at something fascinating on the floor in front of us. I couldn't see his face too well because the glasses were reflecting light from the window, but the rest of his face seemed impassive.

"Is that why you're here, Mr. Abbey? You want to write a biography?"

"Yes. I'd like to try."

"All right." He took a deep breath and went back to looking at the floor. "Then I'll tell you what I've told the others. I personally would love to see a biography written of the man. From what little I know, he led a fascinating life. Not so much so when he got older and lived in Galen . . . but every literary figure should have his portrait done. But when Marshall became famous, he loathed the notoriety that went along with it. I've always been convinced that that was part of what killed him so early—people from all over hounded him, and he just wasn't able to handle it. At all. Anyway, his daughter . . ." He stopped and licked his lips. "His daughter, Anna, is a very strange woman. She's never really forgiven the rest of the world for the fact that her father died so early. He was only forty-four, you know. She lives alone now, out in that big awful house in Galen, and refuses to talk to anyone about anything that has to do with him. Do you know how long I've tried to wangle the manuscript of his novel out of her? Years, Mr. Abbey. You know about his novel, don't you?"

I nodded. The learned biographer.

"Yes, well, good luck. Besides the fact that it would make her a small mountain of money—not to sound mercenary—I think that whatever he wrote should be printed and read. He was the only full-fledged genius I ever came up against in this business, and you can quote me. For God's sake, his fans are so devoted to him that some book dealer downtown told me the other day that he sold a copy of *Peach Shadows* for seventy-five dollars!"

Ahem.

"No, Mr. Abbey, she won't listen to me or to anyone else. Marshall never told her before he died that the book was finished, although in his letters to me he implied that it was. But to her it's unfinished, *i.e.* unpublishable. So I've begged her to let me put it out with a long note saying that it's incomplete, but she just closes her little bee-stung eyes and disappears back into Baby Anna Land, and that's the end of it.

"But I must also tell you that Marshall never wanted a biography written, so naturally she's obeyed that request too. I sometimes think that she's trying to hoard what's left of the man from the rest of the world. She'd probably take all of his books off people's shelves if she could." He scratched his white, steel-wool hair. "But really—not publishing the novel, not allowing a biography, never talking to the journalists who've gone out there to write articles on him . . . She's trying to squirrel him away from the rest of the world, for Christ's sake!" He shook his head and looked at the ceiling. I looked at it too and didn't see anything. It was quiet and comfortable, and both of us were thinking about this remarkable man who was such a big part of both of our lives.

"What about the possibility of writing a biography that *wasn't* authorized, Mr. Louis? I mean, there must be ways to find out about him without having to go through her. Anna."

"Oh, it's been tried. A couple of years ago an eager-beaver grad student from Princeton came through here on his way out to Galen." He smiled a private smile and took his glasses off. "He was an outrageously pompous ass, but that was all right. I was interested to see how he'd fare up against the mighty Anna. I asked him to write if anything happened out there, but I never heard from him again."

"And what did Anna say?"

"Anna? Oh, her usual. Wrote me a venomous letter telling me to stop sending snoopers out to dig around in her father's life. Nothing new, believe me. In her eyes, I'm that New York Jew who exploited her father right into his grave." He turned both hands palms up and shrugged.

I waited for him to say something more, but he didn't. I rubbed my hand on the coarse canvas arm of the couch and tried to think of another question. Here was the man who had known Marshall France—talked with him, read his manuscripts—so where were all of my questions? Why was I suddenly at a loss?

"I'll tell you a little about Anna, Thomas. Maybe it will give you an idea of what you'd be up against if you tried this book. I'll tell you just one instance in my never-ending love affair with the lovely Anna." He pushed off the couch and went over to his desk. He opened a small black lacquer box—the kind you see in Russian gift shops—and took out a cigar that looked like the twisted roots of a tree.

"Years ago I went out to Galen to talk with Marshall about a book he was working on. It turned out that it was *The Night Races into Anna* and that he was right in the middle of it. I read what he had and liked it, but there were parts that needed work. He'd never done a novel before, and it was turning out to be much more serious than any of his other work." He puffed his cigar and watched the tip grow orange. He was one of those people who like to tell a story in fits and starts—always stopping just when they've reached a crucial point and know their audience is panting for them to go on. In this case, Louis had his intermission just after he said that he told Marshall France that something he wrote "needed work."

"Did he mind hearing that?" I scrunched around in my seat and tried to act as if I could wait all day for his answer. I was also framing in my mind a part of the biography where I would say, "When asked if France minded editorial suggestion, his long-time editor, David Louis, chuckled around his De Nobili cigar and said . . ."

Puff. Puff. A long look out the window. He tapped the ashes into the ashtray and took a final look at the cigar, held out at arm's length. "Did he mind? Criticism, you mean? Absolutely not at all. I never knew how much he listened to me, but I never had any hesitation telling him when I thought that something was wrong or needed work."

"And was that often?"

"No. In almost every case, his manuscripts came in to me as finished products. I did very little editing on Marshall's work after the first book. Usually just some punctuation mistakes and sentence shifting.

"But let me get back to this novel. When I was out there, I took a couple of days to read it carefully and take notes. Anna was about . . . oh, maybe twenty or twenty-two by then. She had just dropped out of Oberlin and was staying home most of the time, in her room. From what Marshall said, she had gone there for their music school because she had had the makings of a concert pianist, but somewhere along the line she gave that up and scuttled back to Galen."

His tone of voice was hard to describe—objective but with little bits of anger sprinkled throughout.

"Now, the interesting thing is, she'd been involved in some sort of mysterious goings-on in college, and something had gone wrong or someone . . ." He rubbed his ear and sucked in one of his cheeks. "*That's* right! Someone had died, I think. Her boyfriend? I'm not sure. Naturally Marshall wasn't any too clear about it, because it was his daughter in the middle of it. Anyway, she was home on the next train.

"When I was out there, I'd see her flit around through the house in her black silk dresses and hair down her back. She'd be hugging a copy of Kafka or Kierkegaard to her chest. I kept getting the impression that she carried them title out so that whoever looked her way would be sure to see what she was reading.

"Marshall had these three cats named One, Two, and Three. He'd had them in the house only a short time, but they owned the place. They'd walk across his desk when he was working, jump up on the table when we were eating. I never knew whom he liked more, Anna or them. His wife, Elizabeth, had died a couple of years before, so it was just the two of them and those three cats in that monstrous old house together.

"One night after dinner I was sitting out on their porch reading. Anna came out with a cat under each arm."

Louis got off the couch again and sat on an edge of his desk, facing me, about six or seven feet away.

"I have to act this out or you won't get the full effect. Now, I'm sitting where you are, Thomas, and Anna's where I am, okay? She's got the two cats up under her arms, and all three of them are glowering at me. I tried to smile, but they didn't react, so I went back to the book. All of a sudden I heard the cats screech and hiss. I looked up, and Anna was looking at me as if I were the bubonic plague. I'd always thought she was eccentric, but this was insanity." He was standing and had curved his arms out from his body, as if he were holding something. The cigar was clenched in his teeth, and his forehead and eyes were screwed up. "Then she came over to me and said something like, 'We hate you! We hate you!' "

"What did you do?"

An ash fell on his lapel and he brushed it away. His face relaxed.

"Nothing, because that was the strangest part of all. I could just make out Marshall standing behind the screen door. He had obviously seen and heard everything. I kept looking at him, naturally expecting him to do something. But all he did was stand there for another minute, and then he turned and went back into the house."

After that strange little nugget, Louis asked if I wanted coffee. The girl with the Virginia Woolf T-shirt came and went, and in the meantime we chit-chatted about nothing. His Anna story had been so odd and unbelievable that for a time I was stymied for something to say. I was glad for the coffee diversion.

"Who was Van Walt?"

He stirred some honey into his coffee. "Van Walt. Van Walt

was another Marshall France mystery. According to him, the man was a recluse who lived in Canada and didn't want to be disturbed by anyone. Marshall made that so clear that we finally said all right, and as a result, whatever dealings we had with him were worked through France."

"Nothing else?"

"Nothing else. When a writer as important as Marshall says to leave him alone, we leave him alone."

"Did he ever talk about his childhood, Mr. Louis?"

"Please call me David. No, he rarely said anything about his past. I know that he was born in Austria. A little town called Rattenstein."

"Ratten*berg*."

"Yes, right, Rattenberg. Years ago, I was curious about it, so one time when I was in Europe I went there.

"The whole town is on a river that rushes by, and it's nice because just off in the distance are the Alps. It's all very *gemütlich*."

"And what about his father? Did he ever say anything about his father or his mother?"

"No, not a thing. He was a very secretive man."

"Well, what about his brother, Isaac—the one that died at Dachau?"

Louis was about to take a drag when I said that, but he stopped the cigar inches from his lips. "Marshall didn't have any brothers. That's one thing I certainly know. No, no brothers or sisters. I distinctly remember his telling me that he was an only child."

I got out my little pocket notebook and flipped through it until I got to the information that Saxony had given me.

" 'Isaac Frank died in—' "

"Isaac *Frank*? Who's Isaac Frank?"

"Well, you see, the person who does research for me"—I knew that if Saxony ever heard me refer to her like that, she would kill me—"found out that the family name was Frank, but that he changed it to France when he came to America."

Louis smiled at me. "Somebody led you down the garden path on that, Thomas. I probably knew the man better than anyone outside of his immediate family, and his name was *always* Marshall France." He shook his head. "And he didn't have any brothers. Sorry."

"Yes, but—"

He raised his hand to cut me off. "Really. I'm telling you this so that you won't waste your time on it. You can spend the rest of your life in the library, but you won't find what you're looking for, I promise you. Marshall France was always Marshall France, and he was an only child. I'm sorry to say that it's as simple as that."

We talked a little longer, but his obvious disbelief of what I'd said cast a pall over further conversation. A few minutes later we were standing in the door. He asked me if I thought I'd try writing the book anyway. I nodded but didn't say anything. He halfheartedly wished me luck and told me to stay in touch. A few seconds later I was going down in the elevator, staring off into space, and wondering about everything. France/Frank, David Louis, Anna . . . Saxony. Where the hell had she gotten that stuff on Martin Frank and a dead brother who never lived in the first place?

5

"Do you think I'm lying?"

"Of course not, Saxony. It's just that Louis was so damned adamant about there not being any brother and France's name not being Frank."

I was at a booth on Sixty-fourth Street that had no door and smelled suspiciously like bananas. I'd called Saxony long distance after getting four thousand quarters in a drugstore. She listened quietly to my adventures with Louis. She never got angry when I hinted at the possibility that her information was all bullshit. In fact it seemed that she was almost relaxed. She was talking in a new low, sexy voice.

I was a little wary of her calmness. There was a long silence while I watched a cabdriver throw a newspaper out the window of his cab.

When she spoke again her voice was even quieter. "There's one way that you can check on this Martin Frank part, Thomas."

"How's that?"

"The undertaker he worked for   Lucente. He's still in business downtown. I checked a Manhattan telephone directory a few days ago. Why don't you go and ask him about Martin Frank? See what he has to say about it."

Her voice was so smooth and sure of itself that I obediently asked her for the Lucente address like a good little boy and hung up.

Things like *The Godfather* and *The American Way of Death* make the job of undertaker sound profitable, if not pleasant, but one look at "Lucente and Son Funeral Home" and you'd have second thoughts.

It was down in a corner pocket of the city near Little Italy. It was next to a store that sold fluorescent madonnas and stone saints that you put in your garden to give it a taste of Italy. When I first walked by Lucente's I missed it completely because the doorway was small and there was only a tiny sign in the lower corner of the front window announcing the family business.

When I opened the door I heard a dog yapping way off in the back somewhere, and the place was lit by a yellow light from the street that cut in through the half-drawn venetian blinds. A green metal chair and desk—the kind you see in an Army recruiting office—a chair facing the desk, a year-old calendar announcing August from the Arthur Siegel Oil Company of New York—that was all. No soft music for the bereaved, no muted Oriental carpets to hush the sound of feet, no professional ghouls gliding around, trying to make you more "comfortable." It all came back to me from the days of my father's funeral.

"Ah! Zito!"

The only other door in the room flashed open and an old man came out in a hurry. He flung both arms up in the air, and looking back over his shoulder into the room he'd just come from, kicked the door shut.

"What can I do for *you?*"

For a moment I asked myself how I'd feel if my mother had just died and I was coming to this place to make the arrangements for her. A crazy old man comes flying out, cursing . . . Some funeral home. But later when I thought about it, I had to admit that I sort of liked it. It wasn't fake-y or put-on.

Lucente was short and wiry. His face was tobacco brown and he had white hair cut in a to-the-bone crew cut. No nonsense there. His eyes were powder blue and bloodshot. I thought that he must be in his seventies or eighties, but he looked strong enough and still full of beans. When I didn't say anything, he looked annoyed. He sat down behind the desk.

"You wanna sit down?"

I sat, and we looked at each other for a while. He clasped his hands in the middle of the desk and nodded, more to himself than to me. I watched his eyes and realized that they were too small to contain all the life that was behind them.

"Yes now, sir, so what can I do for you?" He slipped open a desk drawer and brought out a long yellow pad and a yellow Bic pen with a black cap.

"Nothing, Mr. Lucente. I, uh, I mean, nobody's died in my family. I'm here to ask you a few questions, if I may. About someone who once worked here for you."

He uncapped the pen and began drawing lazy circles on the top of the paper, one overlapping the next. "Questions? You wanna ask me about someone who worked for me?"

I sat up straight in my chair and couldn't find anyplace to put my hands. "Yes, you see, we've discovered that a man named Martin Frank worked here for you years ago. Around 1939 or so? I know that that's quite a long time, but I was wondering if you'd remember him or anything about him. If it's of any help, not long after he was here he changed his name to Marshall France and later became a very famous writer."

Lucente stopped drawing his circles and tapped the pen on the pad. He looked up once, expressionless, then turned in his chair and yelled over his shoulder.

"Hey, Violetta!"

When there was no answer, he scowled, dropped the pen on the desk, and got up.

"My wife's so old now she don't even hear the water running no more. I gotta turn it off for her half the time. Wait a minute." He scuffled to the door, and I saw for the first time that he was wearing a pair of plum-colored corduroy bedroom slippers. He opened the door but didn't go into the room. Instead he screamed for Violetta again.

A steel-wool voice rasped back, "Wha'? Whadya want?"

"You remember Martin Frank?"

"Martin *who?*"

"Martin *Frank!*"

"Martin Frank? Ah ha ha ha!"

Lucente was smiling crazily when he turned again and looked at me. He pointed off into the dark room and shook his hand as if he'd just burned it on something.

"Martin Frank. Yeah, sure, we remember Martin Frank."

6

The long train ride back gave me a lot of time to think about Lucente's story. Violetta, who I assumed was his wife, never came out of the other room, but that didn't keep her from yelling things to the old man. "Tell him about those two midgets and the trains!" . . . "Don'a forget the butterflies and that cookie!"

Apparently the first day on the job, Lucente brought in some man who'd jumped off a building and who'd been scraped up with a shovel and shoved in a box. According to the undertaker, his new employee took one look at the body and threw up. They tried it a few more times, but the same thing happened. However, Mrs. Lucente was a cripple, so they put him to work in their apartment cleaning and cooking and doing the laundry. Needless to say, it was pretty depressing at first to hear that the author of my favorite book in the world was kept on at the job because he cooked a mean lasagne.

But then one day Lucente was working on a beautiful young girl who had killed herself by overdosing on sleeping pills. He was halfway through the job when he stopped for lunch. When he returned, the woman's arm was on her stomach and she held a big chocolate-chip cookie in her hand. Next to her on a small side table was a glass of milk. Lucente thought it was a great joke—this kind of black humor was traditional in the funeral business. A few weeks later, a mean old woman from down the block died in her sleep. A big yellow-and-black butterfly was taped to her nose the morning after they brought her to the funeral home. Lucente laughed again, but I felt differently: perhaps Marshall France had been creating his first characters.

The new apprentice not only got over his nausea, but he soon became a highly valued assistant. He bought a copy of *Gray's Anatomy* and studied it constantly. Lucente said that after six months Frank developed an extraordinary ability to model an expression on a face that was as lifelike as any the old man had ever seen.

"That's the hardest thing, you see. Making them look alive is the hardest thing there is. Did you ever look in a casket? Sure, one look and you know they're dead. Big deal. But Martin had it, if you know what I mean. He had something that made even me jealous. You looked at one of his jobs and you'd wonder why the hell the guy was lying down in there!"

While he was in New York, Frank spent most of his time with the Lucentes, either at work or in their apartment behind the funeral home. But on Sunday, every Sunday, he went out with the Turtons. The Turtons were midgets. He met them when he happened into their candy store one day. The three of them loved trains and fried chicken, so every week they'd have a big fried-chicken dinner at a restaurant and then go over to Grand Central or Penn Station and get on a train to somewhere nearby. The Lucentes never went with them on these jaunts, but when Frank returned in the evening he would tell them about where they'd gone and what they'd seen.

Lucente never really understood why Frank quit. The longer he worked, the more fascinated he seemed by the job, but one day he came in and said that he'd be leaving at the end of the month. Said that he was going out to the Midwest to live with his uncle.

One of the kids on the hall was standing in front of my apartment when I got home. "There's a woman in your apartment, Mr. Abbey. I think she got Mr. Rosenberg to let her in."

I opened the door and dropped my briefcase on the floor. I kicked the door shut and closed my eyes. The whole place smelled of curry. I hate curry.

"Hello?" a voice called.

"Hi. Uh, hi. Saxony?"

She came around the corner carrying my old wooden stirring spoon. It had a few kernels of rice stuck to it. She was smiling a little too hard and her face was very flushed. I guessed it was half from cooking, half from nervousness.

"What are you up to, Sax?"

The spoon had moved slowly down to her side, and she stopped smiling. She looked at the floor.

"I thought that since you were in the city all day, you probably didn't have much to eat, with all that racing around . . ." Her voice petered out, although the spoon came up again and she waved it around in the air like a sad magic wand. Maybe she wanted it to finish her sentence for her.

"Oh, God, look, never mind. It's really nice of you!"

We were both totally embarrassed, so I beat a hasty retreat to the bathroom.

"Do you like curry, Thomas?"

Halfway through the meal my tongue was a five-alarm fire, but I winked back the tears and nodded and pointed my fork at my plate a couple of times. ". . . love it." It might have been the worst meal I'd ever eaten in my life. First her banana bread, then the curry . . .

In his mercy, God made her buy Sara Lee brownies for dessert, which, after three glasses of milk, calmed the fires in my mouth.

When the dishes were cleared, I began telling her about my cabdriver experience. I had gotten to where Tuto ordered me out of his car when she bit her lip and looked away.

"What's the matter?" I was tempted to say something like, "I'm not boring you, am I?" But by then I knew it was wrong and unnecessary.

"I . . ." She looked at me, then away, at me, away. "I was really happy here this afternoon, Thomas. I came over right after I talked to you on the phone. I was really happy being here, cooking. . . . Do you understand what I mean?" Her glare dissolved back into lip biting, but she was watching me very carefully.

"Yes, well, sure. I mean, of course I understand. . . . *Boy,* that curry was excellent, Saxony."

Later, when I gave her the big book on puppets, she took one look at it and started to cry. And then she wouldn't pick it up: she got out of her chair and came over to me. She put her arms around my neck and hugged and hugged me.

We started necking, and moved over to the bed. We began undoing each other's clothes as fast as we could. But it wasn't fast enough, so we separated and undid our own buttons. Although her back was turned to me, I stopped when I saw her pull her shirt over her head. I love to watch a woman undress. No matter if you're going to make love to her or you're peeking at her through a window, there's something tingly and wonderfully exciting about it.

I put my thumb on the back of her neck and slowly ran it down the bump-bridge of her spine. She looked over her shoulder and gave a little grimace. "Can I ask a favor?"

"Of course."

"I'm very shy about undressing in front of someone. I'm sorry, but do you think you could close your eyes or look away while I do it?"

I leaned across the bed and kissed her shoulder. "Sure. I get embarrassed about that too."

It was perfect. I hate taking off my pants in front of a woman I don't know. So this was great—I'd turn my back to her, pull off my pants while she pulled off hers, we'd both slip under the covers at the same time, turn off the light for a little while . . .

RRRrriiinnnggg!

I'd just stepped out of my boxer shorts when the phone rang. No one ever called me, especially not at twelve o'clock at night. The phone was on the other side of the room, so, naked, I sprang for it. Saxony let out a whoop, and unconsciously I turned and faced her. Her green panties were down around her knees, and from the look on her face, she didn't know whether to push them down or pull them back up.

"Thomas, where have you been? I've been trying to get in touch with you for days!"

"Ma?"

"Yes. The only time I can ever get you is in the middle of the night. Did you get those pants that I sent you from Bloomingdale's?"

"Pants? Ma . . ." I put my hand over the mouthpiece and looked at Saxony. "My mother wants to know if I got the pants she sent me from Bloomingdale's."

Sax immediately looked at the panties in her hand and then at me. We both started laughing. I got off the phone as fast as I could.

For the next few weeks we poked around more and more together. We went down to New Haven to see a play, drove all the way to Sturbridge Village for dinner one night, and sat out a freak hailstorm in a little cottage my mother owned on the Rhode Island shore.

One afternoon she sheepishly asked if she could go to Galen.

"Yes, but only if you promise to go with me."

Part Two

Part Two

1

"Saxony, you can't take all of those suitcases! What do you think this is, *Wagon Train?*"

All she needed was an ancient steamer trunk to complete her lineup. There was a delicate yellow-and-red wicker basket, a scruffy knapsack that bulged like a bratwurst, an old brown leather suitcase with brass locks and edges. She'd topped it all off with several things just back from the dry cleaner's in plastic wrap on metal hangers.

She scowled at me and walked around to the back of the station wagon. She flipped down the gate and laid the first of her many things in.

"Don't you hassle me, Thomas. I've had one lousy day so far, okay? Just don't hassle me."

I tapped my fingers on the steering wheel, looked at my new haircut in the rearview mirror, and wondered whether it was worth a fight. For a week I'd been telling her that I wanted to travel as light as possible on this trip. Since we had been together almost every day after my New York trip, I'd come to believe that she had about three shirts and two dresses and a white smock that looked like a peasant castoff. At one point I wanted to buy her an Indian dress she admired in a store window, but she wouldn't let me, even when I insisted. "Not yet," she said, whatever that was supposed to mean.

So what did she have in those bags? Another nightmare grew in my mind—groceries and a hot plate! She was going to cook our meals all the way to Galen! Banana bread . . . curry . . . apple tea . . .

"What've you got in those things anyway, Sax?"

"There's no reason to yell!"

I looked at her in the mirror and saw her with her hands on her hips. I thought of how nice those hips were without any clothes on them.

"Okay, I'm sorry. But how come you're taking so much?"

I heard gravel crunch, and then she was standing by my door. I looked up at her, but she was busy undoing the straps on the wicker basket.

"Just look."

It was full of handwritten notes, magazine clippings, blank yellow pads, yellow pencils, and the fat pink erasers she liked to use.

"This one is my work bag. Am I allowed to take it?"

"Sax . . ."

"The duffel bag has all of my clothes in it. . . ."

"Look, I wasn't saying . . ."

"And the suitcase has some marionettes in it that I'm working on." She smiled and clicked the latches shut on the bag. "That's the one thing that you'll have to get used to around me, Thomas: wherever I go, I always carry my life around with me."

"I would hope so."

"Oh, you're very funny, Thomas. So clever."

June graduation ceremonies had taken place several days before, so the campus of my school was summer-green and silent and kind of sad when we drove away. Schools without students are always strangely ominous to me. All the rooms are too clean and the floors too polished. When a phone rings it echoes all over the place, and it will go eight or nine times before someone feels like answering it or the caller realizes that everyone's gone and he hangs up. We passed a huge copper beech tree that was a great favorite of mine, and I realized that I wouldn't sit under it again for a long time.

She reached over and turned on the radio. "Thomas, are you sad that you're leaving?"

The last part of "Hey, Jude" was on, and I remembered the girl

I was dating on Nantucket when the song first came out in the sixties.

"Sad? Yes, a little. But I'm pretty glad, too. After a while you discover that you're talking and moving in a trance. Do you know that I taught *Huckleberry Finn* for the fourth time this year? It's a great book and all, but it was getting to the point where I wasn't even reading the stuff anymore. I didn't have to be able to teach it. That kind of thing's not good."

We sat and listened to the song finish. I guess the station was doing a Beatles retrospective, because "Strawberry Fields Forever" came on next. I drove up a ramp onto the New England Thruway.

"Did you ever want to be an actor?" She pulled a thread off the sleeve of my shirt.

"An *actor?* No, not after my father, hell no."

"I remember being madly in love with Stephen Abbey after I saw him in *The Beginners.*"

I snorted but didn't say anything. What person in the world wasn't in love with my father?

"Don't laugh at me—it's true!" Her voice was almost indignant. "I'd just gone into the hospital for the first time, so my parents got me a little portable television set. I remember the whole thing very clearly. It was on *Million Dollar Movie*, which showed the same old film every afternoon for a week. I watched every showing of both *The Beginners* and *Yankee Doodle Dandy.*"

"*Yankee Doodle Dandy?*"

"Yes, with James Cagney. I was madly in love with both James Cagney and your father when I was in the hospital."

"How long were you in there?"

"The hospital? For four months the first time and two the second."

"And what did they do—skin grafts and that kind of thing?"

She didn't say anything. I looked over at her, but there was no expression on her face. I hadn't meant to pry, and as the silence continued, I felt like apologizing, but I didn't.

A big thunderstorm was brewing up over the hills in front of us, and we drove into a lowering curtain of smoky pearl clouds. I looked in the rearview mirror and saw the sun still shining down on where we'd just come from. I knew that most of the people back there had no idea of what they were in for later that afternoon.

"When did you fall out of love with my father?"

"Thomas, do you really want to know about when I was in the hospital? I've never liked to talk about it, but if you'd like to know, I'll tell you."

She said it with so much conviction in her voice that I didn't know what to answer. She went on before I had a chance to say anything.

"The first time was horrible. They'd put me in these baths so that all of the dead skin would come off and the new could start to grow. I remember that there was this stupid nurse named Mrs. Rasmussen who took care of me and always talked to me like I was a moron. I don't remember much else about it except that I was scared and hated everything. I guess I've blocked a lot out. The second time was a lot of therapy, and everyone seemed much nicer. It's probably because they knew I'd be walking again. When I was in there, I discovered that people treat you much more . . . I don't know, humanely, when they see that you're going to be all right again."

A snake of yellow lightning skittered across the clouds, followed closely by one of those quick cracks of thunder that make you jump a little in spite of yourself. The radio had become almost pure static, so I switched it off. Big marbles of rain began to fall, but I held off turning on the windshield wipers until the last moment. My side window was down, and I could feel the dying heat and heaviness on the air. I thought about a little Saxony Gardner sitting bolt upright in a hospital bed with her little-kid legs bandaged all the way up and down. The picture was so sad and sweet that it made me smile. If I'd had a kid like that, I would have bought her so many toys and books that she would have suffocated under them.

"What was it like being the son of Stephen Abbey?"

I took a deep breath to put her off for a minute. In the time that we'd been together she'd asked me very few questions about my family, and I was damned grateful.

"My mother called him Punch. Sometimes he'd walk off a set in the middle of the day, come home, and take us all out to someplace like Knott's Berry Farm or the beach. He'd run around and buy us all hot dogs and Coke and ask us if this wasn't the best time we'd ever had in our lives. He got pretty manic sometimes, but we loved it all. If he got too crazy, then my mother would say, 'Take it easy, Punch,' and I'd hate her for it. He always had to be the life of the party when he was around, but since he was around so little then, we all ate him up."

The rain came down in transparent curtains, and you could hear it slooshing up under the wheels. I was driving in the slow lane, and whenever someone passed us there was so much water flung across the windshield that the poor wipers could barely keep up with it. The lightning and thunder were simultaneous now, so I knew that the storm was right over us.

"He took me to the studio once when they were filming *A Fire in Virginia*. In a way, it was one of the greatest days of my life, I guess. All I remember about it was that someone was always asking me if I wanted an ice cream, and that later I fell asleep and was carried into his dressing room. When I woke up he was standing over me like a white mountain, smiling that famous smile. He had on an all-white shirt and a huge cream panama hat with a black band." I shook my head and tapped out a tune on the steering wheel to swish away the memory. A Grand Union trailer truck floated by in slow motion.

"Did you love him?" Her voice was quiet and held back, I guess a little afraid.

"No. Yes. I don't know—how can you not love your father?"

"Very easily—I didn't love mine. His greatest dream in life came true when one of his students got into Harvard."

"What do you mean—your father was a teacher?"

"Uh-huh."

"You never told me that."

"Yes. He taught English too."

I slid a quick look at her, and she puffed out her cheeks so that she looked like a squirrel with a lot of nuts in there.

"I guess I shouldn't say this, but he was awful, from everything I remember about him." She put her hands on the dashboard and patted out a kind of soft African beat. She spoke while she patted. "He used to eat sliced pineapple and read *Hiawatha* out loud to my mother and me."

"*Hiawatha?* 'By the shores of Gitchy Gummi,/On the bottom of the lake,/Hiawatha and his buddies/Playing poker for a stake.' "

"Gee, you must be an English teacher too."

The sky was so dark that I switched on the headlights and slowed down to forty. I had often wondered what she was like as a kid. That nice, moony-pale face in miniature. I could see her off in a dark corner of a dark living room playing with her marionettes until nine, when her mother would tell her to go to bed. White socks that were falling down, and black patent leather shoes with gold buckles.

"You know, Thomas, when I was little about the only exciting thing my family ever did was to go to Peach Lake on the weekends in the summer. I used to get sunburned."

"Oh, yeah? Well, the only exciting thing that ever happened to me was reading *The Land of Laughs* and drinking Hires root beer out of a big glass bottle. Whatever happened to Hires root beer in a big glass bottle?"

"Oh, come on, you can't tell me that your life out there with all of those famous people wasn't neat. You don't have to try to make me feel better."

"Better? That has nothing to do with it. At least you had a normal father! Look, being his son was like living in this birdcage. You couldn't open your mouth without everyone being fake-nice to you or telling you how much they liked your 'Papa's' movies! What the hell did I care about his movies? I was a little kid, for Christ's sake! All I wanted to do was ride my bike."

"Don't shout."

"I don't have to . . ." I wanted to say something more, but I saw the turnoff for a roadside rest stop so I took it instead. It was dark as night outside as I crept down the exit ramp. The parking lot was filled with camper trucks and cars with overflowing luggage racks. Many of them were open to the rain, so the exposed suitcases, baby strollers, and bicycles were totally soaked and shiny. I found a parking space when a white Fiat with Oklahoma plates almost hit me while backing out of it. I switched off the motor and we both sat there while the rain hammered on the roof. Her hands were folded in her lap, but mine still gripped the steering wheel. I felt like ripping it off and handing it to her.

"All right, do you want something to eat or what?"

"Eat? Why? We've only been on the road for an hour."

"Oh, well, I'm sorry, *dear*—I'm not supposed to be hungry, huh? I'm not allowed to eat or anything unless you do, is that it?" I sounded like a kid who's just discovered sarcasm but doesn't know how to use it yet.

"Just shut up, Thomas. Go outside and have a fishburger or something. I don't care what you do. I don't deserve your anger."

There wasn't much else I could do but go. We both knew that I was making more and more of an ass of myself, but by then I didn't know how to stop. If I'd been her, I would have been royally bored by me.

"Do you want any . . . ? Oh, shit, I'll be back in a little while."

I opened the door and stepped right into this monstrous puddle, drenching both my sneaker and sock in one plunge. I looked to see if she'd been watching, but her eyes were closed, hands still folded in her lap. I put my other, dry foot carefully into the puddle and left it there until I felt the cold seeping in. Then I paddled both feet up and down in my new little footbath. Splish splat.

"What . . . are . . . you . . . doing?"

Splish splat.

"Thomas, don't do that." She started to laugh. It sounded so much better than the rain. "Don't be crazy! Close the door."

My back was to her, and I felt her grab a handful of my sweatshirt. She laughed harder and gave a strong tug.

"Will you please get back in here? What are you doing?"

I looked up into the rain, and it was coming down so hard and sharp that it forced my eyes closed. "Penance! Penance! All of my fucking life people have been asking me what it was like to be

Stephen Abbey's son. Every time I try to answer that question, I sound dumber and dumber."

I stopped flapping my feet. I felt so sad, like such an idiot. I wanted to turn around and look at her, but I couldn't. "I'm sorry, Sax. If I had anything to say, God knows, I'd tell you."

The wind was blowing the rain right into my face. A family walked by and gaped at me.

"I don't care, Thomas." The wind gusted and closed my eyes again. I didn't know if I'd heard her right.

"What?"

"I said that I don't care about your father." She touched my back with the flat of her hand, and now her voice was strong and insistent and loving.

I turned around and put my wet arms around her. I kissed her warm neck and could feel her kissing mine.

"Hold me tight, you old sponge. You've already got me soaked." She squeezed tighter and gave my neck a bite.

I couldn't think of anything to say except for a line from France's book *The Green Dog's Sorrow*: "The Voice of Salt loved Krang too. When it was with her, it always whispered."

2

We had planned to make the trip in two days, but suddenly we were stopping at Stuckey's for pralines, Frontier Town or Santa Claus Village or Reptile City whenever we saw them advertised, and anywhere in general if we were in the mood.

"Wait a minute. Do you want to see . . . hold it . . . the site of the Battle of Green River?"

"I don't know. Sure. What war was it in?"

"What's the difference? Five miles to go. Sax, what's your fa-vorite France book?"

"It's a toss-up between *Pool of Stars* and *Land of Laughs*."

"*Pool of Stars?* Really?"

"Yes, I think my favorite scene of all is in there. The one where the girl goes down to the beach at night. When she sees the old man and the white bird scooping those blue holes out of the ocean."

"Jeez, I couldn't say what my favorite scene is. Something out of *Land of Laughs,* though. Definitely. But I'd have trouble choosing between a funny scene and a magical one. In many ways I like the funny scenes more now, but when I was little those battles between the Words and the Silence . . . phew!"

"Thomas, don't drive off the road."

Sometimes we pulled off the highway into a parking area and perched on the hot hood of the car, watching everyone fly by. Neither of us would say a word, and there wasn't any urge to keep moving, to get there.

The first night out, we stayed in a little town just west of Pittsburgh. The people who ran our motel raised black-and-tan coonhounds, and after dinner we took a few puppies out onto the front lawn and let them bite us for a while.

"Thomas?"

"Uh-huh? Hey, catch him before he gets away."

"Listen to me, Thomas, this is serious."

"Okay."

"Do you know this is the first time I've ever been to a motel with anyone?"

"Is that right?"

"Uh-huh. And you know what else? I'm very pleased." She handed me a puppy and stood up. "When I was younger and used to think about my burns all the time, I never thought any man would ever want to go to a motel with me, the way I looked."

The next morning when we were about to leave, the woman came out of the office and gave us these beautiful lunches she had packed, complete with beer and Milky Way candy bars. She whispered something to Saxony and then went back into the office.

"What'd she say?"

"She said that you were too skinny and that I should give you my Milky Way."

"You should."

"Nothing doing."

The whole trip went like that—one nice thing after another—so by the time we got to St. Louis and saw the Saarinen Arch, we were both a little rueful that we'd already come this far. We stopped in the middle of the day in Pacific, Missouri, and wandered around the Six Flags amusement park there. That night we went back to our air-conditioned motel room and made love. She kept saying my name over and over again. I'd never been with anyone who'd done that. Things were so nice now. I looked in all the dark corners of my life and wondered which one of them had something up its sleeve. . . . No answer. Not that I was expecting one.

3

I pulled into a Sunoco station and a pretty blond girl with a bright red St. Louis Cardinals baseball cap came out of the garage.

"Fill it up, please. Also, how far is it to Galen?"

She bent down and put her hands on her knees. I noticed that her fingernails were short and that two of them were completely blackened. As if something heavy had fallen on them, the blood came up from the finger underneath and stayed.

"Galen? Oh, 'bout four miles. You go straight down this road to the junction and turn right, and you'll be there in a few minutes."

She went back to filling the tank, and I looked at Saxony. She was smiling, but she was obviously as nervous as I was.

"Well . . ." I flipped my hand in the air.

"Well . . ." She dipped her head in agreement.

"Well, kid, we're almost there."

"Yes."

"*The* Land of Laughs . . ."

"Marshall France Land."

The road had long gradual dips and rises, and the ups and downs felt good after the straight monotony of the turnpike. We passed a true-to-life railroad dining car, a lumberyard where the fresh smell of cut wood was in and out of the car in a second, and a veterinarian's office with the harsh sound of scared and sick dogs barking crazily from within. At the junction there was a stop sign that had been riddled with bullet holes and BB dents that had rusted orange. A kid was standing next to it, hitchhiking. He looked harmless enough, although I admit that a couple of scenes from *In Cold Blood* flashed through my mind.

"Galen."

We told him that we were going there too and to get in. He had a kind of limp Afro of red hair, and every time I looked in the rearview mirror I saw him either looking me straight in the eye or his burning bush of hair blocking my view.

"You guys are going to Galen? I saw that you've got Connecticut plates." He pronounced it "Con*nect*-ticut." "You didn't come all the way out here to go to Galen, didya?"

I nodded pleasantly and looked him over in the mirror. A little positive eye contact. The old stare-him-down game. "Yes, we did, as a matter of fact."

"Wowie, Connecticut to Galen," he said sarcastically. "Some trip."

I had had so many twerps like him in class that his rudeness didn't bother me. Boondocks hippie. All he needed was a "KISS" T-shirt and his underpants showing above his blue jeans to make him complete.

Saxony turned around in her seat. "Do you live there?"

"Yeah."

"Do you know Anna France?"

"Miss France? Sure."

I chanced another look in the mirror, and his eyes were still on me, but now he was contentedly chewing a thumbnail.

"You guys are here to see her?"

"Yes, we've got to talk to her."

"Yeah? Well, she's okay." He sniffed and moved around in his seat. "She's a hip lady. Very laid-back, you know?"

All of a sudden we were there. Coming over a small rise, we passed a white house with two thin pillars and a dentist's shingle hanging from a lamppost on the front lawn. Then there was the Dagenais Lawnmower Repair Service in a blue-silver tin shack, a

Montgomery Ward outlet store, a firehouse with its big doors swung open but no fire trucks inside, and a grain store that was advertising a special this week on the fifty-pound bag of Purina Dog Chow.

This was it. This was where he had written all of the books. This was where he had eaten and slept and walked and known people and bought things like potatoes and newspapers and gas for his car. Most of the people here had known him. Had *known* Marshall France.

The main part of the town was on the other side of some railroad tracks. As we approached the crossing, the safety bars started to descend and a bell began its warning. I was delighted by the reprieve. Anything that would postpone our seeing Anna France was welcome. I've always liked to stop and watch trains go by. I remember the cross-country trips that my mother and I frequently made on the Twentieth Century and Super Chief when my parents were still married.

When we got to the lowered bars I switched off the engine and rested my arm on the back of Saxony's seat. It felt hot and clammy. It had turned out to be one of those summer days when the air feels like soft lead and the clouds can't decide on whether they want to downpour or just move on.

"You can let me off here."

"Can you tell us where Miss France lives?"

He stuck his skinny arm between our two seats and jabbed his index finger forward while he talked. "Go to the end of this street. It's about three blocks. Then you take your right onto Connolly Street. Her house is number eight. If you miss it, just ask anyone around there. They'll tell you. Thanks for the ride."

He got out of the car, and when he walked away I saw that he had colorful patches sewn onto both of his back pockets. One of them was a hand giving you the finger, the other was of a hand giving you the V-for-peace sign. Both patches were red, white, and blue, and the fingers had stars all up and down them.

The train turned out to be a slow-moving two-hundred-car-long freight. A passing parade of Erie Lackawanna, Chesapeake & Ohio, Seatrain . . . Loud, even clickety-clicks, the different sounds each car made when it passed. Then the coziness of the little brick-red caboose when it passed and a guy in its high square window was reading a newspaper and smoking a pipe, oblivious of the world. I liked the whole thing.

When the train was gone, the red-and-white-striped bars began rising slowly, almost as if they were tired and weren't in the mood to go up. I started the engine and bumped the car up and over the tracks. I looked in the mirror and saw that there was no one behind us.

"You see? That's the difference between here and in the East."

"What is?"

"We were just at that crossing for what, five or eight minutes, right? Well, in the East if you were there half that long there would be a line of cars ten miles long waiting to go. Here . . . well, just look behind us." She did, but she didn't say anything. "You see? Not a car. Not one. That's your difference."

"Uh-huh. Thomas, do you realize where we are on this earth? Do you realize that we are actually here?"

"I'm trying not to think about it yet. It makes my stomach ache." An understatement. I was quickly on my way to being terrified of talking to Anna France, but I didn't want Saxony to know that. I kept thinking of every word David Louis had said about her. Witch. Neurotic. To avoid any more conversation, I rolled my window down all the way and took a deep breath. The air smelled of hot dust and something else.

"Hey, look, Sax, a barbecue! Let's have some lunch."

A big green canopy had been set up in an open lot between Phend's Sporting Goods and the Glass Insurance Company. Underneath the canopy about twenty people were sitting at redwood picnic tables, eating and talking. A hand-painted sign in front announced that it was the annual Lions Club barbecue. I parked the car next to a dirty pickup truck and got out. The air was still and redolent with the smell of woodsmoke and grilled meat. A slight breeze pushed by. I started to stretch, but when I happened to look toward the eaters I stopped in mid-flight. Almost all of them had stopped eating and were looking at us. Except for one nice-looking woman with short black hair who was hurrying by with a couple of boxes of hamburger rolls in her hands, they were all frozen in position—a fat man in a straw hat with a sparerib held near his open mouth, a woman pouring an empty Coke can into a full cup, a child holding a stuffed pink-and-white rabbit over his head with two hands.

"What is this, *Ode on a Grecian Urn?*" I mumbled to no one.

I watched the woman with the rolls spear open a box with a barbecue fork. The freeze on the rest of them lasted maybe ten long seconds, and then a loud engine noise which turned out to be a truck carrying a palomino horse broke the spell. One of the men behind the grills smiled and waved us over with a greasy spatula.

"There's plenty here, folks. Come on over and support the Galen Lions."

We started over, and the man nodded his approval. There was space on one of the benches, so Saxony sat down while I went over to the smoking grills.

My new pal scraped grease off the silver bars into the fire and called over his shoulder for more ribs. Then he looked at me and tapped the grill. "Connecticut, huh? You came all this way just to taste my spareribs, huh?"

He had on a puffy white cooking glove that was stained grease-brown on the palm. I smiled stupidly and laughed through my nose.

"Now, you see, I got the ribs and Bob Schott over there's got the hamburgers. If I were you, though, I wouldn't eat 'em, because Bob's a doctor and he might try to poison you so he'll have a couple of new customers later."

Bob thought that was the funniest thing he'd ever heard. He looked around to see if everyone was laughing as hard as he was.

"But now, you take some ribs from me, and you'll know what good is, because I own the market here and this meat is fresh off the truck this morning. It's the best stuff I've got." He pointed at the grilling ribs. They were basted in a red sauce and dripped hot grease onto the coals, which in turn gave off an almost continual sizzle. They smelled great.

"Sure, Dan, sure. You know that they're just the ones you couldn't sell last week."

When I looked over my shoulder at Saxony to see how all these knee-slappers were going down with her, I was surprised to see her laughing.

"Us dopes's keeping you from eating, friend. What would you and your lady like?"

Dan, the master of ceremonies, was shiny-bald except for some short brown hair on the sides of his head. His eyes were dark and friendly and set into a fat, red, unwrinkled face that looked as if it had eaten a lot of spareribs over the years. He had on a white T-shirt, rumpled tan pants, and black work boots. Overall he reminded me of an actor who died a couple of years ago named Johnny Fox, who was infamous for beating his wife but who nevertheless always played the part in cowboy movies of a cowardly small-town mayor or shopowner. The kind who's afraid to challenge the Dalton gang when they come into town looking to tear everything apart.

My father used to bring home men like Johnny Fox. They always looked astonished that he had actually invited them to dinner. He would come in the front door and yell to Esther, our cook, that there'd be another for dinner.

If I was in the room with my mother, she'd inevitably groan and look at the ceiling, as if the answer were written up there. "Your father's found another monster," she'd say, and then push herself wearily up and out of her chair so that she'd at least be standing when he appeared in the doorway with his new pal in tow.

Looking sheepish and naughty at the same time, he'd boom out, "Look who's in for dinner, Meg, Johnny Fox! You remember Johnny, don't you?"

Johnny would tiptoe forward and shake her hand as if she were an electric eel about to strike. They were all petrified of her and sensed, despite her invariable politeness, that she couldn't stand having them in her house, much less at her table. But the meals went well. There'd be talk about the movies they were working on, gossip, tidbits from their world. Then, when we were done,

Johnny (or whoever) would beat as hasty a retreat as possible out the door, thanking Mother obsequiously for the delicious meal. Once a cameraman named Whitey, who'd brained his wife with a toaster and got thirty days for it, fell back over the rubber welcome mat and sprained his ankle trying to get out.

When they'd gone, the folks would move into the living room, where Father would light up a Montecristo cigar and she would go to her place by the window, where, with her back to him, she'd begin the battle.

Matter-of-factly she'd say, "Isn't he the one who beats his wife [robbed a diner, raised killer dogs, ran Mexicans over the border]?"

He'd whoosh out a long gray fan of smoke and look at the cigar, a happy man. "Yes, that's right. He just got out of the pokey two weeks ago. Bryson was afraid we'd have to get someone else to play the mayor. It's lucky his wife decided not to press charges."

"Yes, isn't it?" She tried to shoot out a cynical flame, but her tongue or heart wasn't in it, and as a result her words came out sounding like she was really glad for Johnny.

"An interesting guy. An interesting guy. I worked with him about five years ago on a picture. He spent the whole time either drunk or trying to put the make on this ugly script girl we had."

"Delightful. You pick up all the sweetie pies, Stephen."

This would go on for the time it took him to smoke his cigar. Then he'd either move up behind her and put his hands on her waist or walk out of the room. Whenever he did that, she'd turn around and stare at the doorway a long time.

"Ribs or a burger?"

"Excuse me? Oh, ribs! Yes, ribs will be fine."

Dan scooped up some red sizzlers and put them onto an over-sized yellow plate along with two dinner rolls. The grease from the ribs ran across the plate and started soaking into the rolls.

"That'll be two-fifty, and no charge for the entertainment."

I got two Cokes and went back to the table. A gray old woman with lined, sunken cheeks and a brown-black tooth in the front of her mouth was sitting next to Saxony and talking low and fast. I thought that was sort of odd, but Saxony listened intently to whatever the other was saying, and when I put the food down in front of her she didn't move. A little miffed, I picked up one of the ribs. It was burning hot and I dropped it on the table. I didn't think that I'd made that much noise, but when I looked up everyone was staring at me again. God, how I hate that. I'm the kind of person who'll order a steak and when the waiter brings fish instead, I'll take it just to avoid making a scene. I hate arguments in public, birthday cakes brought to you in restaurants, tripping or farting or anything out in the open that makes people stop and stare at you for the longest seconds in existence.

I gave the people around me my "Ain't I a dummy?" smile, but it didn't do any good. They looked and looked and looked. . . .

"Thomas?" Good old Saxony to the rescue.

"Yes!" I think I answered loud enough to curdle cream. She picked up the rib and put it back on my plate.

"This is Mrs. Fletcher. Mrs. Fletcher, Thomas Abbey."

The old woman stuck her hand out over the table and gave me a strong, pumping shake. She looked about sixty-eight or-nine. I saw her running the town post office or popcorn and candy concession at the movie theater. She didn't have the dry snakeskin of a person who's old and lived out in the sun all her life. More white, an inside-living white that had begun to go gray like an old postcard.

"How d'ya do? I hear you're out here to stay maybe for a while?"

I looked at Saxony and wondered how much she had told Mrs. Fletcher. She winked at me in between bites of sparerib.

"That you might want to rent a place?"

"Well, yes, maybe. It's just that we don't know how long we'll be here, you see."

"That doesn't make any difference. I've got so much room downstairs in my house that I could rent it out for a bowling alley. Twice." She took a black-and-gold-plastic cigarette case out of her handbag. Unsnapping it, she pulled out one of those hundred-millimeter-long cigarettes and a black Cricket lighter. Lighting up, she took a huge first drag that quickly burned down into a long ash. It drooped more and more as she talked, but she refused to tap it off.

"Dan, these ribs look good. Can I have a plate of them?"

"Sure, Goosey."

"Notice he calls me Goosey? All of my friends call me that."

I nodded and didn't know whether it would be rude to start eating again while she talked.

"You don't have to worry about not being married or anything with me." She looked at us separately and tapped the ring finger on her left hand. "That kind of stuff's never bothered me. I only wish people'd felt that way when I was a girl. I would have had a great time, believe me!"

I looked at Saxony for her response to that, but she kept looking at Mrs. Fletcher.

The woman stopped as she was about to say something, and drummed her fingers on the table. "I'll rent you my downstairs . . . I'll rent it to you for thirty-five dollars a week. Now, you can't get that kind of price at any motel around here. It's got a good kitchen down there, too."

I was about to tell her that we'd have to talk it over when Dan brought her plate.

"What do you say to thirty-five dollars a week for renting out my downstairs, Dan?"

He crossed his arms over his stomach and sucked air in through his teeth. It sounded like a steam iron.

"You people are thinking of staying in Galen for a while, are you?" I didn't know if I was just paranoid, but I was sure that his voice clicked into being less friendly.

Saxony spoke before I had a chance to. "We're trying to see if we can talk to Anna France. We're very interested in doing a book about her father."

And wasn't there a silence then? Faces that showed a slow, thick interest that moved through the air toward us like smoke on humid air?

"Anna? You say you want to do a book on Marshall?" Dan's

voice rose out over the cooking food, the quietness, the breeze that kept coming up out of nowhere and dying just as quickly.

I was furious with Saxony. I had wanted to poke around the town for at least a few days before I started telling people why we were here. I'd recently read an article about an up and coming writer who lived in a small town in Washington State. The people in the town were tight-lipped about him to outsiders because they liked him and wanted to protect his privacy. Although Marshall France was dead, I was sure all along that the people in Galen would hesitate to talk about him. It was really the first stupid thing Saxony had done. The only thing I could attribute it to was her nervousness at actually being here.

Dan turned around and bellowed to one of his buddies, "The man here wants to do a book about Marshall France."

"Marshall?"

A woman wearing blue jeans and a man's chambray shirt at a table across from us piped up, "On Marshall, you say?"

I felt like standing up on the bench and announcing through an electronic bullhorn, "YES, FOLKS! I WANT TO WRITE A BOOK ABOUT MARSHALL FRANCE. IS IT OKAY WITH YOU?" But I didn't do that. I took a sip of Coke instead.

"Anna?"

I wasn't sure that I had heard him right. His voice sounded like he was calling a name rather than stating it.

"Yes?"

The voice came up from behind me, and I felt my bowels expand and contract.

With my back to Anna France, I lived in that momentary limbo that precedes a drastic change in your life. I wanted to turn around, but I didn't dare. What did she look like, what was her voice like, her eyes, her mannerisms? The realization that I was the closest I'd ever come to Marshall France suddenly crept up behind me at a town barbecue, and I was paralyzed.

"Can I join you people?" Her voice was on my left shoulder like a leaf. I could easily have reached back and touched her.

" 'Course you can, Anna. These people here have been dying

to meet you, from what they say. They came all the way out here from Connecticut."

I heard Saxony slide over on the bench to make way for her. The two of them mumbled hello. I had to look.

It was the woman who'd been carrying the boxes of hamburger rolls. She had short black, glossy-clean hair cut in a kind of monk's bowl that came down over her ears, although the rather large lobes could still be clearly seen. A small nice nose that peaked up a little at the end, eyes that were almost Oriental and either gray or dusty green. Her lips were full and purplish and I was sure that that was their natural color, although sometimes they got so dark you would have thought that she'd been eating some kind of grape candy. She had on a pair of white carpenter's overalls, a black T-shirt, no jewelry at all, and black rubber flip-flop thongs on her feet. All in all, she was great-looking in a kind of hip, clean, youngish Midwestern housewife way. Where the hell was the Charles Addams character David Louis had referred to? This woman looked like she'd just had the family station wagon washed at the Shell station.

She offered me her hand, and it was soft and cool, not sweaty at all, like mine.

"Are you Thomas Abbey?" She smiled and nodded like she already knew I was. She kept hold of my hand. I'd almost jerked it away when she said my name.

"Yes, uh, hello. How'd you—?"

"David Louis wrote and told me that you were coming."

I frowned at that one. Why had he done that? If she was the Medusa he'd made her out to be, knowing what I was here for would only make her seal off whatever cracks into her father's life I might have been able to find snooping around on my own, incognito. I vowed to send Louis a ten-page hate letter at the first opportunity. No wonder no biographer had ever had any luck with her. With him running interference, she had a twenty-mile head start.

"Do you mind if I sit down? I've been hopping around here so today in this crazy heat. . . ." She shook her head, and her monk's cut flipped back and forth like a tight little grass skirt.

I realized that I hadn't properly introduced her to Saxony.

"Ms. France, this is my colleague, Saxony Gardner." Colleague? When was the last time I'd used that word?

They smiled at each other and shook hands, but I noticed that their shake was short and barely touching.

"You're a writer too, Miss Gardner?"

"No, I do the research and Thomas will do the writing."

Why didn't she say "Thomas *does* the writing," rather than put it in the future tense? It would have sounded so much more professional.

I looked at their two faces and tried not to think that Anna was lovely and Saxony was wholesome. Maybe it was just my momentary anger at Sax.

"You want to write a book about my father? Why is that?"

I thought that by now the best thing to do was give it to her straight and see how she reacted. "Because he's the best there is, Ms. France. Reading his books was the only time in my entire life when I was totally gone into the world of the story. Not that it makes any difference, but I teach English at a boy's prep school, and even all of the so-called 'greats' have never affected me the way *The Land of Laughs* does."

She seemed pleased by the compliment but squinted up her eyes and touched me briefly on the hand. "I have told you a million times not to exaggerate, Mr. Abbey." She smiled like a little girl absolutely delighted with herself. The joke and the smile made me delighted with her too.

What the hell was David Louis talking about when he pictured her as some kind of shrewy weirdo who vamped around in black dresses with a candle in her hand? She was pretty and funny and wore Dee-Cee overalls, and from what I'd seen so far, everyone in town knew and liked her.

"It's true, Miss France." Saxony said it so ardently that we all stopped and looked at her.

"Did David tell you, though, how I felt about a biography of my father?"

Saxony spoke. "He said that you were very much against one being written."

"No, that is not quite true. I've been against it because the people who have wanted to write about him have come out here to our town for all of the wrong reasons. They would all like to become the authority on Marshall France. But when you talk to them, it is easy to see that they aren't interested in what kind of man he was. To them he is just a literary figure."

A kind of low-level bitterness moved in over her voice like a cloud bank. She was facing Saxony, so I only saw her in profile. Her chin was angular and sharp. When she spoke, her white teeth came out from under those dark, heavy lips in sharp contrast, but then they went back into hiding as soon as she stopped. She had long sparse eyelashes that looked recently curled. Her neck was long and white and incredibly vulnerable and held the only wrinkles on her face. I guessed that she was either in her forties or late thirties, but everything about her looked firm and healthy, and I could picture her living to a very old age. Unless she had the same weak heart as her father.

She turned to me and started playing with the blue plastic fork they'd given me for my spareribs. "If you had known my father, Mr. Abbey, you would understand why I'm so sensitive about this. He was a very private person. The only real friends he had outside of my mother and Mrs. Lee were Dan"—she smiled and nodded up toward the grocer; he shrugged and looked modestly at his spatula—"and only a few others in town. Everybody knew him and liked him, but he hated being in the public eye and worked very hard to avoid it."

Dan spoke, but only to Anna, not any of us. "The thing he liked to do best was come into my store and sit behind the butcher counter with me on those little wood-stump stools that I keep back there, you know? Once in a while he'd work at the cash register if one of my regular people didn't come in."

What a great beginning for my biography! Open it with France working at the cash register of Dan's store in Galen. . . . Even if the possibility of the book was gone, it was a joy to be sitting here with these people who had been so much a part of his life. I envied all of them incredibly.

"And I could tell when he was back there with ya, Dan. There'd never be no service up front!"

Dan scratched his head and winked at us. There was a thought in my mind that wouldn't disappear. Here was this nice little fat guy, a grocer, who'd probably spent what amounted to years in the company of my hero. What could they have talked about? Baseball? Women? Who got drunk at the firehouse last night? It was an obnoxious and condescending attitude to have, but why couldn't I have switched places with him for even one of those afternoons behind the butcher counter? One afternoon shooting the bull with Marshall France and maybe talking about books and fantasy . . . about the characters in his books.

"Hey, now, Marshall, how did you ever come up with [fill in the blank]?"

He would lean back against a couple of legs of lamb and say something like, "I knew this sword swallower when I was a kid. . . ."

Then we'd turn on the radio and listen to the ball game in that sleepy and calm way that men get when they're bullshitting and looking off into space. We'd talk about Stan Musial's batting average or Fred's new tractor. . . .

I was off in my dream world chatting with France when I heard Saxony say "something-something-something Stephen Abbey." That brought me around, and when my eyes locked back into the scene, Mrs. Fletcher was staring at me with her mouth wide open.

"Your father was Stephen Abbey?"

I shrugged and wondered why the hell Saxony had let that cat out of the bag. Oh, we were going to have a lovely talk later on.

The soft chain-saw whine of a crying baby cut through the air and covered the halt in conversation.

"The man's father was Stephen Abbey."

That did it. Eyes came up, hamburgers went down, the baby stopped crying. I looked at Saxony with instant death in my eyes. Her face fell and she looked away. She tried to get out of it by saying to Anna that since we both had famous fathers, we probably had quite a bit in common.

"If that's true, then my father wasn't in the same league as Mr. Abbey's." Anna looked at me while she said this. Her eyes moved freely over my face. I half-liked, half-didn't-like the inspection.

"Then it is true? Your father was Stephen Abbey?"

I picked up a cold sparerib and took a bite. I wanted to play down my answer as much as possible, so I thought that a mumble through a mouthful of meat would be a good place to start.

"Yes." Chomp chomp. "Yes, he was." I looked hypnotically at the rib and my greasy fingers. Chewing was easy, swallowing wasn't. I *ulked* it down with half a can of Coke.

"Do you remember when me and your father took you to see *The Beginners,* Anna?"

"You did?"

"What do you mean, 'You did?' Of course we did. We went over to that theater in Hermann and you had to go to the bathroom the whole time."

"What was it like, Mr. Abbey?"

"You tell *me,* Ms. France." I gave a two-second nasty-sly smile that she picked up and shot back at me.

"Two people with famous fathers right at the table with us, Dan." Mrs. Fletcher clapped her hands, then, laying them flat on the table, rubbed them back and forth as if sanding it.

"Anna, you gotta get me more rolls again!"

She stood straight up, looked down the front of her overalls, and brushed off some crumbs. "Why don't we talk about this some more, okay? Would you two like to come over to my house for dinner tonight? Around seven-thirty? Eddie told you the address and how to get there, didn't he?"

I was stunned. We all shook hands and she went off. Dinner tonight at Marshall France's house? Eddie? The hippie kid we'd given the ride to? There was no way he could have gotten to that barbecue before we did.

———

We drove Mrs. Fletcher over to her house, which was on the other side of town. It was great. To get there you went up a flagstone walk that cut through a garden of six-foot-high sunflowers, chestnut-size pumpkins, watermelons, and tomato vines. According to her, the only kind of garden she could see was one that you ate. She didn't hold with roses and honeysuckle, no matter how good they smelled.

You climbed four broad wooden steps to the kind of shaded porch you dream of drinking iced tea on in the middle of August. Real Norman Rockwell stuff. There was a white hammock big enough for ten people, two white rocking chairs with green cushions on the seats, and an all-white dog that looked like a baby pig.

"Now, that there's Nails. He's a bull terrier, if you don't know the breed."

"Nails?"

"Yeah—doesn't his head look like one of those wedging nails? Marshall France gave him that name."

I've never been crazy for either dogs or cats, but one look at Nails and it was love at first sight. He was so ugly, so short and tight-skinned—like a sausage about to burst its casing. Eyes on either side of his head like a lizard's.

"Does he bite?"

"Nails? Lord, no. Nails, come here, boy."

He got up and stretched, and his skin got even tighter. He walked stiff-leggedly over to us and lay right down again as if the effort to get there had done him in.

"They raise these dogs in England for fighting. Put 'em in a pen or a pit together and let them tear each other up. People do crazy things, hah, Nails?"

The dog's face was expressionless, although his eyes were following everything. Little brown coal eyes stuck deep into a white snowman's face.

"Go ahead and pet him, Tom. He likes people."

I reached out and hesitantly tapped him twice on the head as if he were a bell at the front desk of a hotel. He moved his noggin up to my hand and pushed into it. I scratched him behind an ear.

I got such a kick out of that that I put my bag down and sat down next to him on the porch. He got up, climbed halfway into my lap, and plopped down again. Saxony handed me her wicker basket and went back down the steps into the garden to look at the tomato vines.

"Why don't you two stay out here for a couple of minutes while I go in and straighten things up?" She moved across the porch and went inside. Nails raised his head but decided to stay in my lap.

After Anna had left us at the barbecue, I told Mrs. Fletcher that we'd like to take her "downstairs" for a few days, and that if things worked out we'd rent it from her by the week. She agreed and told us again that she didn't mind our not being married. I gave her fourteen dollars in advance.

Next to her house was a huge yellow, turn-of-the-century icehouse. It was both ominous and pleasing to look at. Solid and unmoving, yet so out-of-place even in a sleepy little town like Galen, where I was sure you could still get some kind of candy for a penny. The old lady said that they had been using it for storage right up until a few years before, when a couple of rafters rotted through and fell, killing two workmen from town. A "bunch of fags" from St. Louis came down to look at it to see if it would be possible to convert it into an antique shop, but the people in Galen let them know that they didn't want them there or their icehouse converted, thank you very much.

As far as my feelings toward Saxony went, I was so buzzed out by the things that had happened that I didn't think about asking her why she'd revealed so much. But while I sat there petting Nails and looking at the icehouse, I made an assessment of what had been accomplished, and I had to admit that we'd gotten a hell of a lot further in one afternoon in Galen than I'd have ever thought possible. We'd arrived, found a place to stay, met some of the townspeople *and* Anna France in one swoop, and—wonder of wonders— were going to her house for dinner that night. So how wrong had Saxony been? Or was it all luck that had landed us so firmly on our feet in the Land of France?

4

"That's a picture of my husband, Joe. I hope you two don't mind pictures of the dead around you. I'll take it down if you want me to."

Mrs. Fletcher had her hands on her hips and was squinting scornfully at Joe. He looked like Larry of the Three Stooges. I could easily imagine what their life together had been like.

"This was his study, see, when he was alive. That's why I got his picture in here. There's his little TV set, his radio, the desk where he wrote all his policies and letters. . . ." She swept across the room and pointed out his TV, radio, desk. There were diplomas and certificates on the walls, photographs of him holding up a big fish, touching his son's shoulder at the boy's graduation, being made an Elk. There was a green waist-high bookcase against one green wall which was filled with copies of *The Reader's Digest, Popular Mechanics, Boy's Life,* and a few books. One of the certificates on the wall thanked him for being a scoutmaster in 1961. A circular red-and-green rug covered most of the floor, but Nails lay down near me on the exposed part of the dark wood as soon as we entered the room. He and I were getting along like old pals. There was another comfortable-looking rocking chair by the window. Standing there, I could easily see being very content in a room like that. The bay window looked out on the still-sunlit vegetable garden in front.

There were three other rooms besides the study. A bedroom where everything was white as a glacier and smelled like lavender, a parlor with giant old Victorian furniture that hulked everywhere and would probably make me depressed sometime, and a combined kitchen-dining room that was big enough to hold the Democratic Convention. For thirty-five dollars a week, I wondered if they had any openings in English at Galen High School. Move in here with Saxony, get my Missouri teaching certificate, and teach days at the school, research and write the book at night if things finally did work out with Anna. . . . Nails put his head on my foot and brought me back down to earth.

I realized that while dreaming, I had been staring at the bookcase. Suddenly I saw what it was I was staring at, and I hotfooted it over there and started reaching for the book before I arrived.

"Saxony! *The Night Races into Anna.* Look at this!" I had the book and thumbed through it, back to front. "Hey, hey, will you look at this! It has three more chapters than your edition, Sax!"

That brought her over. She snatched it out of my hand.

"You're right, but I don't understand." She turned to ask Mrs. Fletcher, but the old woman was gone. We looked at each other and then I looked out the window, which was just over Sax's shoulder. Dwarfed by the nodding and swaying yellow-and-black sunflowers, our new landlady moved across the garden. She was looking toward the window, toward us.

Saxony sat on the high white bed and kicked off her loafers. "Do you mind if I read it first? I won't be long."

"No, go ahead. I want to take a shower."

But there was no shower. Only one of those seven-or eight-foot-long bathtubs with white lion claws holding white balls for legs. I didn't mind a good soothing soak in tepid water—in fact, after everything that had happened today, it sounded good. There was even a brand-new chunky bar of Ivory soap in the metal tray and a thick purple towel and washcloth slung over the side of the tub.

I was soaping my head and singing a Randy Newman song when she came in. She had the book in her hand and, without saying anything, sat down on the top of the white wicker clothes hamper.

"Are you okay, Sax?"

"Yes. I just didn't feel like reading. I thought I did. Are you mad at me?"

"No. Yes. Yes, I guess I was, back there, before, but everything's worked out so well that I can't be mad any longer."

"Was it because I mentioned your father?"

"Partly. Partly that, and then when you told them about the biography."

She got off the hamper and walked to the sink. She looked at herself in the medicine-chest mirror.

"I thought so. Are you excited about going to this dinner with her?"

She spoke in a monotone that I wasn't used to. She normally had a voice for every mood, and it was easy to tell how she was feeling by the way she spoke. Since she came into the bathroom, though, she'd sounded like a talking computer.

"Of course I'm excited! Do you know that if she quote accepts us unquote, we'll be halfway there?"

"Yes, I know. What do you think of the town?"

"Saxony, will you please tell me what's wrong with you? You sound like *The Night of the Living Dead*. What are you, half asleep? You don't seem to realize that we have been invited to dinner tonight by Anna France, as in *the* Anna France." I guess I was angry and my voice showed it. I caught her eye in the mirror, and she gave me a weak smile. Then she turned around and looked at me and I felt like some sort of dope there in the bathtub with my knees up under my chin and a head full of shampoo suds.

"I know." She kept looking at me and then said it again. "I know." She moved over to the hamper, picked up the book, and left the room.

"What the hell was *that* supposed to mean?" I asked the tub. The soap squiggled out of my hand and fell into the water with a plop.

I finished my bath only half-conscious of what I was doing, because I was trying to figure out what was going on. But when I was done and had dripped my way back into the bedroom, she was up and at 'em again, so I decided to keep quiet.

We wanted to walk to the France house. Mrs. Fletcher was out on the front porch in one of the rocking chairs, shucking corn. Nails was lying next to her, guarding but not eating a big pink-and-white bone. She gave us careful walking directions to Anna's, which turned out to be about six blocks away. Going down the porch steps, I was sure that she was watching our every move, but I didn't turn around to check. It would have been too obvious, and I didn't want to be on bad terms with her. If we decided to stay awhile, her house was too nice and comfortable (and cheap) to make me want to throw it away simply because she was odd and nosy.

The sun was setting on the top of the icehouse, but it looked pale compared to the deep lemon of the building. There were the ghosts of once-black letters on the side of the place that we hadn't seen when we first passed it.

"Hey, will you look at that? 'Fletcher and Family.' I wonder why she didn't tell us before that she owned it?"

"Maybe she was embarrassed to admit to her wealth?" Sax looked at me and squinched up her eyes against the sun.

"What wealth? She rents rooms in her house and owns a closed-up icehouse? I think she didn't want to 'fess up to owning a place where people got killed because of owner neglect."

That idea held the floor for a few silent minutes of walking.

It was the beginning of the evening, and the sky had cleared to cobalt blue with a streak of sharp white airplane exhaust vapor through its center. A lawnmower whined somewhere and the air smelled of cut grass, and of oil and gasoline when we passed Bert Keener's Exxon Station. A guy was sitting in front of the office in a red aluminum lawn chair with a can of beer propped on a pile of old worn tires nearby. Another Norman Rockwell painting, this one titled "Bert's Exxon Station in June." A new white Volkswagen pulled into the station and rolled up to the pumps. The man inside rolled down his window and stuck his head out.

"Get your ass over here, Larry. You gettin' paid to drink beer or what?"

Larry, in the lawn chair, made a face and looked at us before he got up. "These guys that buy these little Kraut cars all get to thinking that they're Hitler, you know?"

We walked past a closed grocery store with particolored stickers all over the windows announcing the weekly specials. I noticed that the prices were cheaper than in Connecticut.

A drive-in hamburger joint was next, with a lot of bright orange everywhere and rock music piped out over its dirt parking lot via a speaker on the roof of the squat, square building. A late-sixties Chevrolet was the only car there, and I noticed that everyone in it was eating big soft-ice-cream cones.

Without knowing it, we had arrived at Anna's street. My stomach, which had been pretty calm until then, said "contact" to the rest of my system, and within milliseconds I was jumpy and scared.

"Thomas . . ."

"Come on, Sax, let's just go. Let's get it over with." I was revving up and knew that I had to keep going or else my knees would start shaking and I'd become tongue-tied.

"Thomas . . ."

"Come *on!*" I took her limp hand from the crook of my elbow and dragged her down the street.

Everyone must have been either eating dinner or out because no one was in sight as we walked toward Anna's. It was almost a little eerie. The houses were mostly white Midwest-solid. Picket fences and aluminum siding and some metal statues on the lawn. Mailboxes with names like Calder and Schreiner, and my favorite— "The Bob and Leona Burns Castle." I could imagine Christmas-tree lights on these places in December. Christmas-tree lights hung over the front doors, and big light-up Santa Clauses on the roofs.

And then there it was. It wasn't hard to make out the house, because I had looked at the magazine picture enough times. Huge, brown, Victorian, full of intricate gingerbread woodwork, and on closer view, small stained-glass windows. Hedges in front that were full and carefully trimmed. Even though it was a kind of dark cocoa brown, the house looked freshly painted.

My grandmother lived in a house like that. She lived to be ninety-four in Iowa and refused to see any of her son's movies. When she died and they went through her belongings, they found eleven leather scrapbooks on his career that went back to his first film. She had wanted him to be a veterinarian. She kept lots of animals in and around her big farmhouse, including a donkey and a goat. Whenever we visited her, the donkey always bit me and then laughed.

". . . go?"

Saxony was in the crook of my arm again and peering at me.

"Excuse me?"

Her expression was tight and flushed, and I assumed that she was as nervous about this as I was.

"Don't you think we should go? I mean, I think it's time, isn't it?"

I looked at my watch without really seeing it, and nodded.

We crossed the street and went up the walk to the house. A screen door, a natural-wood mailbox with just the name in white block letters (what incredible mail must have been in there at one time!), and a black doorbell that was as big as a checker. I pressed it and a deep chiming went off in the back of the house. A dog barked and then abruptly stopped. I looked at the floor and saw a matching brown mat that said "GO AWAY!" I nudged Saxony and pointed to it.

"Do you think she means us?"

That's all I needed. I had thought the mat was a funny idea, and then she had to make it into something else to worry about. What if Anna really didn't want us—

"Hi. Come in. I'd better not shake hands with you. I'm a little greasy from the chicken."

"Hey, look, it's Nails!"

It was. A white bull terrier had shoved its head between Anna's knees and was checking us out with those hilariously tight, slanty eyes.

Anna closed her legs tighter and held its head between them like a punishment stock. The dog didn't move, but I could see its tail wagging behind Anna.

"No, this one is Petals; she's Nails's girlfriend." Anna let her go and Petals came right over to say hello. She was as friendly as the other one. I had never seen bull terriers before today, and then the two of them within a few hours. But it made sense, with Nails just down the street.

A wide hallway led straight to a flight of stairs. Halfway up them, above the landing, two big stained-glass windows beamed Technicolor light across some of the lower steps and the last part of the hall. The walls were white. On the left as you walked in was a big gold fish-eye mirror next to a bentwood hat rack with two slouchy men's hats on them. *His* hats? Had Marshall France actually worn them? To the right of the rack were eighteenth- and nineteenth-century ascension balloon and zeppelin prints in expensive modern silver frames. Next to them, and a big surprise to me because I'd pictured France as a modest man, were framed mock-ups of the Van Walt covers to all of his books. I didn't want to appear too snoopy, so I stopped peeking at the pictures. Maybe later, when we were all more comfortable with each other (if there *was* going to be a later after tonight). I began playing with Petals, who kept jumping up and down by herself in the middle of the hallway. Then she started jumping on me.

"These dogs are incredible. I never really knew of them before today, but now I think I want one!"

"You'll see a lot of them around here. We're a little bull-terrier enclave. They were the only dogs my father ever liked. If she gets to be too much for you, just push her away. They are the world's greatest dogs, but all of them have a tendency to get a little crazy sometimes. Come on, let's go into the living room."

I wondered what she was like in bed but suppressed the thought, since it seemed sacrilegious to do it with the daughter of France. The hell with it—she was sexy and had a great deep voice and she wore the kind of jeans-and-T-shirt clothes that showed she still had a very nice, full figure. Walking into the living room, I pictured her in a Paris atelier living with a crazy Russian painter whose eyes glowed like Rasputin's and who took her fifty times a day in between painting nude portraits of her and drinking absinthe.

In the incredible France living room my first amazed inventory took in: a hand-carved olive-wood Pinocchio with moving arms and legs, six-foot-tall department store mannequin from the 1920's that was painted silver and looked like Jean Harlow with her hair swept up on her head, Navaho rug. Hand puppets and marionettes. *Masks!*

(Mostly Japanese, South American, and African on first glance.) Peacock feathers stuck in an earthenware pitcher. Japanese prints (Hokusai and Hiroshige). A shelf full of old alarm clocks with painted faces, metal banks, and tin toys. Old leather-bound books. Three square wood boxes from a Shanghai tea exporter with yellow, red, and black flowers and fans and women and sampans. A stereo somewhere was playing the score to *Cabaret*. A ceiling fan with wooden blades hung unmoving.

We stood in the doorway and gasped. He wrote the books, and this was his living room, and it all made perfect sense.

"People either love this room when they first come in or they are horrified." Anna pushed between us and went in. We stayed frozen in the doorway, looking. "My mother was very conservative. She liked antimacassars and doilies and tea cozies. All of her things are boxed up in the attic now, because as soon as she died, Father and I transformed this room. We did it over into what we'd envisioned for years. Even when I was very young, I liked the same things that he did."

"But it's great! When I think of all the books and the characters, and then all of this . . ." I spread both arms toward the room. "It's all him. It's completely Marshall France."

She liked that. She stood in the middle of the room, beaming, and told us to come in and sit down. I say "told" because whatever she said sounded either like an order or a definitive statement. She was not an insecure person.

Saxony, however, went right over to a hand puppet that was hanging from a hook on the wall.

"May I try it?"

I didn't think that that was the sort of thing to ask right after you'd come in, but Anna said that it was okay.

Sax reached for it, then stopped and stepped back. "It's a Klee!"

Anna nodded but didn't say anything. She looked at me and raised her eyebrows.

"But it's a Paul Klee!" Saxony looked from the puppet, to Anna, to me, totally flabbergasted. "How did you . . . ?"

"You're very good, Miss Gardner. Not many people know how rare that is."

"She's a puppeteer," I said, trying to get into the act.

"But it's a Klee!"

I wondered if she was trying to imitate a parrot. She took it off the wall and handled it like the Holy Grail. She started talking, but it was so quietly that it was either to herself or to the puppet.

"Sax, what are you saying?"

She looked up. "Paul Klee made fifty of these for his son, Felix. But twenty of the originals were destroyed when the town of Dessau was bombed during the war. The rest of them are supposed to be at a museum in Switzerland."

"Yes, they are in Bern. But Father and Klee had a great correspondence going between them for years. Klee wrote first to tell him how much he liked *The Green Dog's Sorrow*. When Father later told him about his collection, Klee sent him that one."

To me the puppet looked like something from a fourth-grade arts-and-crafts class.

Sax sank into a nearby leather chair and went on communing with the Klee. I looked at Anna and smiled, and Anna looked at me and smiled. For two seconds it was as if Saxony wasn't in the room with us. For two seconds I felt how easy and nice it would be to be Anna's lover. The feeling passed, but its echoes didn't.

"So who are you, Mr. Abbey? Besides Stephen Abbey's son."

"Who *am* I?"

"Yes, who are you? Where are you coming from now, what do you do . . . ?"

"Oh, I see. Well, I've been teaching at a prep school in Connecticut . . ."

"Teaching? You mean that you are not an actor?"

I took one of my deep breaths and crossed one leg over the other. A bit of hairy ankle showed between the cuff and the top of my gray sock, so I covered it with my hand. I tried to laugh off her question/statement. "Ha, ha, no, one actor in the family was enough."

"Yes, *genug.* I feel the same way. I could never be a writer."

She looked at me calmly. Again, that kind of unspoken, just-between-us intimacy was there. Or was I fantasizing? I pulled on my shoelace and undid the bow. I was tying it again when she spoke.

"Which of Father's was your favorite book?"

"The Land of Laughs."

"Why?" She picked an oblong glass paperweight off an end table and rolled it around in her hands.

"Because no one else ever got that close to my world." I un-crossed my leg and leaned forward, elbows on knees. "Reading a book, for me at least, is like traveling in someone else's world. If it's a good book, then you feel comfortable and yet anxious to see what's going to happen to you there, what'll be around the next corner. But if it's a lousy book, then it's like going through Secau-cus, New Jersey—it smells and you wish you weren't there, but since you've started the trip, you roll up the windows and breathe through your mouth until you're done."

She laughed and bent down to pet Petals, who was resting her chunky head on Anna's foot. "You mean that you finish every book that you start?"

"Yes, it's this terrible habit that I have. Even if it's the worst thing that was ever written, once I get started with it, then I'm hooked until I find out what happens."

"That is very interesting, because my father was the same way. As soon as he picked up anything—even the phone book—he would read it until the bitter end."

"Didn't they make a great movie out of that?"

"Out of what?"

"The phone book." I knew it was a terrible joke as soon as I said it, but Anna didn't even attempt a smile. I wondered if she judged future biographers on their sense of humor.

"Excuse me for a minute, will you? I have to go look at the dinner." She left the room to Saxony and me. Petals looked up and wagged her tail but stayed where she was on the floor. Naturally I jumped up and poked around. France or someone in the house liked biographies and autobiographies, because there were so many of them around, the pages bent over and whole sections marked off. It was a strange assortment, too—Richard Halliburton's *The Magic Carpet*, the notebooks of Max Frisch (in German), Aleister Crowley, Gurdjieff's *Meetings with Remarkable Men,* a French priest who fought for the underground in WW II, *Mein Kampf* (in German), the notebooks of Leonardo da Vinci, *Three on a Toothbrush* by Jack Paar.

A cardboard shoebox with Buster Brown on the side contained a collection of old postcards. When I thumbed through them, I noticed that many were of European train stations. I flipped one of the Vienna Westbahnhof over and got the shivers when I looked at the signature printed across the bottom—"Isaac." The date on it was 1933. I couldn't read the German, but I was sorely tempted to steal the card and send it to David Louis in New York. "Dear Mr. Louis: I thought you might like to see a postcard to Marshall France from his nonexistent brother, Isaac."

"Dinner is ready! Come and eat everything before it gets cold."

I didn't realize how hungry I was until we walked in and saw big steaming platters of fried chicken, peas, and mashed potatoes.

"Because this is your first time here, I thought that I would make you my father's favorite meal. When he was alive he was very mad if this wasn't made for him at least once a week. If it had been his choice, we would have had it every day. Please, sit down."

It was a small oval table with three straw place mats. I sat on Anna's right, Saxony on her left. The food smells were driving me crazy. Anna served, loading down my plate with two fat legs, a pile of peas, and a heavy yellow cloud of mashed potatoes. I was on the verge of licking my lips and diving right into them when I picked up my knife and fork and looked at them.

"Yipes!"

Anna looked over, and seeing what was happening, smiled. "I was waiting to see how long it would take you to react. Aren't they crazy? They were Father's too. He had a silversmith in New York make them."

My fork was a silver clown. His head was bent back and the tines of the fork came out of his open mouth. My knife was a long-muscled arm holding a kind of paddle. Not Ping-Pong or anything like that; more sinister-looking—the sort of thing they smack kids with in English public schools. Saxony held hers up to the light, and they were completely different. Her fork was a witch riding a broom. The tines were the brush part, the shaft the broomstick.

"They're incredible!"

"There are enough for six place settings. I'll show you the others after dinner."

As soon as I started eating, I knew it was going to be a long, long meal. I wondered why I was damned to eat horrible food from the hands of interesting women.

Halfway through the unspeakable coffee, she put her napkin down and started talking about France. Now and then she'd pick up her fork and play with it, running it through her fingers as if practicing to be a magician. She watched her hands most of the time, although once in a while she would pause and look at one of us to see, by our expressions, if we understood what she was talking about.

"My father loved living in Galen. His parents sent him to America before the war because they were Jews and they were afraid of Hitler long before most people. Father's brother, Isaac, was killed in one of the concentration camps."

"David Louis told me that your father was an only child."

"Do you speak German, Mr. Abbey? No? Well, there is a little German saying that suits David Louis perfectly. *'Dreck mit zwei augen.'* Do you understand that? 'Garbage with two eyes.' Some people would translate it *'Shit* with two eyes,' but I am feeling charitable tonight." She ran the edge of her fork back and forth over the edge of the table several times. Until then her tone had been calm and amiable, but the "shit" stopped it short. I didn't see her as a woman who cursed much. What came to mind was a picture of Louis in his office, sitting on the canvas couch telling me that bizarre story about Anna and her cats hissing at him with hatred. Her cats. There were no cats. I thought it would be a harmless enough question to ask to clear the air of the "shit" that was still hanging there.

"Don't you have cats?"

"Cats? No, never! I hate cats."

"Did your father have any?"

"No. He hated most animals. Bull terriers were the only kind of furry beasts that he could stand."

"Really? But then how did he know animals so well for his books?"

"Would you like some more coffee?"

I shook my head so hard it almost fell off. She didn't offer Saxony more tea. I was beginning to think that she wasn't crazy for Sax. But was it because of Saxony's personality or because she was another woman? Competing for me? Afraid not. Sometimes you meet a person and as soon as you touch hands with her there's instant dislike, or vice versa. She can be brilliant or beautiful or sexy but you *don't like* her. If that was the case here, then it was going to make things very difficult. I decided not to think about it until Anna agreed to let us do the biography.

We stood up, and Saxony led the way into the other room. It was dark now except for whatever came through the windows from the street. It caught edges and half-shapes of the masks, mannequin, and other things, and was, uh, spooky, to say the least. Anna was just in front of me with her hand on the light switch, but she didn't click it on.

"Father loved the room like this. I used to catch him standing here in the doorway, looking at all of his things in this cat light."

" 'Cat light,' eh? *Green Dog's Sorrow*, eh?"

"That's right. You do know your France, don't you?" She turned on the light, and the things that went bump in the night went back to being things, thank God. I do not like: horror movies, horror stories, nightmares, black things. I teach Poe only because I'm told to by my department chairman, and it takes me two weeks to get over "The Telltale Heart" every time I read it. Yes, I like masks and things that are different and fantastic, but enjoying the almost-real and fearing the monstrous are very different things. Remember, please, that I'm a coward.

Saxony sat on the couch and crossed her legs. Petals put a paw up next to her and then looked at Anna for couch approval. When nothing was said, she took it as a "yes" and worked her way up, one slow leg at a time.

"When he arrived in New York, he went to work for an undertaker. Oh, I'm sorry—would either of you like a brandy or drink of some kind? Some Kahlúa or Tia Maria? I've got everything over there."

We both said no, and she sank back down into her chair.

"All of this is a big secret, though. Very few people know about my father's first job."

I looked at Saxony, but Saxony looked at Anna. Then she spoke for the first time since dinner. "How long did he work for this undertaker?"

It was a loaded question, because Lucente himself had told me the answer when I saw him. Nine months.

"Two years." She had the paperweight in her hands again and was rolling it around and around.

I looked at Saxony, but Saxony looked at Anna.

"What did he do for him?"

"Do?" Anna shrugged and smiled at me as if the question wasn't worth answering and wasn't my friend dumb for asking it.

"Well, he didn't do any normal things because he got sick every time he saw one of the bodies. Really! He said that whenever they called him into the rooms where they did their work, he would take one look and run out for the bathroom! Poor Father, he was never meant to take care of the dead. No, do you know what he did? He cooked. He took care of the kitchen and cleaning the place."

"He never did any work for the man? Not even after he'd been there awhile?"

She smiled warmly at me and shook her head. "*Never*. My father had trouble looking at an animal killed in the road. But you know, I'll tell you a funny story for your biography, Mr. Abbey. Once in a while he would go with them to drive the truck when they picked up a body. This time they got a call to pick up a man whose apartment was on the sixth floor of a walk-up building. There was no elevator. When they got up there they opened the door and the body turned out to be three hundred pounds!"

"Three hundred? What did they use to get him out of there—a forklift?" Despite the fact that she was probably lying about this too, the idea fascinated me.

She liked my forklift. She snorted and actually slapped her knee. "No, not quite. What they did was send Father downstairs to make sure that no one was on the stairs or coming into the building. Then when he called out to them that it was all clear, he started back up. Suddenly he heard this big *bump*. Then *bump bump*. He looked up through the stairwell and saw them rolling the body down the stairs with the toes of their shoes. Can you imagine that? Can you imagine opening the door to that apartment building and seeing a three-hundred-pound body come bumping down toward you?"

"You can't be serious."

She held up the three middle fingers of her right hand, palm-out, and shook her head. "Girl scout's honor."

"They *rolled* him down the stairs? Down *six flights* of stairs?"

"Exactly."

"Well, what'd they do when they got him there? Wasn't he all damaged and everything?"

"Yes, of course, but then they took him back to the funeral parlor and fixed him with makeup and those things they use. The next day at the funeral, Father said he looked as good as new."

Baloney or not, it was a good story, and I could detect a bit of her father's narrative flair.

She put the paperweight back down on the side table. "Would you like to see his study? I think you might be interested."

"Ms. France, you don't *know* how much I'd like to see his study!" I was already halfway out of my chair.

She led the way, Petals second, Saxony, then me. Always the gentleman.

When I was a boy I used to sit with my brother and sister at the top of our red-carpeted staircase and watch my parents get ready to go out for the evening. We would be in our pajamas and fuzzy brown Roy Rogers slippers and the hall light would touch just the tips of our warm toes. The parents were too far away for us to hear what they were saying to each other, but we were cozy and sleepy and they looked so sleek and beautiful. That was about the only time that I ever saw my father as anything more than just "my pop," who wasn't there most of the time and tried to love us too much when he was. I hadn't thought about that in years—one of those little Proustian memories that are so easy to forget but so cherished when you happen across them again. Hiking up the staircase to France's office brought it all back so clearly that I had a momentary urge to sit down on the steps and feel what it was like again. I wondered if Anna had ever done the same thing with her parents.

A light went on before I got to the top. Just as I arrived, I caught sight of the three of them disappearing around a dark corner.

A voice called out, "Are you still there?"

I quickened my step and called back, "Yes, yes, I'm right behind you."

The floor was a blond, bare wood that had been carefully stripped and sealed and reminded me of houses in Scandinavia. No tables or chairs or sideboards here, no pictures on the walls. The house seemed to have separate upstairs and downstairs personalities: pure up, cluttered and crazy down. I turned the corner and saw light spilling out of a narrow doorway. No sound of voices or bodies moving around. I came up to it and walked through and was instantly disappointed. There was literally nothing in the room but a large oak rolltop desk and a swivel chair tucked into the leg hole. There was a green blotter on the desk and an old orange Parker "Lucky Curve" fountain pen. Nothing else.

"It's so empty."

"Yes, it's very different from the living room. Father said that anything distracted him when he worked, so this is the way he wanted his room." A phone that turned out to be behind the door rang, and she excused herself to answer it. Sax went up to the desk and ran her hand over the top of it.

"*Blinded?* What do you mean, blinded? It's impossible. How did it happen?"

I looked at Saxony and knew that both of us were eavesdropping. Anna's face was tight, and she looked at the floor. She looked more angry than upset.

"All right, all right. Stay there and I'll come as soon as I can. What? No, *stay there*." She hung up and ran her hand across her forehead. "I'm sorry, but one of my friends was just hurt in an accident. I have to go to the hospital right away. I'll drop you at your house."

"I'm sorry. Is there anything we can do? Really, we'll be glad to."

She shook her head and looked out the window. "No. No, there's nothing." She turned out the light, and without waiting for us, hurried down the hall toward the stairs.

5

"Are you awake?" She touched me very lightly on the shoulder with one finger.

I rolled over in bed so that I was facing her. The light from the full moon came in through the window and cut long white patches across her hair and pale blue nightgown. Even half-asleep, the color reminded me of looking in France's living room before Anna had turned on the lights.

"Awake? Sax, I'm not only awake, I'm—"

"Please don't be funny with me, Thomas. I don't want you to be funny now, okay? Please?"

I couldn't see her face clearly, but I knew from the tone of her voice what it would look like. Eyes impassive, but her lips would be turned down at the corners, and after a while she would start to blink a lot. It was her silent sign that she wanted to be touched and held. As soon as you did, she clutched you twice as hard, and it made you sad and it made you wonder if you had the strength at the moment for both of you—which was what she was demanding.

"Are you okay, babe?" I cupped the back of her head and felt the clean smoothness of her hair.

"Yes, but just don't talk now. Hold me, please, and don't talk."

It had already happened before. Some nights she would get small and scared, convinced that anything good in her life was about to disappear and she wouldn't be able to stop it. I called it her "night fears." She was the first to admit that they were stupid and that it was pure masochism on her part, but she couldn't help it. She said the worst part was that they'd come most often when she was either completely happy or in-the-pits sad and depressed.

While I held her, I wondered if I'd done something to bring them on this time. I went through a two-second instant replay of the night at Anna's house. Uh-oh; the cold shoulder from Anna. The lousy food. No definite answer on the biography. The casual flirting between Anna and me. What a schmuck I was. I hugged Saxony to me and kept kissing the top of her head. The rubbing and touching and guilt made me want her very much. I rolled her gently onto her back and slid her nightgown up.

6

The next morning the sun sneaked into the room and on across the bed about seven o'clock. It woke me with its heat on my face. I hate to get up early when it's not necessary, so I scrooched around and tried to find a shady spot. But Saxony had Scotch-taped herself to me during the night, so moving was hard.

To top it all off, the door creaked open, Nails trotted in, and leaped up onto the bed. I felt like the three of us were on a life raft in the middle of the ocean, because we were all three huddled up together in the middle of the bed, leaning on the nearest body. I haven't mentioned my claustrophobia before, but sealed in between two hot bodies, the sun frying my head, the sheet wrapped around my feet . . . I decided that it was time to get up. I patted Nails on the head and gave him a little push. He growled. I thought that it was just a little morning grouchiness, so I patted him again and pushed him again. He growled louder. We looked at each other over a thin pink wave of blanket, but bull terriers have absolutely no expression on their faces, so you never know what's what with them.

"Nice Nails. Good boy."

"Why is he growling at you? What did you do to him?" Saxony cuddled a little closer, and I could feel her warm breath on my neck.

"I didn't do anything. I just gave him a little push so that I could get up."

"Wow. Do you think that you should do it again?"

"How do I know? How do I know he won't bite me?" I looked over at her, and she blinked.

"No, Thomas, I don't think so. He likes you. Remember yesterday?" She sounded convinced.

"Oh, yeah? Well, today's today, and your arm's not in jeopardy."

"Then do you plan on staying here all morning?" She smiled and rubbed the flat of her palm across her nose. Thank God she'd snapped back from last night. "Tommy is a chick-en . . ."

I looked at Nails and he looked at me. A standoff. The tip of his prune-black nose poked up from behind one of his paws.

"Mrs. Fletch-er!"

"Oh, come on, Thomas, don't do that! What if she's still asleep?"

"Too bad. I ain't gonna get bit. Niiiice Nailsy, good boy! Mrs. Fletch-er!"

We heard footsteps, and a second before she popped her head into the room, Nails jumped off the bed to greet her.

Saxony started laughing and pulled the pillow over her head.

"Yes? Good morning."

"Good morning. Uh, well, Nails was up on the bed and I gave him a little push because I wanted to get up, you see, and, uh, he sort of growled at me. I was afraid that he might mean it."

"Who, Nails? Naah, never. Watch this." He stood next to her but kept looking at us on the bed. She lifted a foot and gave him a little shove sideways. Without looking at her he growled. He also kept wagging his tail.

"What do you two want for breakfast? I decided to throw it in for you on your first day. I bet you haven't done any shopping, have you, Saxony?"

I sat up and pushed my hands through my hair. "You don't have to do that. It's easy for us—"

"I know I don't have to do anything. What would you like? I make good pancakes and sausages. Yeah, why don't you have my pancakes and sausages."

We decided to have pancakes and sausages. She left the room and Nails jumped back up on the bed. He climbed over my legs and settled down halfway across Saxony's stomach.

"Are you okay this morning, Sporty?" I asked.

"Yes. I just get crazy at night sometimes. I start thinking that everything is going to go wrong, or that you'll go away soon . . . things like that. I've been doing it all my life. I think it's just because I'm overtired now. Usually the next morning everything is okay again."

"You've got a little split personality in you, huh?" I pulled a lock of hair away from her eyes.

"Yes, completely. I know what's going on in me when it happens, but there's nothing I can do to stop it." There was a pause, and she took my hand. "Do you think I'm crazy, Thomas? Do you hate me when it happens?"

"Don't be ridiculous, Sax. You know me by now—if I hated you, I would have gotten away from you. Stop thinking that way." I squeezed her hand and stuck out my tongue at her. She pulled the pillow over her head, and Nails tried to shove his head under there with her.

I looked out the window, and the garden was all sunny and moving back and forth in the wind. Bees hovered over some of the plants, and a redbird lit on the porch railing not three feet away.

Early morning in Galen, Missouri. A few cars drove by, and I yawned. Then a little kid passed, licking an ice-cream cone and running his free hand along the top of Mrs. Fletcher's fence. Tom Sawyer with a bright green pistachio cone. I dreamily watched him and wondered how anyone could eat ice cream at eight o'clock in the morning.

Without looking either way, the boy started across the street and was instantly punched into the air by a pickup truck. The truck was moving fast, so he was thrown far beyond the view from our window. When he disappeared, he was still going up.

"Holy shit!" I snatched my pants off a chair and ran for the door. I heard Saxony call, but I didn't stop to explain. It was the second time I'd seen someone hit by a car. Once in New York, and the person landed right on his head. Going down the porch steps two at a time, I thought how unreal these goddamned things looked. One minute a person's there, talking to a friend or eating a green ice-cream cone. The next thing you know you've heard a fast thump and there's a body sailing away through the air.

The driver was out of the truck and stooped over the body. The first thing I saw when I got there was the green ice cream, half-covered with dirt and pebbles and already beginning to melt on the black pavement.

No one else was around. I came up to the man and hesitantly peered over his shoulder. He smelled of sweat and human heat. The boy was on his side on the ground, his legs splayed apart in such a way that he looked as if he'd been stop-framed, running. He was bleeding from the mouth and his eyes were wide open. No, *one* of his eyes was wide open; the other was half-shut and fluttering.

"Is there anything I can do? I'll call an ambulance, okay? I mean, you stay here and I'll go call the ambulance."

The man turned around, and I recognized him from the barbecue. One of the cooks at the grill. One of the big jokers.

"All this is *wrong*. I knew it, though. Yeah, sure, go get that ambulance. I can't tell nothin' yet." His face was pinched and frightened as hell, but the tone of his voice was what surprised me. It was half-angry, half-self-pitying. There was no fear there at all. No remorse either. It had to be shock: horrible events make people act crazy and say mad things. The poor fool was probably realizing that the rest of his life was now shadowed, no matter what happened to the boy. He'd have the guilt of having run over a child to live with for the next fifty years. God, I pitied him.

"Joe Jordan! It wasn't supposed to be you!"

Mrs. Fletcher had come up from behind us and was standing there with a pink dish towel in her hand.

"I know, goddammit! How many things are going to fuck up before we get this straightened out? Did you hear about last night? How many things've there been already, four? Five? No one knows *nothin'* anymore, nothin'!"

"Calm down, Joe. Let's wait and see. You going to call that ambulance, Mr. Abbey? The number's one-two-three-four-five. Just dial the first five numbers. That's the emergency line."

The boy began gurgling and his legs jumped and twitched involuntarily, like a frog touched by an electric prod in a biology experiment. I looked at Jordan, but he was looking at the boy and shaking his head.

"I'm telling you, Goosey, it wasn't supposed to be me with this!"

As I turned to run to the phone, I heard Mrs. Fletcher say, "Just quiet down and wait."

The pavement was hot under my bare feet, and out of the corner of my eye I saw the melting ice-cream cone again. I ran by Saxony standing on the top step of the porch, holding Nails by his thick leather collar.

"Is he dead?"

"Not yet, but he's in bad shape. I've got to call the ambulance."

When it came, a few people were standing around and watching from a distance. A white police car was in the middle of the street with its row of busy blue lights on the roof flashing back and forth.

The short bursts of people's voices from its radio filled the air with a staccato crackle that was both adamant and annoying at the same time.

We watched from the porch while they gently lifted the flaccid body onto a stretcher and slid it into the back of the van. When it was gone, Joe Jordan and the policeman stood in front of our house and talked. Jordan kept running his hand across the lower part of his face, and the cop rested both hands on the front of his wide black belt.

Mrs. Fletcher moved away from a bunch of onlookers and joined the two men. They talked for several minutes, and then Jordan and the policeman drove off together in the patrol car. Mrs. Fletcher stood there and watched them go. After a while she turned around and waved me over to join her. I walked down the steps and across the warm flagstones.

"You saw it all, eh, Tom?"

"Yes, unfortunately. The whole horrible thing."

The sun was high and directly over her shoulder. I had to squint to look at her.

"Was the boy laughing before he got hit?"

"Laughing? I don't know what you mean."

"Laughing. You know, laughing? He was eating that pistachio cone, but was he laughing too?"

She was totally serious. What the hell kind of question was that?

"No, not that I remember."

"You're *sure* about that? You're sure that he wasn't laughing?"

"Yes, I guess so. I saw him right up until he got hit, but I wasn't really paying that much attention. No, I'm positive about that, though. Why is it so important?"

"But he was touching the fence with his hand, right?"

"Yes, he was touching the fence. He was touching the top of it with his free hand."

She looked at me. I felt very confused and uncomfortable. To get out from under those X-ray eyes, I looked around, and everyone was staring at me with that same impassive gaze that had made me feel so squirmy the day before at the barbecue.

An old farmer in a rust-red Corvair, a teenager with a bag of groceries under his arm, a doughy-looking woman with her hair up in hot pink curlers and a cigarette dangling unattractively from her lip. All giving me the gaze. . . .

About an hour later, Mrs. Fletcher and Saxony went off to shop for groceries. They said they wouldn't be back until the early afternoon. I secretly wanted to go along with them, but they didn't ask me, and I've always felt strange inviting myself to things. Anyway, I thought that it would be good for us to be separated for a while. I wanted to work on some notes that I'd had floating around in my head since we'd arrived. First impressions of Galen and all that. I also wanted to start reading some of the literary biographies we had brought along to see how it was supposed to be done.

I changed into a pair of corduroy shorts, T-shirt, and sandals and got another cup of coffee from the kitchen. Nails followed me everywhere, but I was already getting used to that. I had all but decided that no matter what happened with this book, as soon as I got back to Connecticut I was going to buy one of these loony dogs. Maybe I'd even buy one here and have a relative of one of Marshall France's dogs. If I couldn't have a biography, at least I could have a bull terrier.

I sat down on one of the rocking chairs and put the coffee cup on the floor within easy reach. Nails tried a tentative sniff or two at my java, but I gave him a bop on the head and he lay down. I opened the book and began reading. I had gotten through about half a page when the image of the boy lying in the street floated up into my mind and stayed there. I tried to think of Saxony, of Saxony in bed, of what my book had just said about Raymond Chandler, of how nice a day it was, of what it would be like to go to bed with Anna France . . . but the boy in the street refused to leave. I got up and walked over to the porch railing to see if I could make out the spot where he had been hit. To see if there was still blood or any other sign that an hour ago we'd all been out there watching him die.

I remembered that I'd also been sitting on a porch when I heard that my father had been killed. The night before, I'd been on the living-room floor of Amy Fischer's house with Amy Fischer watching him in *Mr. & Mrs. Time*. I was much more interested in undressing Amy than in his performance, which I'd seen countless times. Since Amy's parents weren't there, she let me do whatever I wanted.

The whole time we were at it, I kept hearing his voice behind me, and I even laughed once or twice because it felt strange screwing in front of my father. The gray-white from the television washed in different, changing patterns over our bodies, and when we were done we lay side by side and watched the end of the film. The next morning Amy decided that we should have breakfast out on the porch. We set the table together, and she even brought out her portable radio so that we could listen while we ate. "Massachusetts" by the Bee Gees was playing, and I was slumped down into the hammock when the news bulletin cut through the song and announced that Stephen Abbey's plane had crashed in Nevada and that there were no survivors. I didn't move when the last part of the song came back on. Amy walked out of the house with a frying pan full of scrambled eggs and Canadian bacon. She called me over to eat. She hadn't heard the bulletin yet, and as I said, you end up doing strange things when something horrible has just happened to you. What did I do? I sat down at the table and ate everything on my plate—I even had seconds on the eggs. When I was done I put my fork down beside my empty orange-juice glass and said, "My father was just killed in an airplane crash." Those were the days in prep school when every other word out of your mouth was cynical, so sweet Amy Fischer shook her head at my bad taste at the breakfast table and went on eating.

Whenever I turn on the television and *Mr. & Mrs. Time* is playing, the first thing that comes to mind is that disgusted look on Amy's face and the way she kept eating her yellow scrambled eggs.

It was several seconds before I realized that a car had stopped in front of the house. I couldn't see the driver, but I could see a big white blob of something pressing its nose against the half-open glass of one of the back windows. The car was an old gold-and-white Dodge station wagon like the one *Leave It to Beaver*'s mother used to cart the family around in. I tried to focus on the driver, but the white bull terrier was now hopping back and forth from the front seat to the back, and I assumed that it was Anna and Petals. The driver's door opened and that perky head of black monk's hair emerged. She shaded her eyes and looked toward the house.

"Hi!"

I waved my book at her and felt embarrassed about my shorts and T-shirt. I don't know why, because I've succeeded so well at repressing my childhood self-consciousness that I'm usually indifferent to what people think of the way I dress.

She stood against the door and talked with one hand cupped to the side of her mouth.

"I came over to see if you two survived last night. I'm so sorry that I had to leave like that."

Petals pushed her nose up against a window and started barking in our direction. Nails perked up his ears but didn't look overly thrilled by the sound. He stayed where he was.

"Oh, that was okay. It was a fine night, Anna. I was going to call and thank you." For the chicken à la Dead Sea Scroll, the bum's rush out the door . . .

"Well, then, I don't feel so guilty. You are telling the truth, aren't you?"

Petals disappeared from the window, and then Anna disappeared down into the car. There was some scuffling and slurred voices, and then the dog was out and flying up the garden path, full tilt. She tried to leap too many porch steps with one bound and fell flat, but she was up in a flash and on her way over to her boyfriend. Nails's indifference disappeared and the two of them waltzed back and forth across the porch in a leaping frenzy of delight and bites. They barked and bit each other's heads and kept falling down every three steps.

"Petals is cuckoo for Nails. Mrs. Fletcher and I take them over to the high-school football field once or twice a week and let them run all of that energy out of their systems."

She stood at the bottom of the porch steps and beamed up at me. She was wearing a scarlet T-shirt that said CODASCO across its front. The shirt accused her of having much bigger breasts than I had originally thought. A pair of faded blue Levi's that were tight in a nice, sexy way, and ratty blue tennis sneakers that were holey and comfortable-looking.

I was about to say something about how good she looked when she pointed at me. "What does your T-shirt say?"

I looked down at it and unconsciously put my hand over the huge white letters. "Uh, 'Virginia Is for Lovers.' I, um, a friend gave it to me."

She stuck her hands in the back pockets of her jeans. "So you are a lover, huh?" She said it with a naughty-nasty smile that made me feel two feet high.

"Yes. Very famous too. I'm written up in *Ripley's Believe It or Not*."

"I don't." Her smile got bigger.

"Don't what?" Mine got smaller.

"Believe it."

Appropriately, Nails chose that moment to start humping Petals, and I was embarrassed but glad for the distraction. I pulled him off. He growled. I think both of them growled.

"Where is Saxony?"

"She and Mrs. Fletcher went shopping."

"That's too bad. I was going to ask if you two would like to come swimming. It's going to be a hot day."

"I'm not really in the mood for it, to tell you the truth. Did you hear about what happened here this morning?" I pointed the book out toward the road.

"The Hayden boy? I know. That was terrible. Did you see it?"

"Yes, the whole thing." I put the book down on the railing and crossed my arms over my chest. The dogs had collapsed a foot away from each other and were panting like little steam engines.

"Then why don't you come out for a ride with me? I'm sure that it will take your mind off things. We'll take the dogs with us."

The two of them jumped right up, as if they understood.

"Okay, sure, that would probably be very nice. Thanks, Anna."

I went back into the house, got my wallet and keys, and wrote Saxony a note. I didn't know how she'd take my not being there when she came back, so instead of rubbing salt into the wound by saying that I was with Anna, I wrote only that I was going out with Nails for a while. Anyway, why not? And why should I feel guilty? Weren't we here to write a book on Marshall France, and so wasn't all contact with his daughter helpful? Bullshit—I felt guilty writing the note because I was excited about whatever was going to happen with Anna today, and not only because she was his daughter.

The car was full of things. Empty cardboard boxes, a yellow garden hose, an old soccer ball, a case of Alpo dog food. The dogs got in back, and Anna pressed a button which lowered the window in the tailgate for them.

"I think that the population of Galen has increased by ten people in the last few years." She took a piece of bubble gum out of her pocket and offered it to me. I said no, and she started peeling it for herself. "Farming is about the only thing that people can do around here, but like so many places, the kids don't want to farm anymore. As soon as they get old enough, they go to St. Louis and the bright lights."

"But you've stayed?"

"Yes. I don't have to work because the house was paid for a long time ago. The royalties from my father's books are more than I need to pay for everything else."

"Do you still play the piano?"

She blew a bubble and it popped almost as soon as it came out of her mouth. "Did David Louis tell you that? Yes, I play once in a while. I had a passion for it at one time, but as I've gotten older . . ." She shrugged and blew another bubble.

She chewed the gum like a kid—mouth open, popping and cracking it until I thought that I would go crazy. Women look terrible chewing gum. Any woman, I don't care who she is. Luckily, she took it and threw it out the window.

"I don't like gum when the taste's gone. Did David tell you about the other man who came here and wanted to do a biography of my father?"

"Yes, the man from Princeton?"

"Yes, what an *ass*. I invited him to dinner and he spent the evening telling me how heuristic *The Land of Laughs* was."

"What does that mean?"

"Heuristic? You're the English teacher, you should know."

"Oh, yeah? I don't even know what a gerund is."

"Isn't that terrible? What's our educational system coming to?"

I rolled down my window and watched a bunch of healthy-looking cows whisk flies away with their big ropy tails. Far off behind them, a tractor worked its way across a flat brown field, and an airplane moved at a pinpoint crawl.

"We'll be there in a few minutes."

"Where? Am I allowed to ask where we're going?"

"No, you'll see. It's a big surprise."

We drove on for three or four more miles, and then, without putting on the blinker, she took a sharp left off onto a narrow dirt road and into a forest so thick that I couldn't see more than fifteen feet into the trees on either side. The car became cooler, and a rich, full smell of wood and shade took over. The road got bumpy, and I could hear rocks banging up into the wheel wells.

"I never thought of Missouri as being very foresty."

Sunlight sneaked in and out of the trees. A deer appeared and disappeared through the trees, and I looked over at Anna to see if she'd seen it too.

"Don't worry, we're almost there."

When she stopped, I looked around but saw nothing.

"Let me guess: your father planted all the trees in this forest, right?"

"No." She switched off the motor and dropped the keys on the floor.

"Uh . . . he used to go walking here?"

"Now you're getting closer."

"He wrote all of his books on that stump?"

"No."

"I give up."

"You didn't try hard enough! Okay. I thought that you would like to see where the Queen of Oil lived."

"Where she lived? What do you mean?"

"Aren't people always asking writers where their characters come from? Father got his Queen from someone who lived in these woods. Come on, I'll show you."

Getting out of the car, I started phrasing the whole passage in my mind for the biography. "The road that led to the Queen of Oil's house snaked its way through a forest which appeared out of nowhere. France had discovered the main character for *The Land of Laughs* in the heart of a woods that should never have been there in the first place."

Boy, that was pretty bad. While Anna led the way into Sherwood Forest, I tried to come up with a couple of other beginnings, but then gave up. The dogs ran everywhere after each other. Anna walked about ten feet in front of me, and I divided my time between watching where I was going and watching where her very nice rear end was going.

"I keep expecting to see Hansel and Gretel out here."

"Just watch out for wolves."

My mind moved over to the time my father went hunting in Africa with Hemingway. He was gone for two months, and when he came back my mother wouldn't let him in the house with all the rhino heads and zebra skins and whatnot he had brought home to be mounted.

"There it is."

If I'd been expecting a gingerbread house with smoke from the chimney that smelled like oatmeal cookies, I was wrong. The house, if you could call it that, was a crudely built wood thing that sagged to one side as if a giant had leaned on it. If there had been glass in the two windows, it was gone now, replaced by pine boards nailed across in an X pattern. There was a crude porch missing several floorboards. The step leading up to it was split in half.

"Watch your step."

"You did say that no one's living here now, didn't you?"

"Yes, that's right. But it was very much like this when she was alive, too."

"And who was *she?*"

"Wait a minute and I'll show you."

She pulled out one of those long old-fashioned keys and stuck it into the lock under the rusted brown doorknob.

"You need a key to get in?"

"No, not really, but it's better this way."

Before I had a chance to ask her what she meant, she had shoved the door in and a huge smell of dampness and clean decay moved out to meet us. She started to go in but then stopped and turned to me. I was right behind her, and when she turned we were face-to-face. She moved back half a step. My heart did a hop when it realized how close we'd been for half a second.

"Stay here for a minute and I will light a lamp in there. The floor is full of holes, and it's very dangerous. Father once sprained his ankle so badly that I had to take him to the hospital."

I thought about holes in the floor and snakes and spiders, and I yawned. I usually yawn when I'm nervous, and it either makes people think that I'm very courageous or stupid. Sometimes I can't stop yawning. When I thought about it, it was ridiculous: one of the great moments of my adult life—going with the daughter of Marshall France to the house of the person who had inspired him to create his greatest character in my favorite book . . . and I was yawning. Before that I was scared, and before that I was thinking about her ass. Not about Anna France, daughter of . . . , but about Anna's ass. How did biographers ever manage to keep their lives separate from their subjects?

"You can come in now, Thomas, everything's all right."

The walls were covered with newspaper turned yellow and brown from dampness and age. The kerosene lamp and light from the open door made the newsprint look like whole colonies of bugs walking around the walls. I'd seen Walker Evans's photographs of Southern sharecroppers who had "decorated" their houses the same way, but when you were faced with the real thing it all became sadder and smaller. A raw wood table was in the center of the room, and two dying chairs were neatly shoved up to it on either side. In one corner was a metal cot with a gray wool blanket folded at the foot and a thin uncovered pillow at the head. That was it—no sink, no stove, doodads, plates, clothes on hooks, nothing. The home of a recluse on a big diet or a madwoman.

"The woman who lived here——"

A voice like a sonic boom pushed its way in from outside. "Who the hell's in there? If you measly little fuckers broke that lock again, I'm going to break your fuckin' heads!"

Footsteps clunked across the wooden porch, and a man came in carrying a shotgun in his left hand like it was a flower he'd picked on the way over.

"Richard, it's me!"

"You little fuckers . . ." He was looking at me and bringing the gun up across his chest when Anna's words penetrated his thick skull.

"Anna?"

"Yes, Richard! Why don't you look before you start cursing at people? This is the third time this has happened. Really, one day you are going to go too far and shoot someone!"

She was angry, and you could immediately see how it affected him. Like a big guard dog that growls and then gets hit on the head by its master, he got all sheepish and embarrassed. It was too dark in there to tell, but I was sure that he was blushing.

In his defense he whined, "Christ, Anna, how'm I supposed to know that it's you in there? Do you know how many times them damn kids have gotten in here—"

"If you'd *look* once, Richard, you would see that the door was unlocked. How many times will we have to go through this? That is why I unlock the door every time!" She took me by the sleeve and marched me past him, out onto the porch. As soon as we were there, she let go.

When he came out, I recognized him from the barbecue too. A red, prickly farmer's face that looked half-tired and half-mean. He had a self-inflicted haircut that wobbled around his big head, a nose and eyes that stuck out too far from his face. I briefly wondered what kind of inbreeding his family had been up to for the past few generations.

"Richard Lee, this is Thomas Abbey."

He nodded absently but didn't offer to shake hands.

"You was at the barbecue yesterday, weren't you." A statement.

"Yes, uh, we were." I couldn't think of anything else to say to him. I wanted to, but I was blank.

"Richard's mother was the Queen of Oil."

I looked at Anna as if to say, "Are you kidding me?" but she nodded to reaffirm what she'd said. "Dorothy Lee. The Queen of Oil."

Richard smiled and showed an incongruously bright white set of perfect teeth. "That's right." He pronounced it "rat." "And if I didn't know your father as good as I did, Anna, I woulda said that he had something going on with my mama. You know what I mean—those two spent more time out here in this house than any of us ever did."

"Father would walk out here from town two or three times a week to see Dorothy when he was writing *The Land of Laughs*. He would put on his black sneakers and walk in the fields by the side of the road. No one would ever offer him a ride because they knew how much he liked the walk."

Richard leaned his shotgun against the wall and scratched his stubbly chin. "And my mama knew exactly when he was coming, too. She'd have us go out and pick a big bowl of berries, and then she'd sprinkle them with powder sugar. When he got out here the two of them'd sit out here on the porch and eat the whole damn bowlful. Right, Anna?"

"Hey, you're the one who wants to write the book on Marshall, aren't you."

"That's what we have been talking about, Richard. That's why I brought him out here to see your mother's cabin."

He turned toward the open door. "My papa built this for her so's she could come out here and live a little in the woods. There were so many kids in my family that she said she needed a place to rest up once in a while. I couldn't blame her. I got three sisters and a brother. But I'm the only one left living in Galen now." He looked at Anna.

"Thomas, I'm sorry, but I have an appointment in town in half an hour. Would you like to stay here or come back with me?"

I couldn't see hanging around in the woods and jawing with Richard, even though I knew that I'd want to talk to him later if Anna ever okayed the book. I'd guessed that she would after dinner at her house and this little trip, but she still hadn't said anything definite one way or the other, and I was still too chicken to push her for a definite answer.

"I guess I'd better go back with you in case Saxony is there."

"Are you afraid she'll worry about you?" Her voice verged on being a taunt.

"Oh, no, not at all. I—"

"No, don't worry. We will have you back in time. Back in time for your tea. Richard, what about you? Do you need a ride?"

"No, I got my truck, Anna. I gotta get a couple of things out here. I'll see you all later." He started to go inside, but then stopped and touched her sleeve. "That Hayden thing's bad, isn't it? After last night, that's the fourth thing that's gone wrong. And now, one so close after the other . . ."

"We'll talk about it later, Richard. Don't worry about it now." Her voice was a quiet monotone.

"Worry? How the hell *don't* you worry? I pissed in my pants when I heard. That poor sucker Joe Jordan's up shit creek."

I watched Anna's face during the exchange, and it hardened more and more as Lee talked on.

"I said that we would talk about it later, Richard. Later." She held up a hand as if to push him away. Her lips had tightened.

He started to say something more but stopped, mouth open, and looked at me. Then he blinked and smiled as if something had dawned on him that made everything clear. "Oh, right! Jesus, listen to me and my big mouth!" He smiled and shook his head. "I'm sorry, Anna. You watch out for her, buddy, she can get pretty damn grouchy on you sometimes."

"Come on, Thomas. Good-bye, Richard."

The path was wide enough for us to walk side by side.

"Anna, I don't understand some of what's going on here."

She didn't stop and she didn't look at me. "Like what? You mean about what Richard was saying?" She pushed a hand through her short hair, giving me a glimpse of sweaty forehead. I love to see sweat on a woman. It's one of the most erotic, inviting things I can think of.

"Yes, what Richard was saying. And then Mrs. Fletcher kept asking me this morning if the Hayden boy was *laughing* when he got hit by the truck."

"Was there anything else?"

"Yes, there was. That man who hit him, Jordan? Joe Jordan? He kept saying that it wasn't supposed to be him, and that nobody knew anything anymore." I didn't want to push her, but I did want to know what was happening.

She slowed down and kicked a stone up the path. It hit another and caromed off into the woods. "All right, I'll tell you. Some terrible things have happened in town in the last six months. A man was electrocuted, a store owner was shot in a holdup, an old woman was blinded last night, and then this thing with the boy today. Galen is Sleepy Town, USA, Thomas. You can see that already, I'm sure. Things just don't happen here. We're the kind of place people joke about when they talk about hayseeds. You know—'What do you people do around here for fun? Oh, we fish illegally or go down to the barbershop and watch them give haircuts.' Suddenly, these nightmares are happening."

"But what did Jordan mean when he said it wasn't supposed to be him?"

"Joe Jordan is a Jehovah's Witness. Do you know anything about them? They think that they are the chosen few. God would never let this happen to one of them, and besides that, what would you say if you had run over a child and killed it?"

"The boy died?"

"No, but he will. I mean, he probably will, from what I've heard."

"All right, that makes sense, but then what was Mrs. Fletcher talking about when she asked me if the kid was laughing before he got hit?"

"Goosey Fletcher is Galen's crazy old lady. You've seen that already, I'm sure. She orders everyone around and asks crazy questions and is perfectly at home in her nutty little head, God bless her. She was committed to an insane asylum for three years after her husband died."

We had reached the car, and she went around back to let the dogs in. Everything sounded reasonable enough the way she explained it. Yes, it sounded fine. So why did I turn and take a long last look back into the woods? Because I knew that what she had said was somehow a bunch of bullshit.

She dropped Nails and me off at Mrs. Fletcher's and said that she would give me a call in a day or two. She wasn't brusque, but she wasn't adorable, either.

As I reached the porch, Saxony loomed up into view behind the screen door.

"Ah, darling, you are a vision in wire mesh!"

"Were you with Anna?"

"Wait a minute." I unclipped Nails from his leash and he sat down on the top step. "Yes. She took me out to the Queen of Oil's house."

"What?" She opened the door and came outside.

"Yes. Some old woman named Dorothy Lee who was supposedly the inspiration for the Queen. She lived in an old dilapidated shack about three or four miles out of town in this big forest. Anna came by and asked if I'd like to see it. I did until Dorothy Lee's son appeared and almost shot us for trespassing. Richard. He reminded me of Lon Chaney Junior in *Of Mice and Men*. 'Tell me 'bout the rabbits, George.' One of those guys, you know?"

"What was the house like?"

"Nothing. A rickety dump decorated with old newspapers. Very uninspiring."

"Did Anna say anything more about the book?"

"No, not a word, dammit. I think she's into this big teasing thing, you know? She'll tell me all these things about her father and always phrase it, 'Here's something else for your book.' But she's never yet said whether she will let me do it or not."

Saxony shifted her stance and tried to sound nonchalant when she spoke. I loved her for the failed effort. "What do you think of Anna? I mean personally?"

I fought a smile down and reached out and ran my hand down her freckly cheek. I saw that she had gotten some sun when she was out shopping. She pulled away and caught hold of my hand in hers. My smile came up anyway. "No, really, Thomas, come on, don't be funny. I know that you think she's pretty, so don't lie about it."

"Why would I lie about it? And she certainly isn't what David Louis painted her. Christ, he had me thinking that we were about to rendezvous with Lizzie Borden."

"So do you like her?" She kept hold of my hand.

"Yes, so far I do." I shrugged. "But I'll tell you something, Sax. I also think that there's some kind of big weirdness going on around here that I don't like much."

"Like what?"

"Like, did you know . . . ?" I stopped at the last moment and lowered my voice to a whisper. "Did you know that Goosey Fletcher was in the booby hatch for three years?"

"Yes, she told me about it when we went shopping today."

"She did?"

"Uh-huh. We started talking about movies because of your father, and she asked me if I'd seen *One Flew Over the Cuckoo's Nest*. I said yes, and she told me that she'd been in an asylum once. She said it like 'So what?' "

"Hmm." I took my hand back and played the dog leash through my fingers.

"But what's the matter with that?"

"Did you buy stuff for lunch?"

"Yes, all kinds of good things. Are you hungry?"

"Starved."

I make the world's most delicious grilled cheese sandwich, bar none. While I flitted around the kitchen whipping us up a couple of masterpieces, I filled her in on my woodland idyll with Anna.

"How great, you got whole-wheat bread! Now, now, now, a lee-tle boot-er . . ."

"Do you really think that Richard Lee would have shot you?"

"Saxony, I not only think so, I've got sweat stains to prove it. That man was not kidding."

"Thomas, you said that David Louis told you that crazy story about Anna screaming at him to get out, and that she wrote him mean letters whenever he sent someone out here to write about her father?"

"Louis didn't send anyone out, Sax, he would just answer their questions. They came out of their own accord, like us."

"All right, they came out on their own. But didn't he say that when they did come out, she would send him letters telling him that it was all his fault and that he had no right doing it?"

I nodded and slapped the spatula on the counter.

"All right, then tell me this: Why is she being so nice to you? If she hates biographers so much, why did she invite us to dinner and then drive you out to the Queen of Oil's house today?"

"That's one of the strange things that I was talking about, Sax. Either David Louis is screwy in the head, or else he just detests Anna France for some reason. Almost everything he said about her so far has proven wrong."

"But remember that she did lie about her father a few times last night, didn't she?" Her voice was triumphant.

"Yes, she did. She welcomed us with open arms and then started lying when she was talking about him." I flipped the spatula in the air and caught it by the handle. "Don't ask me about these things, dear, I only work here."

"It's interesting, you know?" She walked to the cabinet and got out two bright blue plates.

"Yup." I scooped the sandwiches out of the skillet at exactly the right moment and slid them onto a piece of paper towel to take up the extra grease. The secret of the perfect grilled cheese.

7

The next few days nothing much happened. I poked around town and talked to people. Everybody was very nice, but no one told me much that I didn't already know. Marshall France was a good old boy who liked to hang around and shoot the breeze just like any other mortal. He didn't like being famous, no sirree: a good family man who maybe spoiled his daughter a little now and then, but what's a father for?

I went to the town library and reread all of his books. The librarian was an old lady with oyster-shell-pink rhinestone glasses and puffy, rouged cheeks. She bustled around as if she had a million things to do every minute of the day, but I saw that the bustling was all busywork and that what she really liked to do was sit behind her big oak desk and read.

A couple of kids were plagiarizing reports out of the *World Book Encyclopedia*, and a very pretty young woman was glued behind a month-old copy of *Popular Mechanics*.

I went over all the France books with a mental magnifying glass to find parallels between them and Galen, but the search was uneventful. I assumed that what France did when he wrote was to take a grain from something real and then drastically reshape it for his own purposes. So Mrs. Lee had been a blob of human clay that he had sculpted into the Queen of Oil.

When I was done investigating, I pushed away from the desk and rubbed my face. I was working in the magazine room, and when I came in I'd noticed a surprisingly good selection of literary magazines on the periodical shelves. I got up to get a copy of *Antaeus*. The librarian caught my eye and crooked her finger for me to come over to her desk. I felt like the bad kid who's been caught making noises in the back of the stacks.

"You're Mr. Abbey?" she whispered sternly.

I nodded and smiled.

"I'll make up a temporary card for you if you'd like. Then you can take books out instead of having to read them in here."

"Oh, that's no problem, thank you anyway. It's a nice room to work in."

I thought my charm would at least make her smile, but she kept a kind of prim frown. She had those little vertical lines under her nose that come from a lifetime of pursed lips. Everything on her desk was orderly too. Her hands were crossed in front of her, and she didn't move or drum or twiddle them when she talked. I was sure that she'd kill anyone who put a book back on the wrong shelf.

"There have been people who came before to write about Marshall, you know."

"Yes?"

"Anna didn't like any of them, especially the man who wanted to write the biography. He was so rude . . ." She shook her head and clicked her tongue.

"Was that the man from the East? The man from Princeton University?"

"Yes, he was the one who wanted to write the biography of Marshall. Can you imagine? They tell me that Princeton is an excellent university, but if they're turning out graduates like that man, they wouldn't get my vote."

"Do you happen to remember his name?"

She cocked her head to the side and raised one chubby hand from the desk. Tapping her chin with a finger, she never took her eyes off me.

"His name? No, I never asked him and he never offered it to me. He came in here like Mr. Mucky-Muck on a high horse and started asking me questions without so much as a please." If she were a bird and had had feathers, she would have ruffled them then. "From what I've heard, he was that same way with everyone in town. I always say that you can be rude, but don't be rude on my doorstep."

I could picture the toad from Princeton with his little Mark Cross briefcase, a Sony tape recorder, and a deadline on his thesis, going from person to person trying to pump them for information and getting exactly nowhere because they didn't feel like being pumped.

"Would you like to see one of Marshall's favorite books, Mr. Abbey?"

"I would love to, if it isn't too much trouble for you."

"Well, that's my job, isn't it? Getting books for people?"

She came out from behind the desk and moved toward the back shelves. I assumed that she was heading toward the children's section, so I was taken aback when she stopped at the shelf marked "Architecture." She carefully looked all around to see if anyone was nearby. "Between you and me, Mr. Abbey, I think she's going to let you try. From everything I've heard, she's going to let you."

"Oh, yes?" I wasn't sure I knew what she was talking about. Her voice had fallen back to its front-desk whisper.

"Do you mean Anna?"

"Yes, yes. Please don't talk so loud. I'd put money on it that she'll let you try."

It was heartening news even if it did come from such a strange source. What I couldn't understand was why we had to come all the way back here for her to tell me that she thought Anna was going to let me write the book.

Somebody came around the corner and looked at us. The librarian reached out and took a book about railroad stations off the shelf.

"This is the one I've been looking for! Here you are." She opened the back cover of the book, and sure enough, France had taken it out five or six times. Very few other names were on the card. When the other person got the book he wanted and left, the librarian closed the train-station book and slid it under my arm. "Walk out with it like this. That way no one will suspect that we've been talking back here." She looked around and peered through a shelf to the next aisle before speaking again. "It's Anna's decision is all I know. We all know that. But it's hard not to be impatient. Ever since——" The sound of approaching feet stopped her in mid-sentence again. This time for good, because a young woman with a little girl in tow came up and asked for a book on raising goldfish that she hadn't been able to find.

I took my book back to the table in the magazine room and skimmed through it. Picture after picture of American railroad stations.

The guy who wrote the accompanying text was a little over-enthusiastic about things like the "grandeur" of the Wainer, Mississippi, "antebellum masterpiece," with its three ticket windows instead of one. But I spent some time with my nose in the book because I could envision France doing it and because, for whatever reason, it was a subject that interested him. I remembered Lucente talking about his Sunday train rides and the postcards of train stations at his house. On my third time through I flipped past Derek, Pennsylvania. A half-second later my eyes widened and I frantically turned back, almost afraid that it might not be there when I got to it. But it was. Someone had penciled extensive notes all along the border of the page. I had seen France's handwriting only a couple of times, but this was it. The same careful up and down letters. The notes had nothing to do with either Derek, Pennsylvania, or its train station. In true artistic fashion, it looked like my man had been inspired and had written his inspiration down on the first scrap of paper he could find.

It was a description of a character named Inkler. I couldn't make out some of the words, but essentially Inkler was an Austrian who decided to walk around the world. To raise money for his journey, he had picture postcards printed up of himself and the white bull terrier he would take along for company. Underneath the picture it stated Inkler's name, where he came from, what he intended on doing, how far it was (60,000 kilometers), that it would take four years, and that the card was his way of raising money for the trip. Would you please donate a little to this worthy cause?

There were notes on what he would look like, the name of the dog and what it looked like, which places they would pass through, and some of their adventures along the way. The entry was dated June 13, 1947.

I copied all of it down on my pad. For the first time, I felt I had really come across buried treasure. There was no Inkler in any of the France books, so I was one of the only people in the world who knew about this particular France creation. I was so greedy about it that for a moment or two I deliberated on whether or not to tell Saxony. It was mine and Marshall France's. Marshall's and mine. . . . But goodness prevailed and I told her. She was excited too, and we spent a happy second day in the library poring over all of the other books that he liked, according to the librarian. We made no other discoveries, but little friend Inkler would end up being quite enough to handle.

The next day, we were in the kitchen having breakfast when I wondered out loud where France got the names for his characters. It was something I especially liked in his books.

Saxony was halfway through a piece of toast smothered in orange marmalade. She took another bite and mumbled, "The graveyard."

"What are you talking about?" I got up and poured myself another cup of the hideous chamomile tea she'd bought. My mother used to soak her feet in chamomile tea. But it was either drink that or else some kind of decaffeinated health-food coffee from Uranus that Saxony had gotten on Mrs. Fletcher's suggestion.

She brushed her hands together and a hail of breadcrumbs flew everywhere. "Yes, from the graveyard here. I took a walk through town the other day to get the lay of the land. There's a very nice church down past the post office that reminded me of one of those old English churches that you see in calendar pictures or on postcards. You know the kind—dark and dignified, a stone wall going around it. . . . I got interested, so I wandered up and noticed a small graveyard behind it. When I was a child I used to do a lot of gravestone rubbings, so I'm always interested in them."

Sitting down at the table, I wiggled my eyebrows up and down like Peter Lorre. "Hee . . . Hee. Heeee! So am I, my dear. Rats and spiders! Spiders and rats!"

"Oh, stop it, Thomas. Haven't you ever done stone rubbings? They're beautiful. *Thomas*, will you stop drooling? Your imitation is marvelous, okay? You're a wonderful vampire. Do you want to hear about this or not?"

"Yes, my dear."

She put two more pieces of whole-wheat bread into the toaster. The way she ate, I sometimes wondered if she had been starved in a previous existence.

"I was wandering around, but something was wrong, you know? Just off, or wrong, or not right. Then I realized what. All of the names that I saw there on the stones, or almost all of them, were the names of characters in *The Night Races into Anna.*"

"Really?"

"That's right. Leslie Baker, Dave Miller, Irene Weigel . . . All of them were there."

"You're kidding."

"Nope. I was going to go back with a pad and write all the names down, but then I thought that you would probably want to go too, so I waited."

"Saxony, that is fantastic! Why didn't you tell me about it sooner?"

She reached over the table and took my hand. The longer we were together, the more it seemed that she liked to touch and be touched. Not always a sexy or loving touch, but just contact. A little electrical connection for a second or two to let the other know that you're there. I liked it too. But business was business and France business was big stuff, so I made her gulp down what was left of her toast and we headed out to the graveyard.

Fifteen minutes later we were standing in front of St. Joseph's Church. When I was little I had a lot of Catholic friends who crossed themselves whenever they went past their church. I didn't feel like being left out, so they taught me how, and I did it too whenever we went by the church together. I was with my mother one day in the car. She drove by St. Mary's, and like the good little Catholic I wasn't, I unconsciously crossed myself in full view of her horrified Methodist eyes. My analyst went crazy for weeks after that trying to dig out of me where the impulse came from.

While Saxony and I stood there, the front door opened and a

priest came out of the building. He moved quickly down the steep stone steps and, giving us a clipped, formal nod, moved on by in a hurry. I turned and watched him slide into a burgundy Oldsmobile Cutlass.

Saxony started toward the church and I followed. It was an especially nice day. The air was cool and a strong wind had been gusting and whipping through the trees, raising summer dust every-where. Overhead, it zipped all of the clouds by as if they were in a speeded-up movie. The sun was a sharp and clear seal in the middle of a cobalt-blue envelope.

"Are you coming? Don't worry, the little men under the graves won't bite you."

"Yes, ma'am." I caught up with her and took her hand.

"Look." She pointed to a gravestone with her foot.

"Hah! Brian Taylor. How do you like that! And look—Anne Megibow. Boy, they are all here. Why don't you start taking names down, Sax, and I'll have a look around."

To tell the truth, I wasn't happy with the discovery. Romantic or not, I wanted my heroes to be struck by inspiration in every aspect of their work. Stories, settings, characters, names . . . I wanted it all to be completely their own—to have come only from them; not a graveyard or a phone book or a newspaper. This some-how made France look too human.

Once in a while some crazily devoted fan got by the security guard at our house in California. My father's favorite story was the "Woman Who Rang the Doorbell." She rang it so long and hard that my old man thought that there was some kind of emergency. He made it a point never to answer the door, but this time he did. The woman, holding an eight-by-ten photo of him, took one look at her god and staggered back off the front step. "But why are you so *short?*" she wailed, and was dragged away in tears.

Saxony was right about the gravestones: they were intriguing and lovely in a sad way. The inscriptions told the stories of so much pain—babies born August 2, died August 4. Men and women whose children all died long before they did. It was so easy to envision a middle-aged couple sitting in a dumpy gray house somewhere, never talking to each other, pictures of all their dead sons and daughters on the mantelpiece. Maybe the woman even called her husband "Mister" for all the years that they were married.

"Thomas?"

I was setting a squat glass jar of flowers straight on someone's headstone when Saxony called. I guess that they had been orange marigolds once, but now they looked like tired little crepe-paper balls.

"Thomas, come here."

She was off on the other side of the graveyard, which sloped downward in her direction. She was squatting by one of the graves and balancing herself with one hand flat on the ground behind her. I got up from where I was, and my knees cracked like dry sticks of wood. Mr. Physical Fitness.

"I don't know if you're going to be very happy about this. Here's your friend Inkler."

"Oh no."

"Yes. Gert Inkler. Born 1913, died 19 . . . Wait a second." She reached out and rubbed her hand across the face of the gray-pink stone. "Died in 1964. He wasn't that old."

"That's what you get from walking around the world. Dammit! I was sure that we'd made this great discovery. A Marshall France character that never appeared in any of his books. Now all he turns out to be is some stiff in the local graveyard."

"You sound like Humphrey Bogart when you talk like that. 'Some stiff in the graveyard.' "

"I'm not trying to sound like him, Saxony. Excuse me for being so unoriginal. We're not all great creators, you know."

"Oh, be quiet, Thomas. Sometimes you pick fights just to see if I'll snap at your bait."

"Mixed metaphor." I stood up and rubbed my hands on my legs to get the dirt off them.

"*Sorry,* Mr. English Teacher."

We threw halfhearted insults back and forth until she saw something behind me and stopped. In fact, she not only stopped, her whole face shut down like an airport in a snowstorm.

"This is a nice place to have a picnic."

I knew who it was. "Hiya, Anna."

This time she wore a white T-shirt, brand-new tan khakis, and her scruffy sneakers: a cutie.

"Why are you two out here?"

How did she know that we were there? Chance? As far as I knew, the only one who had seen us was the priest, and that was only a few minutes before. Even if he had called her and told her, how had she gotten there so quickly—by rocket ship?

"We're doing some research. Thomas discovered where your father got the names for the characters in *The Night Races into Anna*. He brought me out here to show me."

My head swiveled around on my neck like Linda Blair's in *The Exorcist. I* discovered?

"And were you surprised?"

"Surprised? Oh, at this? Yeah. No. Uh, yeah, I guess so." I was trying to figure out why Saxony had lied. Was she trying to make me look good in Anna's cool eyes?

"Who are you visiting? Gert Inkler? Father never used him in a book."

"Yes, we know. The man who walked around the world. Did he ever do it?"

The smile slid right off her face. And Christ, could her eyes get small and mean. "Where did you hear about that?"

"Railroad Stations of America."

My answer didn't bring the sunshine back. Her look reminded me of the way she had treated Richard Lee in the woods the other day. It wasn't the same kind of fire-and-brimstone fury that David Louis had portrayed, but kind of a turn-to-ice, stone-cold anger.

"The librarian in town gave me a book that your father liked. The one on train stations in America? I skimmed through it and found a description of Inkler in one of the margins. I have it at home if you'd like to see it."

"You two are really doing your homework on this already,

aren't you? But what if I don't authorize the biography?"

She looked straight at me first, then flicked her eyes over my shoulder to Saxony.

"If you weren't going to let us do it, then why have you been so nice to us all this time? David Louis said that you were a monster."

Good old Saxony. Tactful, sensitive, always there with the right compliment at the right time. The born diplomat.

I was tempted to put my hands over my head to protect myself against the Battle of the Titans, but astonishingly it never came. Instead, Anna sniffed, shoved her hands down into her pockets, and nodded like a doll with its head on a spring. Up and down and up and down . . .

"Saxony, you are right. I must admit that I do enjoy taunting people sometimes. I wanted to see how long you would wait before you became annoyed with my little games and just *asked* if you could do it."

"Okay, can we do it?" I wanted the question to sound forceful, convinced, but it crawled out of my throat as if afraid of the daylight.

"Yes, you can. The book is all yours if you want to write it. If you aren't too mad at me, I'll help you in whatever ways I can. I'm sure that there are ways that I can help."

I felt a surge of triumph. I turned to Saxony to see how she'd taken it. She smiled, picked up a little white pebble, and threw it at my knee.

"Well, Miss Sporty?"

"Well what?" She picked up another pebble and threw it.

"Well, I guess we're all set." I reached out and took her hand again. She squeezed it and smiled. Then she turned and smiled at Anna. France's daughter stood there in all of her adorableness, but that moment was for Saxony and me, and I wanted her to know how happy I was that it had come and that she was there with me.

8

"Be careful that you don't break your neck going down these stairs. One of Father's favorite unkept promises was that he would fix them one day."

Anna had the flashlight, but she was in front of Saxony, who was in front of me. As a result, all I saw of the weak yellow beam was a straight snake of it here and there as it darted around their legs.

"Why do all basements smell the same?" I reached out to touch the wall for balance. It was crumbly and damp. I remembered the smell out at the Lee house in the woods.

"What's the smell?"

"Like a funky locker room after the team has taken a lot of showers."

"No, that's a clean smell. Basements smell secretive and hidden."

"Secretive? How can something smell secretive?"

"Well, I know it doesn't smell like a locker room!"

"Wait a minute, here is the light."

A click and then the same kind of piss-yellow light illuminated the large square room.

"Be careful of your head, Thomas, the ceiling is low in here."

I hunched down and looked at the room. An army-green furnace loomed over in a corner. The walls were rough plaster and uneven. The floor was a step away from being dirt. There weren't many things down there besides some tied bundles of old magazines. *Pageant, Coronet, Ken, Stage, Gentry*. I'd never heard of any of them.

"What did your father do down here?"

"Wait a minute and I'll show you. Follow me."

When she moved, I noticed for the first time an open doorway that apparently led to another room. A snick of a light switch and we went in.

There was a school blackboard on the wall about three feet high and maybe six feet long. A chalk holder was attached to one end of it, and it was filled with long, brand-new sticks of white chalk. It made me feel right at home. I had to restrain a mad urge to go up there and diagram a sentence.

"This is where he began all of his books." Anna picked up a piece of chalk and started to doodle in the middle of the board. A kind of crude, not very good rendition of Snoopy from the *Peanuts* comic strip.

"I thought that you said he worked upstairs?"

"He did, but only after he had mapped out all of his characters here on his board."

"He did it for every book?"

"Yes. He would hide down here for days and create his next universe."

"How? In what way?"

"He said that he always had a main character in mind. For *The Land of Laughs* it was the Queen of Oil, Richard Lee's mother. He would put her name at the top of the board and start listing other people's names under it."

"Names of real people, or ones that he had made up?"

"Real people. He said that if he thought of the real people first, then the things he wanted to use from their personalities came right to his mind."

She wrote "Dorothy Lee" on the board and then "Thomas Abbey" under it. She drew arrows from both of our names out to the right. Then she wrote "The Queen of Oil" next to the first, "Father's Biographer," next to mine. Her handwriting was nothing like her father's—it was squiggly and wide and messy, the kind I'd comment on at the bottom of an essay after I'd read it.

Then under "Thomas Abbey—Father's Biographer," she wrote: "Famous father, English teacher, Clever, Insecure, Hopeful, the Power?"

I frowned. "What do you mean by 'the Power?' "

She waved the question away. "Wait. I'm doing it the way he did it. The things that he didn't know about, or didn't know if he wanted to use, he would put a question mark next to."

"Are all the rest of the things up there me too? Insecure, hope-ful . . ."

"If I were my father, I would write down what I felt about you and what I thought was interesting enough to use. These things are just my own impressions. You aren't angry with me, are you?"

"Who, me? Nooo. Not at all. Nooo. Not a—"

"Okay, Thomas, you made your point."

"Nooo. Not—"

"Thomas!"

Anna looked at Saxony. I guess she didn't believe me. "Is he mad at me?"

"No. It's just the 'insecure' and 'famous-father' parts that got him, I think."

"You have to remember too that I'm me and not my father. If he were going to use you, he might have seen totally different things about you."

"Seriously, Anna, I think this would be a really nice beginning to the book. In the prologue, I'd simply describe your father coming down those creaky stairs by himself, turning on the lights, and start-ing to work on one of the books by doing this thing at the black-board. The whole first few pages are both the beginning of his book and the beginning of mine. What do you think?"

She put the chalk down for the first time and erased Snoopy with the flat of her hand. "I don't like it."

"I think it's an excellent idea, Thomas." I didn't know whether Sax said it because she did like it or because she wanted to pick a fight with Anna.

"But you don't like it, Anna."

She turned from the board and dusted her hands against each other. "You don't really know anything yet, Thomas, and you're already trying to come up with all of these clever little tricks to use. . . ."

"I wasn't trying to be clever, Anna. I honestly thought that—"

"Let me finish. If I am going to let you do this book, you have got to do it carefully and beautifully. Do you know how many terrible biographies I've read that don't even begin to bring their subject back to life, much less make them interesting or intriguing? You cannot imagine how important it is that this book be well done, Thomas. I'm sure that you care enough about my father to want to do it right, so any kind of cleverness is out. Any kind of cleverness or shortcuts or paragraphs that begin with 'Twenty years later . . .' There can't be any of that. Your book has to have it all, or else he won't . . ."

Her tirade had been so kooky and heartfelt and loud that I was taken off-guard when she stopped in mid-sentence.

I swallowed. "Anna?"

"Yes?"

Saxony interrupted. "Anna, are you sure that you want Thomas to write this book? Are you really sure?"

"Yes, now I am. Positive."

I took a deep breath and let it out loudly, hoping it would somehow break the tension that was hovering in the air up around A-bomb level.

Saxony went to the blackboard, picked up some chalk, and began drawing a cartoon near where our names—Mrs. Lee's and mine—were written. I knew she was a good artist from the sketches I had seen of her puppets, but she outdid herself with this one.

The Queen of Oil—a very good, quick rendering of the famous Van Walt illustration—and I stood over the gravestone of Marshall France. Up above us, France looked down from a cloud and worked puppet strings that were attached to both of us everywhere. It was certainly well done, but it was also a disturbing picture in light of what Anna had been saying.

"I don't think you are positive, Anna." Saxony finished sketching and put the chalk back in the holder at the end of the board.

"Oh, you don't?" Anna's voice was low. She watched Sax intently.

"No, I don't. I think a biography is very much a writer's interpretation of his subject's life. It shouldn't just be 'he did this and he did that.' "

"Did I ever say that it should be?" Anna's voice dropped its urgency and sounded . . . amused.

"No, but you have already made it pretty clear that you want to call all the shots on it. I get the distinct feeling already that you want Thomas to write your version of the life of Marshall France, and not Thomas Abbey's."

"Come on, Sax. . . ."

"No, you come on, Thomas. You know that I'm right."

"Did I say anything?"

"No, but you were about to." She licked her lips and then rubbed the side of her nose. Her nose got itchy when she got really angry.

"That's a rather rude thing to say, Saxony, considering who I am and how much I have at stake in this matter, wouldn't you say? Yes, of course I am biased. I *do* think the book should be done in a certain way. . . ."

"What'd I tell you?" Saxony looked at me and nodded ruefully.

"I did not mean it that way. Don't misinterpret what I'm saying."

Both of them had their arms crossed, *locked,* over their chests.

"Hey look, ladies, cool it. I haven't even started on page one yet, and you're already at battle stations." They wouldn't look at me, but they were listening. "Anna, you want the book with everything in it, right? So do I. Sax, you want me to write it my way. So do I. So will someone please tell me what the big problem is here? Huh? What is it?"

While I talked, I kept thinking that it was the kind of scene my father would play. Maybe a little too hammy, but enough to stop their attacks.

"All right? Okay, look, I want to make a proposal. May I have the floor? Yes? Okay, here it is: Anna, you give me all the information I need to write the first chapter of the book *my* way. However long it takes me, you can't look at it—any of it—until I'm finished and satisfied with it. When I'm done, I'll give it to you and you can do whatever you want with it. Cut it, rearrange it, throw it out . . . I don't know, maybe you'll even like the way

I've done it. Anyway, if you don't, and end up hating it, then I promise I'll work as closely with you as you want after that. I won't tape you or anything, but it'll be a collaborative effort of the three of us from start to finish. I'm sure this idea is totally unprofessional and any publisher would pull out his hair if he heard about it, but I don't care. If you agree to it, then that's the way we'll do it."

"And what happens if I like the first chapter the way it is?"

"Then I get to write the whole thing my way and bring it to you when I'm done."

How much fairer could I be? If she hated my first chapter, we would work together from the very beginning. If she hated the final product, then she would have the right to—gasp—throw it all out and have either me or someone else start it again. I didn't want to think about that prospect.

"All right." She picked up the black felt eraser and disappeared Saxony's drawing in two sharp swipes.

"All right, Thomas, but I am going to give you a time limit: one month. One month to work completely on your own, and then the first chapter has to be done. There isn't much time to spare these days."

Saxony spoke before I had a chance to. "Okay, but then you've got to give us access to everything we want. No more holding back and no more lying about things."

Anna arched an eyebrow at that one. I half-admired, half-despaired at Saxony's bluntness.

"If you are going to do it chronologically . . . I assume you are? I will give you everything about him until his arrival in America. You won't be covering more than that in your first chapter."

9

And that was that. True to her word, books and diaries, letters and postcards poured out of the France house. It was all we could do to keep track of them in the beginning, much less make sense of them.

France had apparently saved everything, or else someone did it for him and gave it to him later in his life. There was a manila envelope bulging with uninteresting children's drawings of horseys and cows. The master, age four. A notebook with ratty-looking old wildflowers and weeds pressed in the pages, which all fell out when you held the book at any kind of angle. In a child's unsteady script, all of the remaining weeds and petrified petunias were labeled in German. One shoebox contained old gold-and-red cigar bands, matchboxes, canceled boat and train tickets. Another had more of those old picture postcards that he seemed to like so much. Lots of them were of the mountains and old *hüttes* where the climbers stayed. It was amazing to see the kind of clothes they wore then for hiking—the women in long, Daisy Miller dresses and fruit-salad hats, men in tweed knickers that ballooned at the knees and comical Tyrolean hats with swooping feathers on the side. All of them looked at the camera with either maniacal smiles or my-wife-just-died frowns. Never the in-between expression that you so often get in modern photographs.

The postcards were from school friends and family, according to Anna. In the shoebox was a little brown school notebook which on further inspection turned out to be a record of postcards received. It was hilarious, especially when you remembered that it was being kept by an eight- or nine-year-old kid. From whom, from where, the date, even the places where he was when he got each one.

"Anna, why *did* he change his name from Martin Frank to Marshall France?"

"Didn't you see the address on some of those old postcards?

'Marshall France in care of Martin Frank'? When he was about eight years old he made up this character named Marshall France. He was a combination of D'Artagnan, Beau Geste, and The Virginian. He told me that he refused to be called by any other name for years. Everyone he knew had to call him Marshall or else he refused to answer." She chuckled. "He must have been an obsessive little boy, huh?"

"Yes, well, that's fine and all, but why did he make that his name when he came to America?"

"To tell you the truth, Thomas, I don't really know for sure. You must remember though that he was a Jew running from the Nazis. Maybe he thought that if they ever got around to invading the United States, with a Gentile name like France there was less of a chance that he would be caught." She bent over to tie one of her shoelaces. I could barely hear her when she spoke. "Whatever the reason, it's perfect for you, isn't it? He became one of his own characters, right? *Very symbolic*, Doctor." She tapped her temple with a finger and told me that she would see me later.

Saxony and I spent at least a week looking over everything. We talked for a long time afterward, and although we argued over a couple of things, we did agree that France had been one strange little boy.

We talked about the best way to go at writing the test chapter. I had had a creative-writing instructor in college who brought a small child's doll to class the first day. He held it up in front of him and said that most people would describe the doll from only the most obvious angle if they were asked to do it. He drew an invisible horizontal line from his eye to the doll. But the real writer, he went on, knew that the doll could be described from any number of different, more interesting angles—from above, below—and that that was where good creative writing began. I told the story to Sax and said that one of those strange angles was what I was looking for here. She agreed with that too, but we ended up having a gigantic fight about what strange angle. She said that if she were writing the book, she would begin by describing a funny little boy sitting in his room in an Austrian Alpine town making careful entries in his postcard book. Then she would have him go out and pick flowers for his flower book, draw a picture of a cow, etc. An indirect way of saying that the kid was artistic, eccentric, and sensitive from Day One of his life.

I thought it was an okay idea, but since Anna had pooh-poohed mine about coming down the stairs to begin *The Land of Laughs*, I was afraid that she would torpedo Saxony's for being too "clever" too. Sax growled but then agreed that it might be too creative for Anna.

I wasted a few more days being tired and confused and depressed. Saxony steered clear of me and hung around out in the garden with Mrs. Fletcher. She liked the old woman a lot more than I did. Where she saw good old Missouri honesty, I saw a lot of hot air and conservatism. We didn't talk about her because we knew that the subject would cause a fight. So suffice it to say that Hot Air Fletcher gave me the idea for the first line of the book.

I had given up one morning and was sitting on the top step of the porch watching the two women fool around with the tomato plants. The day was cloudy and thick, and I was hoping for a monster thunderstorm to come through and clean off the world.

Good old Nails ambled up the stairs and sat down next to me, panting out a kind of quick "Kaa-kaa-kaa" sound. We watched the tomato pickers and I put my hand on his rock head. Bull terriers have rocks for heads; they only pretend that they are skin and bones.

"Do you like tomatoes, Tom?"

"Excuse me?"

"I asked ya if ya liked tomatoes?" Mrs. Fletcher straightened up slowly and, shading her eyes, looked over toward Nails and me.

"Tomatoes? Yes, I like them very much."

"Well, you know Marshall? He hated 'em. Said that his father made him eat them all the time when he was a boy, and ever since then, he wouldn't touch one. Wouldn't eat ketchup, tomato sauce, nothin'!" She dropped a handful of fat red ones into a wooden bushel basket that Saxony was holding for her.

Suddenly I knew that I had the first sentence and an idea for the chapter.

Saxony came into the bedroom an hour later and, sliding her hands over my shoulders, leaned down and asked what I was doing. Although it was totally unnecessary and theatrical, I snatched the first page that I'd written out of my notebook and handed it to her without stopping my scribbling.

" 'He didn't like tomatoes.' That's going to be the beginning of your book?"

"Read on." I kept writing.

" 'He didn't like tomatoes. He collected picture postcards of railroad stations. He found names for his characters in a small Missouri graveyard. He began his books on a school-size blackboard in a musty room in his basement. He kept everything he had ever accumulated as a child, and when he came to America from Europe, changed his name to that of an imaginary character he had created when he was a boy. He spent his free time working in a grocery store as a clerk at the cash register. . . .' "

She stopped, and after a moment's silence as deep as a canyon, I stopped pretending to write.

"Do you see what I'm trying to do? Put it all in a gun and blast it straight out at the readers. Let them catch whatever they want from that first shot and then I'll go over all of it slowly and carefully in the chapters that follow. I'll tell Anna all that, but why not let this chapter grab the readers by the neck and literally drag them into France's life? That's what we've been avoiding the whole time, Sax. Sure, we said that he was a strange kid, but he was also a goddamned strange man! He's the perfect eccentric artist. Look at his house, this little town he loved, the books he wrote! We have been dancing clear of that fact all along because we didn't want to admit to ourselves that our man was a weirdo. But what an incredible weirdo!"

"How do you think Anna will react to your calling her father that, Thomas? She would put him on Mount Olympus if you gave her half a chance."

"Yes, I know that there's that too, but I think that if I do it right, she'll understand what I'm trying to get at."

"You're willing to take that kind of chance?"

"Hey, Sax, you were the one who said that it had to be my book above anyone else's!"

"Yes, that's right."

"Well, then, this is the way I want to do my book. I know it now, and I've got to write it this way."

"Until Anna sees it."

"Come on, Sax. A little moral support now and then, huh?"

The thunderstorm that I wanted came through and decided to stay. For the next week it rained on and off. Saxony went to the library and brought back an armload of famous children's books. She said that the librarian had told her to tell me, "I told you so."

We had decided to read and reread as many of the classics as we could in case there was anything there for comparison or contrast with the work of the King, as I called him.

The Hobbit, The Lion, The Witch and the Wardrobe, Through the Looking Glass . . . Half of our time was spent out on the porch reading in Mrs. Fletcher's damp wicker chairs. The rain was mild and pleasant and turned everything either blue or shiny green.

Our landlady must have known how involved we were, because she wasn't around much. For that matter, neither was Anna, whom we didn't see at all after she delivered the boxes of France memorabilia. She had told me to call her if I needed her, but I didn't.

Between the reading, writing, the rain, and fooling around with Saxony (she said that bad weather made her feel sexy, and so our sex life got better and better), the days were full and passed like an express. Before I knew it, I had finished *The House at Pooh Corner, Charlie and the Chocolate Factory, The King of the Golden River,* and the first draft of my chapter. It had taken a little over two weeks. We celebrated that evening with Shake 'n Bake chicken, a bottle of

Mateus rosé, and my father's *Train Through Germany* on television, which was one of his better flicks.

The next day I woke up and felt so good that I leaped out of bed and did twenty push-ups on the floor. For the first time in a very long time, I didn't need a map to see where I was going. It was damned nice.

After my push-ups I sneaked over to the desk and flicked on the little Tensor lamp that I'd bought at Wade's Hardware Store in town. There were the pages. *My* pages! I knew that I would end up rewriting them a dozen times, but that didn't matter. I was doing exactly what I wanted with whom I wanted, and maybe, just maybe, Anna France would actually like them and . . . I didn't want to think about that part yet. I would do it first and see.

I heard sniffing sounds from the other side of the door. It creaked open and Nails came in. He jumped up on the bed and lay down. He usually joined us now for his last forty winks before getting up for good in the morning. Mrs. Fletcher had a nice old battered love seat for him out in the hallway, but since we had arrived he'd taken to spending more and more time with us, both day and night. One night we were just about to make love when he jumped up and ran his freezing nose up my bare leg. I banged my head on the side of the bed and lost my erection somewhere between fury and laughter.

I looked over my shoulder and saw that he had once again perched on Saxony's chest. She was smiling and trying to push him off, but he wasn't having any of it. He made no attempt to move. He closed his eyes. Out to lunch. I walked over from the desk to the bed.

"Beauty and the Beast, huh?" I patted his head. "Hi, Beautiful."

"Very funny. Don't just stand there like that. He's crushing me!"

"Maybe he's a sex maniac and is really giving you some kind of nasty dog caress."

"Thomas, will you please just get him off me? Thank you."

After he had been shifted-wrestled over to my side of the bed (his head right on my pillow, no less), Saxony locked her hands behind her neck and looked at me. "Do you know what I've been thinking?"

"No, Petunia, what have you been thinking?"

"That after you finish this book you should do a biography of your father."

"My father? Why would I want to do a book about him?"

"I just think that you should." Her gaze shifted away from me up to the ceiling.

"That ain't no reason."

Her eyes slid back to mine. "Do you really want me to tell you?"

"Yes, of course I do. You've never said anything about this before."

"I know, but I've been thinking recently about how important he is in your life, whether you know it or not. Look, do you realize how often you talk about him?" She held up her hand to stop me from saying anything. "I know, I know—he drove you crazy and most of the time he wasn't even around. Okay. But he's *in* you, Thomas. More so than any kid-parent relationship that I've ever known. Whether you like it or not, he's staked out a big part in your guts, and I think it would be very important for you to sit down sometime soon and just write about him. It doesn't matter if it turns out to be an actual biography or just your memoirs. . . ."

I perched on the edge of the bed with my back to her. "But what good would it do?"

"Well, I never understood a lot of things about my mother, you know? I've already told you about her."

"Yes, you said that she could make anyone feel guilty about anything."

"That's right. But then one day my father told me that her mother had committed suicide. Do you know how many things became clear to me after that? How much made sense? I didn't actually *like* her that much more, but I suddenly saw a different person."

"And you think that if I find out about my father's life, then it'll make my relationship with him clearer to me?"

"Maybe, maybe not." She reached around and put her hand on my leg. "I do think, though, there's too much unresolved stuff that has ended up making you love and hate him at the same time. Maybe if you really dug into who he was, it would clear the runway for you. Do you understand what I mean?"

"Yes, I guess so. I don't know, Sax. I don't really want to think about it now. There's too much else that has to be done these days."

"Okay. I'm not telling you to drop everything and do it this minute, Thomas. Don't take it the wrong way. I just think that you should consider it."

"I will. Sure."

Nails shoved his nose into her neck, and that got her up and out of bed fast. I was glad that the conversation ended there.

The sun was out, and after breakfast we decided to take a walk into town. It was still early, and everything glistened like wet glass from the dew and the leftover rain. By now we more or less knew a few people—store owners and others—who waved when they drove by. That was another pleasant thing about living in a small town: there weren't enough of you around so that you could afford to ignore anyone. You might have to buy a cabbage from one of them or have him work on your car that afternoon.

When we got to the library, my friend "I told you so" was walking toward us on the other side of the street. I assumed that she was about to open the library. "There you are! The hermit. Wait there a minute. Let me cross." She looked so carefully both ways, you would have thought that she was crossing the San Diego Freeway. A Toyota puttered by, driven by a woman I had often seen in town but didn't really know. But she waved too.

"I've got some more books for you, Mr. Abbey. Are you ready for them?" The rosy rouge on her cheeks made me very sad for some reason.

"Thomas hasn't finished *The Wind in the Willows* yet, Mrs. Ameden. As soon as he does, I'll bring the whole bunch back to you and pick up the new ones."

"*The Wind in the Willows* was never one of my favorites. How can you have a hero who is a greasy little frog?"

I cracked up. She looked at me sternly and shook her blue-gray head. "Well, it's the truth! Frogs, little creatures with hair on the tops of their feet like the hobbit. . . . Do you know what Marshall used to say about that? 'The worst thing that can happen to a man in a fairy tale is to be turned into an animal. But the greatest reward for an animal in one is to be turned into a man.' Those are my sentiments exactly.

"Anyway, don't get me going on that subject. How is your book going?"

The more we talked with her, the more it seemed that everyone knew everything about everyone in that town: the librarian knew about the test chapter, how much information on France his daughter had given us, and the one-month deadline. But why? Sure, like Anna, the townspeople had a kind of claim on France, since he had spent so much of his life among them, but did Anna tell them everything because of that, or was there some other, more cloudy reason?

A picture flashed across my mind—Anna, naked and tied with leather straps to a bar in someone's basement playroom, being whipped again and again with a bullwhip until she told all of the deadpan Galen faces around her what they wanted to know about Saxony and me.

"Did you give him the train-station postcards too?"

"No, never! Aaugh, yes, yes, I gave him everything!"

Then (this is the same picture), the plywood door explodes and I come flying in with two Bruce Lee kung-fu chains whirling around in my hands like airplane propellers.

". . . the house?"

"Thomas!"

I started and saw that the two women were waiting for an answer from me. Saxony squinted daggers and sneaked in a killer pinch under my arm.

"I'm sorry. What were you saying?"

"He *is* a writer, isn't he? Head floating around in the clouds . . .

just like Marshall. Did you know that Anna took away his car keys a couple of years before he died? He bumped into more trees with that old station wagon. Dreaming, he was. Just plain old dreaming."

Everyone had at least ten Marshall France stories to tell. Marshall behind the wheel, Marshall at the cash register, Marshall and his hatred for tomatoes. It was a biographer's paradise, but I had begun to wonder why they had paid so much attention to him, and why there was so much contact among them. I kept thinking about Faulkner in Oxford, Mississippi. From what I had read, everybody in that town knew him and was proud that he lived there, but it wasn't any big deal to them—he was just their well-known writer. But the way people talked about Marshall France, you would have thought that he was either a miniature God in a kind of down-home way, or at the very least the brother that they were closest to in the family.

We decided to skip the library and finish our walk into town instead, partly because I didn't feel like looking at any books that morning, and partly because there were a few places that I hadn't visited for a few days.

The Abbey Guided Tour began with the bus station with its flaking white park benches outside and bus schedules posted right above them so that you almost had to sit in someone's lap to find out when the St. Louis express came through. A fat, pretty woman sat behind the tiny Plexiglas window and sold you your ticket. How many movies began with dusty bus stops like this in the middle of nowhere? A Greyhound comes slowly down Main Street and stops at Nick and Bonnie's Café or the Taylor bus depot. Above the windshield where the glass is tinted green, the sign says that this one is going to Houston or Los Angeles. But along the way it's stopped in Taylor, Kansas (read Galen, Missouri), and you want to know why. The front door hisses open and out steps Spencer Tracy or John Garfield. He's either got a battered suitcase in his hand and he looks like a bum, or else he's dressed in fit-to-kill city clothes. But either way, there is no reason in the world for him to be way out here. . . .

Favorite place number two was a macabre store a couple of steps down from the bus depot. Inside, hundreds of spooky white plaster statues: Apollo, Venus, Michelangelo's *David*, Laurel and Hardy, Charlie Chaplin, jockeys holding hitching rings in one outstretched hand. Christmas wreaths waited in ghostlike rows for people to buy them. The man who owned the place was an Italian who did all the work in the back of the store and who rarely appeared when you came in to look around. I had seen only two or three of his pieces in people's houses or out on their lawns in all of the time that I had been in Galen, but I assumed that he made enough money from them to survive. What was so ominous about it was the total whiteness of everything. When you entered the store, it was like stepping into clouds, only here they were John F. Kennedy and crucified-Christ clouds. Saxony hated the place and always went to the drugstore instead to see if any new paperback books had come in. I had vowed to myself that before we left, I would buy something from the guy just because I spent so much time wandering around in his joint. Not that there was ever anyone else in there.

"Hey, Mr. Abbey! I was hopin' that you'd be in soon. I got somethin' for you that I done special. Wait here."

The owner disappeared into his workroom and came out a few seconds later with a wonderful small statue of the Queen of Oil. Unlike the others, this one had been painted to match the colors of the book illustration.

"Fantastic! It's wonderful. How did you—?"

"Naah, naah, don't thank me. It was strictly a commission job. Anna came in here about a week ago and told me to make it up for you. You want to thank anyone, thank her."

Very cleverly, I slipped the statue into my pocket and decided for the time being that I'd hide it from Sax. I wasn't in the mood for a heavy discussion. I had a couple of minutes before I had to meet her at the drugstore, so I popped into a phone booth and rang up Anna's number.

"France." Her voice sounded like a sledgehammer on an anvil.

"Hello, Anna? This is Thomas Abbey. How are you?"

"Hi, Thomas. I'm fine. What's happening with you? How is the book going?"

"Good, okay. I finished the first draft of the chapter and I think it turned out all right."

"Congratulations! Mr. Tom Terrific! You're way ahead of schedule. Are there many surprises?" In an instant her tone of voice switched from hard to coy.

"Yes . . . I don't know. I guess so. Listen, I just went to Marrone's, and he gave me your present. I love it. What a great idea. I'm very touched."

"And what did Saxony think of it?" Her voice moved again, back to shifty.

"Um, well, I didn't show her yet, to tell you the truth."

"I didn't know if you would. But why don't you go ahead and tell her that it is a present to both of you. Tell her that it's a little something for having finished the chapter. She wouldn't get mad at you for that, would she?"

"Why would I do that? You gave it to me, didn't you?"

"Yes, I did, but please don't misunderstand." Her voice stopped and hung there out in space, indicating nothing.

"Yes, but look, if you gave it to me as a present, I wouldn't think of sharing it." I realized that I sounded offended.

"But you wouldn't really be sharing it. You and I would know . . ."

We actually went on and had an argument about it. The upshot was that I was disappointed, to be totally honest. Maybe getting it had created all kinds of Anna-and-me fantasies in my head. Then hearing her brush it off so lightly was a cold shower over everything. Anyway, she said that Petals had an appointment at the veterinarian for shots, so the rest of the conversation was short. At the end she repeated that she would be glad to help if we needed anything more, and then she was gone. I hung up but didn't take my hand off the black receiver once it was hooked back in its cradle. What the hell was I doing? I had just that morning been thinking about how nicely my life was going, then two hours later I was slamming phones down because I couldn't fool around with Anna France.

I left the booth and trotted over to the drugstore.

"Hey, Sax, what's up? What are you doing?"

"Thomas! Eek, you're not supposed to see any of this."

The man behind the counter stood in front of her and smiled beatifically at me. He had a couple of mascara containers in his hand.

"Since when did you start wearing mascara, Sax?"

"I'm just *trying* it, don't get excited."

I wanted to tell her that I liked her eyes the way they were, but I didn't want to sound like a character out of *My Little Margie* in front of the druggist. He had a little white name tag on his jacket: Melvin Parker. He reminded me of one of those Mormon missionaries that come to your door preaching the gospel.

Behind us something banged and I turned around to see Richard Lee finish off a quart bottle of Coke in one loud glug.

"Hiya, Mel. Hiya, Abbey. Hello there." The last was for Saxony. He said it so gallantly that I expected him to tip his baseball cap. I felt a little ping of jealousy.

"Mel, come over here a minute, will ya?"

The druggist walked over to "Prescriptions" and Lee joined him there. Mel reached under the counter and brought out a gigantic red-and-white box of unlubricated Trojan condoms. Lee hadn't said a word to him about what he wanted.

I don't want to sound like an elitist, but Trojans were the kind of rubber you kept in your wallet for three years when you were twelve or thirteen because they were so strong and thick. The word was that nothing short of a truck driving through one could put a dent in it. And yes, they were strong, but when the magic moment arrived and you actually used it, it was like screwing inside the Graf Zeppelin.

Lee bent closer to Parker and whispered something long and low in his ear. I tried not to pay attention but it was either them or Saxony's eyelashes in the counter mirror.

" 'Now if I can only find my goddamn keys I'll drive us both outta here in my bulldozer!' " I assumed that it was the punch line to a dirty joke, because Lee reared up like he'd been stung by a wasp in the fanny.

The two of them had a good laugh, although Lee's was more forced and rough and went on much longer than Parker's.

The Trojans disappeared into a brown paper bag and were paid for with a dirty twenty-dollar bill.

Putting the bag under his arm, Lee got his change and turned toward me. I have a bad habit of judging people as soon as I meet them. Unfortunately I'm wrong about them a lot of the time. I'm also stubborn, which means that if I don't like a person right away—even if he is an angel in disguise—it takes a hell of a long time for me to see that I'm wrong and to begin dealing with him differently. I didn't like Richard Lee. He looked as if he walked around all day in his underpants and took baths on alternate Thursdays. There were gold sleep nuggets in the corners of both of his eyes, which is the kind of thing that makes me want to reach out and wipe them away. Like a crumb on someone's beard that he hasn't noticed.

"I heard that Anna's letting you do the book. Congrats to you!"

My heart melted a little when he stuck out his big mitt for a shake, but then it froze again when I saw him leering at Saxony.

"Why don't you two come over to my house tonight? I can show you pictures of my mother and some other things like that. Why don't you come over and have dinner? I think we got enough for all of us."

I looked at Sax and vaguely hoped that she would come up with an excuse. But I knew that I had to talk to this man sooner or later because of the importance of his mother.

"It's fine with me. Thomas? We're not doing anything, as far as I can remember."

"No. Yeah. No, that's great. That would be terrific, Richard. Thanks a lot for asking."

"Good. I'm going fishing this afternoon, and if we're lucky we'll be having fresh catfish right off the line."

"Hey, that's great. Fresh catfish." I tried to nod enthusiastically, but if my expression betrayed me it was only because I was thinking about the whiskers on catfish.

He left and then Saxony decided to buy the Max Factor. I went to the counter to pay. While he rung it up, Mel the Druggist shook his head. "Personally, I never liked catfish. The only reason they're always so fat is that they eat anything. Real garbage fish, you know? That will be two-oh-seven, sir."

There were crosses on top of crosses. Jesus bled all over the room from fifty different places, each showing him suffering some new kind of agony. The whole house smelled of frying fish and tomatoes. Except for the couch I sat on, which smelled like wet dogs and cigarettes.

Lee's wife, Sharon, had the kind of innocent but odd pink face that you often see on midgets. She never stopped smiling, even when she tripped over their bull terrier, Buddy, and fell down. The daughters, Midge and Ruth Ann, were just the opposite: they slumped around the place as if the air were too heavy for them.

Richard brought out his handgun collection, his rifle collection, his fishing-pole collection, and his Indian-head nickel. Sharon brought out a photo album of the family, but most of the pictures were either of dogs they had had through the years or, for some reason, pictures of the family when they were injured. Richard smiling at his leg in a thick white cast, Midge merrily pointing to an ugly blue-black eye, Ruth Ann on her back in what was obviously a hospital bed, and in apparent pain.

"My God, what happened there?" I pointed to this one of Ruth Ann.

"When was that? Let me think. Ruth Ann, do you remember when I took that one of you?"

Ruth Ann scuffed over and breathed on my head while she looked at it. "That's when I slipped that disk in gym, Daddy. Don't you remember?"

"Oh, that's right, Richard. That one's of the slipped disk she got."

"Hell yes, now I remember. That cost me about three hundred bucks to put her up in the hospital. All they had down there was a semiprivate room, but I put her in anyway. Didn't I, Ruth Ann?"

Tobacco Road-y as they sounded (and looked and were), you could tell that they liked each other very much. Richard kept putting his arm around the girls or his wife. They loved it; whenever he did, they would snuggle up into him with little peeps of delight. It was bizarre to think of this bunch together in their sad white house looking at pictures of Ruth Ann in traction, but how many families do you know that are happy and enjoy each other's company?

"Dinner's ready, everyone."

As guest of honor, I got the biggest catfish, its mouth open in a final rictus. Stewed tomatoes and dandelion greens were there too. No matter how much I cut or pushed the catfish to the farthest corners of my plate, I couldn't lose it. I knew that the battle was lost and that I would have to eat some.

"Have you got a lot of work done on your book?"

"No, we're really just beginning. It will probably take quite a long time."

The Lees looked at each other across the table, and there was a pause of a couple of seconds.

"Writing a book. That's something I'd never do. In school sometimes I liked to read."

"You read now, Richard. What are you talking about? You've got all kinds of subscriptions." Sharon nodded at us as if to reaffirm the truth of what she had said. She hadn't stopped smiling once, even when she was chewing.

"Yeah, well, Marshall sure could write though, huh? That guy had more damned stories in his little finger . . ." He shook his head and picked up a drooling tomato from his plate. "I think you've gotta be a writer when you've got so many crazy ideas and stories to tell. You'd blow up if you didn't get them down. What do you think, Tom?" He put the whole tomato in his mouth and talked through it. "Some guys got stories, all right, but all they got to do to keep from explodin' is to tell them. Talk them out and then they feel okay again. Like Bob Fumo, right, Sharon? This guy Bob can tell you the damnedest stories all night long and then wake up the next morning and tell you a hundred more. But he just tells them and then he's done. I guess guys like you have got it a lot worse, huh?"

"And a lot slower." I smiled at my plate and pushed some more of the fish around with my fork.

"Slower's right, boy. How long do you think it'll take you to finish off this one about Marshall?"

"It's really very hard to say. I've never written a book before, and there are a lot of things that I'll have to know before I can really get going on it."

Again there was a pause in the conversation. Sharon got up and started to clear the table. Saxony offered to help but was quickly smiled down.

"Did you hear that that Hayden boy that got hit out in front of your place the other day died?" There was no expression on Richard's face when he said it. No concern, no pity.

But I felt a whomp in my stomach, both because I had seen it happen and because it was a little boy who had been happy two seconds before he had been splattered all over the road.

"How are his parents handling it?"

He stretched and looked at the kitchen door. "They're okay. There's not much you can do about it, you know?"

How can people do that? When a boy gets killed, how can you not want to punch something or at least shake your fist at God? Farmers and guys like that are of another breed, sure, they see death all the time, everybody's heard that story, but human is human, dammit. How do you not mourn the death of a child? I hoped that Lee was just being stoic.

"My God, I just remembered something! Anna *told* me that he would die. Isn't that strange?"

Saxony, who had devoured her fish, tomatoes, and dandelion

greens, twiddled a spoon. "What do you mean, she told you? How could she know that he'd die?"

"Don't ask me, Sax. All I remember is that she said he would. I mean, it wasn't any kind of big Svengali thing—he was in very bad shape when they picked him up."

"What do you think Anna is, Tom, the Amazing Kreskin? Did you ever see that guy on *Johnny Carson*? The magician? You can't believe what he does up there. . . ."

The kitchen door swung open and Sharon came in with a big hot pie on a black metal tray.

Now. This is what I saw, and you can draw your own conclusions. But I did see it. No, Saxony said she didn't. She thought I was crazy when I told her afterward; then she got really solicitous when I kept insisting that it was true. It *was* true.

There is a character in *The Green Dog's Sorrow* named Krang. Krang is a mad kite that has decided that the wind is its enemy. It begs to go up every day so that it can continue its war on its constant battlefield, the sky. The Green Dog falls in love with the face painted on the kite. When he runs away from the house where he lives, the house where "Yawns owned everything that men thought was theirs," he steals Krang from the closet, ties her white string to his collar, and the two of them go off together.

The first thing I saw when Sharon Lee came out of the kitchen was Sharon Lee. I blinked, and when I looked again, I saw Krang coming out of the kitchen holding a hot pie on a black metal tray. The Van Walt illustration: the wide empty eyes that betray the joy in the mouth's full, happy smile. The red cheeks, red lips, circus-yellow skin . . . At first I thought that it was some kind of remarkable mask that the Lees owned. And I'd thought that they were dumb? Anyone who owned a mask like that, much less put it on at that perfect moment, was brilliant. Nutsy-brilliant, but brilliant. It was like a Fellini movie or a funny-bad dream that you don't really want to wake up from even though it is frightening.

"That's incredible, Sharon!" I said it twelve times too loudly, but I was astonished. Then I looked to my right to see how Saxony was taking it. She frowned at me.

"What's incredible?"

"Sharon! Come on, Sax, it's amazing!"

She looked past me and smiled in Krang's direction. "Yes, yes!" she finally piped up, but then muttered to me under her breath, "Don't overdo it, Thomas, it's only a pie."

"Yeah, ha ha, pie-shmy. Very funny."

"Thomas . . ." Her smile went away and her voice had a warning in it.

Something was wrong. I whipped around and saw good old Sharon cutting the pie. Not Krang. Not a single Krang in the house. Not nobody but smiling Sharon Lee and her famous hot peach pie.

"I guess that that Tom wants a big piece, huh, Richard?"

"I guess that that's about the loudest hint I ever heard. Maybe you should give him the whole thing, honey, and make up a batch of popcorn for the rest of us!"

They all laughed, and Sharon served me an enormous piece. My mouth hung open. It *was* Krang, dammit. The same everything from the Van Walt illustration. I checked it out later to be sure. I checked it several hundred times later.

But there was no mask either. It was Sharon and then it was Krang and then it was Sharon. I was the only one who saw it happen. I was the only one it happened to. If I had been working night and day on the biography, it would have made a kind of sense: Biographer A leaps into the life of Author B and gets so deeply into it that soon he's seeing B's characters all over the place. Okay, okay, the idea has been overcooked a million times, but in my case I hadn't even started the book yet, really, much less been at it for a long time.

I had lunch with Anna a couple of days later when Saxony went off shopping again with Mrs. Fletcher.

I told her about my "vision," with a dismal chuckle.

"Krang? Just Krang? No one else?" She passed me the scrambled eggs.

"Just Krang? Jesus Christ, Anna, at this rate, next week I'll have all of the characters riding Nails around the backyard."

Petals heard his name and her tail thumped twice on the floor. She was sitting next to Anna, waiting for any table scraps that might come her way.

Anna ate some chutney and smiled. "I guess Sharon Lee isn't much like Krang, is she?"

"Hardly. The only things that they've got in common are those vacuous smiles."

"I'll tell you something though, Thomas, that might make you feel better. Did you know that Van Walt was my father?"

"Van Walt was your . . . You mean to say that your father illustrated his own books? Those are all his drawings?"

"The real Van Walt was a childhood friend of his who was later killed by the Nazis. Father took his name when he started doing the drawings for the books."

"So, hypothetically, Sharon Lee in some kind of crazy way might have been the inspiration for Krang?"

"Oh, yes, it's possible. You said yourself that they have the same smile." She brushed her lips with her napkin and put it down next to her plate. "Personally, I think it's a good sign for you. Father is becoming your little dybbuk, and now he'll haunt you all the time, night and day, until you finish his book."

I looked at her over the fresh white tablecloth. She fluttered her eyes, laughed, and slipped Petals a piece of egg under the table. It took me a moment to realize that her looking at me like that gave me a terrific erection.

If this story were a forties movie, then the next shot would be of a big calendar. Its pages would begin to flip by a day at a time, Filmland's way of showing you that time is passing. I worked like a dog, cleaning and cutting and polishing. On alternate days I loved it and hated it. Once I got up in the middle of the night after making long, exhausting love with Saxony. I walked over to the desk and just stared like an idiot at the damned manuscript in the moonlight. I gave it the finger for at least a minute before I got back into bed without feeling any better. I wanted it all to be so good—better than anything I had ever dreamed of doing. In a way, I secretly knew that it was a kind of last chance for me. If I didn't give it everything I had, it would make much more sense to go back to Connecticut in my station wagon and teach *The Scarlet Letter* to tenth-graders for the rest of my life.

In the meantime, between researching and reading and our constant discussions, Saxony had found time to begin work on a new marionette. I didn't pay much attention, I must admit. We got into the habit of getting up early, eating a light quick breakfast, and then disappearing into our respective hideaways until lunchtime.

I finished-finished two days before my month was up. I capped my Montblanc, quietly closed my notebook, lined the pen up right alongside it. I put my hands on top of the book and looked out the window. I asked myself if I wanted to cry. I asked if I wanted to jump up and dance a few jigs, but that got vetoed too. I smiled and picked up the big chunky Montblanc. It was shiny black and gold and weighed much more than a fountain pen should have. I had corrected a few million essays with it, and now it had written part of my book. Good old Montblanc. Someday they would have it under glass in a museum with a white arrow pointing to it. "This is the pen Thomas Abbey used to write the France biography." I felt like I'd float right up out of my chair and around the room on the slightest breeze. My mind lay down and put its hands behind its head. It looked up at the sky and felt pretty good. Pretty goddamned good.

"You're really done."

"I'm really done."

"Completely and totally?"

"The works, Saxolini. Everything." I jigged my shoulders and still felt as if I weighed two pounds.

She was sitting on a high chromium stool, sanding what looked like a rough wooden hand. Nails was under the table snuffling around a big bone we'd gotten him the day before.

"Wait a minute." She put the hand down and got off the stool. "Go out of the kitchen for a little while. I'll call you when I want you to come back in."

Nails and I went out on the porch. He dropped the bone where

I stopped, and lay down on top of it. I looked out at the still garden and empty street. I literally had no idea of what day it was.

"Okay, Thomas, you can come back in now."

Without a word from me, Nails picked up his bone and walked to the screen door. He waited there with his nose pressed to the wire mesh. How did he know things like that? Nails the Wonder Dog.

"I'm not completely done with it yet, but I wanted you to have it today."

From one of the photographs of Marshall France, she had carved a meticulously detailed mask of the King. The expression on his face, the color in his eyes, his skin, lips . . . it was all awesomely real. I turned it over and over in my hands, looking at it from every conceivable angle. I loved it but was also very spooked by it.

A Queen of Oil from Anna, a Marshall France from Saxony, my chapter done, and the fall had just about arrived—my favorite season of the year.

Anna loved the first chapter.

I gave it to her and spent an hour quivering and twitching and hopping around her living room, touching everything in sight and sure that she would hate everything that I had written and would want me out of town on the next freight. When she came back into the room with it stuffed up under her arm like an old newspaper, I knew that it was curtains. But it wasn't. Instead she walked over, handed it to me, and kissed me hard on both cheeks as the French do.

"Wunderbar!"

"It is?" I smiled, frowned, tried to smile again, but couldn't.

"Yes, it most certainly is, Mr. Abbey. I didn't know what you were doing when I first began reading, but then the whole thing opened up like those Japanese stones that you throw in water and they suddenly blossom up like moonflowers. Do you know what I mean?"

"I guess so." I was having trouble swallowing.

She sat down on the couch and picked up a black silk pillow

with a yellow dragon on it. "You were right all along. The book must open up like a peacock's tail—whoosh! It would have been wrong for it to start in Rattenberg. 'He was born in Rattenberg.' No, no. 'He didn't like tomatoes.' Perfect! The perfect beginning. How did you know that? He hated tomatoes. He would have howled, *howled* with laughter if he had known that his official biography would begin like that. It is wonderful, Thomas."

"It is?"

"Stop saying, 'It is?' Of course it is. You know that as well as I do. You've caught him, Thomas. If the rest of your book is this good"—she waved the manuscript at me and then kissed the damned thing—"he'll be living and breathing again. And you will have done it for him. I am not going to say another word about how I think it should be written."

If it had ended there, the credits would have come up over a picture of young Thomas Abbey taking his manuscript from the alluring Anna France, walking out of the house and down the road to fame and fortune and the love of a good woman. A Screen Gems Production. The End.

What happened instead was, two days after that, a freak late summer tornado whipped through Galen and made a total mess of everything. One of the only human casualties was Saxony, who got a compound fracture of her left leg and had to be taken to the hospital.

The townspeople were unruffled by the tornado, although the Laundromat was leveled, as were parts of the elementary school and new post office. Whether it was Midwestern stoicism or what, no one moaned or groaned or made much of a fuss about it. A couple of times people told me that you had to expect that kind of thing out here.

I missed having Saxony around, and I moped through the house for a couple of days doing nothing, but then I forced myself to create a daily schedule that would be both comfortable and productive. If nothing else, I knew that she would have yelled at me if she found out that I wasn't working on the book while she was in the hospital.

I got up around eight, had breakfast, and worked on the book until noon or one. Then I made up a couple of sandwiches and drove over to the hospital in time to have a leisurely lunch with Sax. That lasted until about three or four, when I went home and either did some more work if I was in the mood, or started preparing my bachelor dinner. Mrs. Fletcher offered to cook for me, but that meant having to eat with her. After dinner I would type up what I'd written that morning, then round off my day with some television or reading.

The second chapter went very slowly. It was the one where I first started retracing my steps through France's life. I knew that it would be best to go back to his childhood, but the question was, where in his childhood? Begin at the beginning with him howling in the cradle? Or as a kid collecting postcards, à la Saxony's idea? I wrote up two or three involved outlines and read them to her, but we agreed that none of them fit. I decided to change my tack—I would just begin writing, as I'd done with the first chapter, and see where it took me. I'd base it on his days in Rattenberg, but if it wandered off, I'd let it go, like a divining rod. If worse came to worst and it got crazy, I could always throw it out.

At night, in between shows like *The Streets of San Francisco* and *Charlie's Angels,* I also began thinking about doing the book on my father. Since Saxony had mentioned it, I realized how often I did talk and think about him. Literally every day some kind of Stephen Abbey ectoplasm materialized, whether it was an anecdote, one of his films on television, a quality in him that I'd remember and then recognize in myself. Would I be exorcised of Stephen Abbey if I wrote about him? And how would my mother react? I knew that she was in love with him long after he drove her away with his manic looniness. If I wrote about him, I'd want to tell everything that I remembered, not like those offensive "I Remember Daddy" things that famous people's kids write all the time and are usually the worst kind of phony adoration or ghost-written hatred and abuse. I called my mother to wish her a happy September 1 (a little tradition we had), but I didn't have the nerve to broach the subject.

I was sitting in the kitchen at the table one night writing

down some memories when the doorbell rang. I sighed and capped my pen. I had filled four sides of my long yellow paper and felt I'd only gotten started. I gaped at the pad and shook my head. "Life with Pa-Pa," by Thomas Abbey. I got up to answer the door.

"Hi, Thomas, I've come to take you out on a midnight picnic." She was dressed all in black, ready for a commando raid.

"Hi, Anna. Come on in." I held the door open, but she didn't budge.

"No, the car is all packed and you have to come with me right now. And don't say that it's eleven o'clock at night. That is when picnics like this get started."

I looked to see if she was kidding. When I saw that she wasn't, I turned off all the lights and got my jacket.

The days were cooler, and some of the nights were pure fall-cold. I'd bought a bright red mackinaw at Lazy Larry's Discount Center. Saxony said that I looked like a cross between a stoplight and Fred Flintstone in it.

The moon was a werewolf's delight—full, gravel-white—and seemed half a mile away. The stars were out too, but the moon held center stage. I stopped before I got to the car and stared up at it while I buttoned every button on my coat. My breath misted white on the still air. Anna stood on the other side and propped her black elbows on the roof of the car.

"I can never get over how clear the sky is out here at night. They must have filtered out all of the impurities."

"Ninety-nine and forty-four one-hundredths pure Missouri sky."

"Exactly."

"Let's go. It is cold out here."

The station wagon smelled of apples. I turned around and saw two bushel baskets filled with them on the backseat.

"Can I have an apple?"

"Yes, but watch out for worms."

I decided not to have an apple. She smiled. In the car's blue darkness, her teeth were as white as the stripe on the road.

"What's a 'midnight picnic'?"

"You aren't allowed to ask any questions. Sit back and enjoy the ride. You'll see everything when we get there."

I did what I was told. I let my head fall back on the seat and looked down my nose to the night road moving by.

"You have to be careful out here at night. There are always cows or dogs or raccoons on it. I once hit a female opossum. I got out of the car and ran back, but it was already dead. What was worse was that all of these little baby possums came crawling out of her stomach pouch as soon as I got there. Their eyes were still closed."

"Nice."

"It was ghastly. I felt like such a murderer."

"Uh, how's old Petals? Nails sends her his love."

"She's in heat, so I have to keep her locked away for two weeks now."

The road snaked up and down and around. I was tired, and the heat blowing up from the floor made my eyelids feel like heavy velvet curtains.

"Thomas, can I ask you a question?"

"Sure. Can I turn down the heat?"

"Yes, press the middle button. Do you mind if it's personal?"

I pressed the wrong middle button, and the blower huffed into high gear. She reached down, and going over my hand, pressed the right one. The huff died away, and I could hear the sound of the engine and the wheels for the first time.

"What's your personal question?"

"What is your relationship with Saxony?"

Here we are—Saxony safely ensconced in the hospital, my little black night commando at the wheel right beside me . . . I could have answered her question so many different ways. What did I want her to think—that I was a happily unmarried man? That I was just passing time with Sax until the right someone came along? That I wanted Anna to be the right someone, even if that was taking the whole thing too far?

"My relationship? Do you mean do I love her?"

All alone. If something happened out there between the two of us that night, no one would ever know. There was no way Saxony would be hurt if I told a small lie about what went on in that darkness. Impossible. It was eleven o'clock at night, Anna was there and I was there and Saxony wasn't there . . . and what I ended up saying was, "Yes, Anna, I love her." Then I sighed. What the hell else could I do? Lie? Yes, I know I could have, but I didn't. Aren't I wonderful?

"Does she love you?" She kept her hands on the top of the steering wheel and her head facing forward.

"Yes, I guess so. She says she does." With that, I felt something in my body let go and deflate. It made me feel calmer and less on edge. As if the jig was up and my main energy center could shut down for the rest of the night because I wouldn't be needing it anymore.

"Why are you asking, Anna?"

"Because I'm interested in you. Is that so surprising?"

"That depends. Professionally interested or personally?"

"Personally." That was all. That was all she said in this Lauren Bacall-deep "if-you-need-anything-just-whistle" voice. "Personally." I didn't dare turn to her. I closed my eyes and felt my heart beat throughout the upper part of my body. I wondered if I would die someday of a heart attack. I wondered if I was about to have a heart attack. Two seconds before, I had been about to fall asleep.

"Uh, what am I supposed to say to that?"

"Nothing. You don't have to say a word. I was only answering your question."

"Oh." I took a deep breath and tried to find a comfortable position on the plastic seat for both me and my eleven-foot-long erection.

I am pretty inept at seducing women. For years I thought that the best way to do it was to have three-hour-long heart-to-heart talks where you ended up saying right out front that you wanted to go to bed with her. That way wasn't completely successful, however, especially when I was in college and the girls that I liked were mostly "intellectuals" who carried around copies of *Nausea* or Kate Millett and used a Renoir postcard to mark their place.

The great problem that arose then was that I would have drunk so much image-building black coffee or poisonous espresso that if the magic moment ever did arise, I would have to keep slipping off to the toilet to piss it all out. I'm sure that I also bored any number of them to tears, because one day a girl said, "Why don't you stop talking so much bullshit and just *take* me?" It was a good lesson at the time, although I often tried it later and was pushed away more often than I was welcomed. As a result, even at this late date I never knew if (1) a woman wanted me or not, (2) if she did, how I was supposed to "take her," (3) . . . It's not necessary, because I think the picture is pretty clear. Luckily, with Saxony it had been mutual—and, God, I was thankful for that. But Anna? Anna France, sweet-mama daughter of my hero? Was she saying here that she wanted me, or was she flirting and trying to see how far she could go before I made my move and she would have to shoot me down?

"Anna?"

"Thomas?"

"I don't know what you want me to do. I don't know if you're saying what I think I'm hearing. Do you know what I mean?"

"Yes, I think so."

My hand was shaking when I lifted it toward her. It was my left hand. I chose it because if she didn't want me to touch her she could push it away and I'd have it back on my side of the seat quicker. Then I didn't know where it should go when it reached her, now that it was halfway there. Her knee, breast, arm? But it knew that it had to go to her face. Slowly, still shaking, I touched her cheek and found it hot. She took my hand in hers, and bringing it around to her lips, kissed it. She squeezed it tightly and brought it down to rest on her right knee. I felt as if my head was about to explode. We rode the rest of the way to her "picnic" like that.

The best description would be to say that Anna totally gave herself to me. Not that she was into any kind of bondage or kinky stuff, but when I made love with her I instantly got the feeling that she would let me do anything I wanted to her, or that she would do anything I asked her to. She didn't leap around or set fire to the ceiling, but she was so *there* that sometimes I felt I had gone all the way through her and would have to work all the way back before either of us was done, much less satisfied. Later, when I asked her if this had been the real purpose of the picnic from the beginning, she said yes.

I even got her to talk a little about herself that night. Making love brought down some of the barriers, and by the time the sun began to come up (we had adjourned to her double sleeping bag, which we put near the car on a high hill that overlooked meadows and cows), I knew that she'd gone through much of the same famous-father crap that I had. She kept repeating that her experiences were nothing compared to mine, but her stories about playmates, high school, special treatment from others, etc., rang so many bells that my head almost fell off from nodding so much.

I told her about myself and didn't feel strange or uncomfortable doing it.

We went to a diner out on the highway, and both of us had a "Trucker's Special" for breakfast—eggs and pancakes, sausages, toast, and all the coffee you could drink. I was famished and ate everything. When I'd finished and looked her way, she had swept her plate clean too, back to its original red and white stripes. She put her hand on my knee and asked Millie, the waitress, for more coffee for both of us. I wanted the other people in the diner to know that Anna France was with me and that only a few hours before we had made love again and again on top of a hill two miles away from there. I was exhausted and happy and I wasn't thinking about Saxony.

After that, until Sax came home, I spent at least part of every night at Anna's. Either she would cook dinner (God forbid) or I would come over later and we would talk or watch television, but then inevitably we ended up in bed. Later on I would stagger out of there at one or two in the morning and drive home in my freezing car.

At the beginning it was an incredible ego trip. Lovely, charming Anna France wanted me. The great-looking daughter of Marshall

France wanted me, *me,* not the son of Stephen Abbey. That had happened more than once with other women—as soon as they knew who I was, it was like a switch being thrown in them: if I can't have the father, then why not the son? Do you know what it's like to screw someone who you know is not doing it with you but with someone you represent?

With Anna I assumed that if there was any other, more blood-less reason, it was that I was her father's biographer, and liking what I'd already turned out, she wanted me to continue writing at the same pitch. Her body, if I really wanted to be cruel and cynical, was being thrown in as an added incentive to do a good job.

I didn't want to think about all of the complications that were due to hit the fan momentarily. I worked in the morning, and worked well, visited the hospital in the afternoon, and went to France at night.

The doctors had had to put some kind of special pin in Saxony's leg, which prolonged her stay in the hospital. The news made her very depressed, although I did what little I could to cheer her up. I brought her everything that I had written and asked her to proof-read it and make corrections and suggestions. She asked for a box of big black Dixon Beginners pencils and made her comments every-where on the manuscript. She had turned into an excellent editor, and more often than not our thoughts were on the same wavelength. When she wasn't at it with her pencil, she was reading biographies of everyone—Andrew Carnegie, Einstein, Delmore Schwartz—and taking pages of notes on them. I'm sure that the nurses thought that we hated each other, because we argued all the time. She would sit propped up in bed with her big white cast sticking out from the sheets and lecture me from a black-and-white school notebook she kept. I had a matching notebook (another couple of treasures from Lazy Larry's), and I'd make an occasional note in mine, though not as often as she said I should.

I don't know if she felt helpless there or if she sensed something different in me. Whatever it was, although she was often crabby and short, she seemed more fragile and fallible than I had ever seen her. It made me love her like crazy, but the love didn't keep me away from Anna.

I had never felt so high and explosive before in my life. Every, every day had twenty different reasons for being there. Getting into bed late at night, I could hardly fall asleep—tired as I was—because the thought of tomorrow was so exciting. I loved leading all of my different lives—writer, researcher, Anna's lover, Saxony's man. But I knew too that that totally convenient world would end any moment, and that then I might be jumping around as if the floor were on fire, trying to salvage whatever I could. Ask me, though, about the most incredible time in my life, and unquestionably it was those weeks in the fall in Galen before the winter and the dead began.

Part Three

1

La-de-da-de-da—I was waltzing on over to Anna's one night, a little earlier than I'd told her I'd come. Saxony was due back in a couple of days, but I still wasn't going to worry about that until the time came. I got to within a house of Anna's when I saw her porch light go on and the front door open. She came out with Richard Lee. They were laughing and she had her hand on his shoulder. He was facing away from her, but at the last minute he turned around and took her in his arms. They kissed right under the light. It went on and on and on. Richard Lee. For God's sake—*Richard Lee!* When they pulled apart, he put both hands on the front of her white blouse, and she laughed at something he said. She lifted one of his hands to her mouth and kissed it. He turned and walked down the porch steps. Petals followed him all the way to his truck, which was parked just in front of the house.

"So tomorrow's okay, Anna?" he bellowed over the roof to her.

She nodded and smiled. He slapped the top of the truck happily and laid a patch of rubber in the street as he pulled away.

When I "arrived" a few minutes later, she seemed pleased that I was there so early. Her cheeks also seemed flushed as hell. I dragged her up to the bedroom and made love to her as if she were a tackling dummy. When we had finished it wasn't two seconds before I was over her again and working even harder. We very rarely said anything when we fucked, but this time I asked her if she was doing it with other men.

She rocked and moved under me, and her fingers squeezed and pinched me wherever they were. Her eyes were closed and her mouth was open in a lovely sensual smile.

"Yes. Yes. Yes." She squeezed my neck very tightly and groaned in my ear. She didn't open her eyes but she kept smiling. I know because I was watching.

"Who?" I had her breasts in my hands, rubbing her plum-colored nipples roughly with my thumbs. I didn't know if I wanted to hurt her or screw her to death or run away or what.

"Yes. Yes. Yes." She rocked and nodded and spoke all at the same time. The words moved with her hips.

"Who?"

"Richard Lee." Her eyes stayed closed. "You-and-Richard. Oh! You-and-Richard!"

Why the hell did it have to be him? Why had she chosen that slob in a baseball cap? Had he bought that huge box of Trojans that day to use on Anna? A hundred cheap rubbers jamming away in her?

She said nothing more about it, but I was sure that she would have answered any other questions I had about "them." That openness only confused me more. I spent the night there for the first time.

2

"Home again! Are you in seventh heaven?"

She was on those old-timey wooden crutches. Her face had a hospital pallor. She hobbled over to our bed, put the crutches across it, and sat down hard. The springs sproinged and spinged.

"Could I have a glass of water please? Nails, will you please *stop?*"

He had been dancing around the room ever since she came in. At first she had been tickled by his joy at seeing her, but it quickly turned into full-blown anger when he kept getting in her way. I didn't say anything, although I thought she was being a little over-sensitive about the whole thing. He couldn't help being happy.

"I bought you some tomato juice, Sax. Would you like me to fix you up a Virgin Mary? We've got some Worcestershire sauce and pepper."

"I feel so tired already. God, it's so stupid. I just got out of the hospital about ten minutes ago and I feel like collapsing."

I went over and sat down next to her. I put my hand where her knee had turned to hardened plaster. "Listen, that happens all the time when you're in bed for a long time. Your body just gets used to being horizontal. It's no big deal. What do you think you have to do, go out and run the Boston Marathon?"

"Tell me all about it, will you, Thomas? Like maybe I don't know what it's like to be in a hospital? Like maybe I haven't spent half of my goddamned life in one?"

"Take it easy, Sax. Don't have a coronary."

I fled the room at the first possible chance, Nails hot on my heels. I hadn't seen her this edgy since the first day we'd met and I'd wanted to buy the France book from her.

The kitchen was drowning in sunlight. It was cold as hell outside, but our apartment was toasty-warm, and the sun coming in made it feel alive and cozy.

I got out a glass and held it up to the light; Saxony had a fetish about eating off either dirty plates or silverware. The glass passed the Abbey inspection and I went to the refrig for the can of tomato juice—her all-time favorite drink.

Clump-clump-clump from the other room, and then she was in the doorway, leaning heavily on her crutches.

"Thomas?"

"Yes, my buddy?" I speared the can with an opener and turned it so that I could punch a hole on the other side.

"I hated being in that hospital. I'm sorry if I'm stupid and wrought-up now, but I'm just so glad to be back here with you and Nails and everything that it's all coming out of me the wrong way. I'm being a bitch and I'm sorry."

I put the opener down and looked at her. The doorway made a big white frame around her in her pine-green dress. Her face looked both tired and guarded at the same time. A flash of Anna, naked and under Richard Lee, crackled across my mind.

"Sax, do you want to make love? I mean, would it make you feel better if we did? More relaxed? Maybe that's the best way to break the ice. Just not say anything more and go right to bed. Get it all out of us."

"Could you do it with this thing on me? Wouldn't it be too hard? That's another thing I was worrying about when I was in there." She looked at the floor and shook her head. "You have so much damned time to think about stupid things, and then you create all kinds of new worries. I was afraid that we wouldn't be able to do our funny business for months with this thing on my leg."

I picked up a spoon and held it in my hand like a cigar. I wriggled my eyebrows like Groucho Marx. "My little dandelion, the only thing hard will be keeping me away from you once this tango has begun!" I wriggled my eyebrows again and tapped the ash off my cigar. I had no desire to make love. "Say the secret word and the bird comes down and pays you fifty dollars!"

I went over, and bending at the knees, hefted her up and over my shoulder. She felt warm and heavy and soft, and she smelled like clean laundry. I did a Tarzan hoot and, stumbling a bit, wobbled off to our bedroom.

And then how was it? Okay. Good. Fine. No, the exact truth of the matter was that it was all right. Very all right. It had nothing to do with the cast, either.

3

Suddenly everyone in Galen was nice to me. I didn't know whether it was because they knew that Anna had liked my first chapter or because they knew that we were lovers (or rather that I was one of her lovers). In any event, I was sure that Mrs. Fletcher knew what was happening, because she often made it easy for me to get out of the house and over to Anna's after Saxony had returned from the hospital.

The two women spent a lot of time together. I often saw them touch or laugh with the familiarity of a mother and daughter. Saxony was giving her wood-carving lessons, and Goosey was teaching her how to cook "country things." I was torn between a kind of jealousy and relief by the relationship. I had never really felt close to any older person, not even to my mother, who was sweet but too neurotic and possessive to put up with for any length of time. But Sax and Goosey giggled and baked and whittled together, and much of the time were like two little girls over in the corner of a room playing those crazy secret games that girls do. I knew about those games because I used to spy on my sister and her friends when they were up to something. They were always so happy and content that I would stomp away from her keyhole or the crack in the door, screaming at the top of my lungs that I'd seen *everything* and was going to tell on them. Not that they were ever doing anything.

In the meantime, over on the other side of town, Anna gave me the run of France's files, and I often spent whole afternoons up there, working at his desk, poring over his early papers, notes, sketches, etc.

Gradually, out of a fog of words I began to get a real picture of the man. The facts that we had originally turned up on him became hollow and unimportant. Where he was born, what he did in 1927, where his family went on their vacations . . . I duly noted it all, but I began to think of these details as his clothes, and what I wanted to do was reach inside and touch the skin beneath. I wanted to know him so well that I could know what kind of thoughts he would have had when he was twelve or twenty-five or forty. Did I want to be him? Sometimes. I wondered if that wasn't true about all biographers. How could you want to immerse yourself in a person's life and not have at least a secret hankering to be that person?

What was so attractive to me about Marshall France? His vision. His ability to create one world after another that silently enchanted you, frightened you, made you wide-eyed or suspicious, made you hide your eyes or clap your hands in glee. And he did it continually. I told all of this to Anna one day, and she asked me what was the difference between her father's books and a good movie, which basically does the same thing to you. In a way she was right, but the difference for me was that I had never seen a movie that came as close to my sensibilities as any of the France books did. He could have been my analyst or greatest friend or confessor. He knew what made me laugh, what scared me, how to end a story just the right way. He was a cook and knew exactly what spices I liked in my meals. When you realize that hundreds of thousands of other people out there felt the same way about the works of Marshall France, you could only marvel at what the man had accomplished.

Sometimes in the afternoon when I came home Saxony wouldn't be there. I never asked her where she went, but I assumed that she was with Mrs. Fletcher. The house would be cold and dark, with only the saddest kind of October-gray light lying tiredly on the floor and on the furniture near the windows. The whole air of the place made me feel wintry and sad. To combat the emptiness that went along with it, I would move madly around, turning on all the lights. I resented her not being there, but I would catch myself for being such a hypocrite. Especially when I had just gotten back from working half the afternoon and making love to Anna the other half.

There was a lot of sex then. I didn't know if I was trying to punish Anna for Richard Lee or trying to show her that I was better. But then I started to see him as only a kind of shadow, his hands appearing out of a darkness. It was what I knew she was doing in return, returning in real life the caresses of this shadow, moaning and moving to him, wanting him. That was what drove the white spike through my imagination every time I thought about her.

It was on one of those absently sad afternoons that I found out about Nails. Anna and I had really gone through the floor with our fucking. It was intense and the orgasm was crazy, but I hadn't done any good work that day, and afterward I felt tired and depressed. I was looking forward to spending the evening with Saxony. We were going to watch a Ronald Colman classic on television that we had been anticipating all week. As a surprise treat, I had stopped at the market on the way home and bought all the fixings for hot-fudge sundaes.

Walking up the steps, I saw that the lights were off in our part of the house. I grimaced and hiked the bag of groceries higher on my chest. Driving home, I had worked out a whole nice, silly scene: flinging the door open, I would race to wherever Sax was. I would tell her to drop everything because "The Great Thomas" had arrived. "Treasures from the Mysterious East, lady." Out would come the chopped walnuts. "Frankincense and myrrh from the Caves of Zanzibar," the maraschino cherries next. Then some other dumb line—the crème de la crème or something—and the fudge sauce would jump onto the counter. I had even gone to two places to find the kind she liked most.

But it didn't make any difference anyway, because she wasn't there. I opened the front door and closed it quietly behind me. The house smelled of dusty heat from the radiators and a kind of damp wood funk that came up from the floors in winter. I started to reach for the light but hung back when I heard someone talking or murmuring in the bedroom. Ah ha! Saxony was having a snooze.

Walking on the toes of my sneakers from the kitchen to the bedroom, I heard a voice murmuring again. It was almost unfamiliar. Almost too high and disconnected for it to be hers. I opened the door as slowly as I could to avoid any creaks it might make. The shades were drawn all the way down. The only thing on the bed was an ethereally white, totally familiar lump with its back turned to me. Nails. Very adorable, but a lousy substitute at the moment for Saxony.

His legs stuck out stiffly in front of him. He twitched a few times and his jaws snapped at the air. I thought he was just having another Nails nightmare. Then he spoke.

"The fur. It is. Breathe through the fur."

A chill needle ran up my spine to my neck. The fucking dog talked. The fucking dog talked. I couldn't move. I wanted to hear more, I wanted to run like hell.

My eyes raced past the corners of the room. We were alone. I was alone.

Willie Morris's memoir of James Jones was on the night table, my other pair of stringy black sneakers was outside the closet door, the dog was on the bed.

"Thomas. Yes, Thomas."

I screeched. I didn't leap in the air when he said my name, but a spasm flicked down my backbone at the same time as I yelped.

There was a flurry of white motion, a couple of sharp barks, and then he was standing on the bed looking at me, tail wagging. He looked like lovely old dumb Nails.

"I heard you!" Scared as I was, I felt like an idiot talking to him like that. He kept on wagging his white whip tail. It slowed for a split second when I said that, but went right back up to its fast windshield-wiper speed.

"Don't you shit around with me, Nails. I'm telling you—I heard you!" What the hell was I doing? He played out the whole bad-doggie bit: the tail went between his legs and his ears pressed down close to his head.

"Goddammit, goddammit, dog. I heard everything. Don't fuck around with me! I heard what you said. 'Breathe through the fur.' "

I was about to say more when he did an odd thing. He closed his eyes for a long time, then sat back on his legs like a frog, looking resigned.

"Well? Huh? Well, say something more. Go ahead. Just don't fool around!" I honestly didn't know what I was saying. He opened his eyes and looked right at me.

"They're home," he said. "They'll be in here in a minute." His voice was clear and understandable, but it sounded like a dwarf's— high and squeezed up through his throat. But he was right. Car doors slammed and I heard the mumble of voices from outside. I looked at him and he blinked.

"But who *are* you?"

He said nothing more. The front door clicked, and seconds later the house was filled with light brown shopping bags, cold cheeks, and Nails's barks.

I wanted to tell someone, but every time I got up enough nerve to talk to Saxony, I remembered the James Thurber story about the unicorn in the garden. A mousy little man discovers a unicorn in his garden. He tells his monstrous wife. She laughs it off the way she laughs off everything he says. The unicorn keeps coming to visit, but it only visits him. In turn he keeps telling the old battle-ax about his nice new friend. Finally she gets fed up and calls for the guys in the white coats with the butterfly nets. The story goes on, and in the end she's the one who gets carted away, but I only thought about it up to that point: where the husband told her once too often about the unicorn and she reached for the telephone and the number of the loony bin.

If not Saxony, then I certainly wasn't going to tell Anna. I had gotten myself into enough trouble when I told her about seeing Krang the Kite on Sharon Lee's face. All I had to do now was add Nails the Talking Dog to my list, and my days as Marshall France's biographer would be over.

But after that, he stayed away from me. He didn't come up on the bed in the morning, didn't follow me around the house any-more. I watched him like a hawk whenever we were in the same room together, but his tight, absent face betrayed nothing but dog eyes and a flash of bubblegum-pink gums whenever he was eating or cleaning himself. He was very much the dog.

Porpoises talked, didn't they? And hadn't they discovered a couple of words in ape language? What about that woman in Africa, Goodall? So what was so strange about a talking dog? These and other stupid rationalizations fluttered across my brain on featherless wings. I had witnessed one of the great wonders of the world, and yet I wondered if it wasn't the way all mad people began down "that" road. Kite faces on women, talking dogs . . . All the things that I knew were a little weird about me stood up, took a bow, and started walking around inside me at top speed: liking my mask collection a little too much, talking about my father so much that I obviously had some kind of fixation about him . . . Things like that.

Nails was killed forty-eight hours later. Every night before bed-time, Mrs. Fletcher fed him and led him out for his last run. No one paid much attention to the leash law in Galen, and wandering dogs were a common sight at all times of the day.

That night a thick winter fog had settled over everything, and the few sounds that seeped in from the street were muffled. Saxony was working on her marionette in the kitchen and I was typing up some notes on Chapter Three when the doorbell rang. I yelled that I would get it and tapped a last key before I got up from my chair.

A young pretty girl I'd never seen before stood on the porch under the bare overhead light. She looked very happy.

"Hi, Mr. Abbey. Is Mrs. Fletcher in?"

"Mrs. Fletcher? I think so." The door to the upstairs was closed. I climbed all the way up and knocked to get her. She came out in her robe and slippers.

"Hi, Tom. What's up? I'm right in the middle of *Kojak*."

"There's a girl downstairs who wants to see you."

"At this time of night?"

"Yes. She's waiting for you at the front door."

"Out in this weather? Give me your arm so I can get down these stairs without breaking my leg."

When we got to the bottom, the girl was standing in the same place.

"Carolyn Cort! What brings you out here tonight?" She rummaged through the pockets of her robe and came up with a battered pink leather eyeglass case. Hooking the fragile-looking spectacles over her ears, she took a step forward. "Huh?"

Carolyn Cort smiled, reached out, and touched the old woman on the elbow. She looked back and forth between the two of us. For a moment I was afraid that she was a Friend of God or a Jesus freak or something, come out in the middle of the night to convert the heathen. "Mrs. Fletcher, you'll never believe this. Nails just got killed! He got hit in the fog!"

I closed my eyes and rubbed the bottom of my face. I felt the fog come up into my nose, and it almost made me cough. I still had my eyes closed when the old woman spoke. Her voice was shrill and excited.

"What's today? Is it right, Carolyn? I can't remember!"

I heard a nervous giggle and opened my eyes. Carolyn was smiling from ear to ear and nodding. "It's exact, Goosey! It's October 24th!"

I looked at Mrs. Fletcher. She was smiling too, just as hard as

Carolyn. She put a hand to her mouth. Her smile sneaked out from beneath the hand and somehow continued to spread.

"Who did it, Carolyn?"

"Sam Dorris! Just as it was supposed to be!"

"Thank God!"

"Yes. Then Timmy Benjamin broke his finger playing *football* with his brothers!"

"The little one? He broke his little finger?" Mrs. Fletcher grabbed hold of Carolyn's sleeve.

"Yes, yes, the little pinkie on the left hand."

They were ecstatic. They hugged and kissed each other as if it was the end of the war. Mrs. Fletcher looked at me and her eyes were brimming with tears. The whole thing was crazy.

"You *must* be the one, Tom. Now it's all going right again." Her face was radiant. Her dog had just been killed and her face was radiant.

"Can I give you a kiss, Mr. Abbey? I mean, only if it's okay with you."

Carolyn gave me a hot peck on the cheek and then twittered away, back into the fog. I didn't know if it was creepier out there or in here.

Mrs. Fletcher gave me another delighted look. "Ever since you started work on his book, Tom, everything here has gone right. Anna knew what she was doing with you, boy." She took my hand and held it in both of hers.

"But what about Nails, Mrs. Fletcher? He was just run over. He's dead."

"I know. I'll see you in the morning, Tom." She waved once when she got to the top of the stairs, and then she closed the door that separated her world from ours.

I went back into our apartment and silently closed the door behind me. Nails was dead. The dog that had talked to me was dead. That was bad enough (or good enough, depending on how you looked at it), but then the joy on both women's faces when Carolyn gave the news . . .

I didn't understand anything, but on the other hand I remembered a section from *The Land of Laughs* where the Queen of Oil says to one of her children:

> The questions are the danger.
> Leave them alone and they sleep.
> Ask them, awake them, and more than you
> know will begin to rise.

"Thomas? Are you there? What happened?"

I saw the yellow light spilling out of the kitchen and I heard Saxony's portable radio tinnily blasting out the new rock song that was being constantly played then. She called it "The Chinese Water Torture Song."

When I walked in, she looked up from her carving and shrugged. "What was that all about?"

4

"Anna?"

She pushed the hair out of her eyes and put one bare arm behind her neck. "Yes?"

"Do you know about Mrs. Fletcher's dog?" I looked at her breasts. The small nipples were still hard and dark in the cold bedroom.

"Yes, I heard that he was run over last night. It's sad, isn't it?" Her voice didn't sound very sad. I didn't know if I wanted to see her face when I asked the next question. The bedroom was dark and shadowy. It smelled of love and old wooden furniture exposed to winter's cold. For the first time I was aware of both the smell and the fact that I didn't like it much.

"I was there when she heard about it." The first two fingers on my right hand started tapping on the part of the blanket down around our waists.

"Hmm?"

"I said that I was there when she heard about it. Do you know what she did?"

She turned her head slowly to me. "What did she do, Thomas?"

"She smiled. She was delighted. She made it sound like it was the best thing she had heard in years."

"She is a crazy old woman, Thomas."

"I know, you keep telling me that. But Carolyn Cort's not crazy, is she?"

"What about Carolyn Cort? How do you know her?" She sounded peeved.

"She was the one who came out to the house to tell Mrs. Fletcher. She was smiling too. She gave me a kiss when she left." I took a handful of blanket and squeezed it.

"God*damn* them!" She sat up in bed and reached to the floor on her side for her sweatshirt and blue jeans. I didn't know whether to move or stay where I was. You didn't want to get in Anna's way when she was mad.

She was dressed in two minutes. When she was done, she stood next to the bed with her hands on her hips and scowled at me. For a moment I thought that she was going to give me a smack or something.

"Petals!" She stared right at me while she bellowed for the dog in a very un-Anna-like voice. "Petals, get in here!" We looked at each other while we waited. I heard toenails clicking on the wooden stairs, then feet padding down the hall rug. Anna walked to the bedroom door and opened it. Petals trotted in and, after a cursory glance at me, sat down on Anna's foot and leaned against her.

"Petals, tell Thomas who you are."

The dog looked at her with that stony blank face.

"Go on, tell him! It's all right—it's time. We have to let him know."

The dog whimpered and dipped its head. It put a paw out, as if it was trying to shake hands.

"Tell him!"

"Wil-Wilma Inkler."

I started to move up and out of the bed. The voice was the

same as Nails's. A dwarf's voice, only this one was more macabre or perverse because it was distinctly feminine. A woman was in there somewhere. Dwarf or bull terrier, it was a woman's voice, loud and clear.

"Tell him what Nails's real name was."

The dog closed its eyes and sighed as if it was in great pain. "Gert Inkler. He was my husband."

"Fucking *A*! The guy in the train-station book! The guy who walked around the world!"

I was talking to a dog. "What am I, nuts? I'm talking to a goddamned dog!"

"I'm not a dog! I'm just one now, but all of that changes today! Today it's over for me! Over! Forever!" Petals was indignant. Her face still had no expression, but she spoke in a higher, more adamant voice. Don't ask me what was going through my head, I couldn't begin to explain. I'm naked, sitting in Anna France's bed, talking with a bull terrier who is saying that she won't be a bull terrier after today.

"Wilma, go out for a while and let us talk. I'll call you back in in a few minutes."

I watched her leave. I felt like a tight ball of yarn was beginning to unravel in my head. I expected to feel dizzy when I stood up, but I didn't.

"Do you understand yet, Thomas?"

I sat back down on the bed, defeated. I had only gotten as far as my white underpants.

"Understand what, Anna? That you've got talking dogs here? No. The fact that you knew that little boy was going to die? No. The fact that people around here celebrate when a dog gets run over? A talking dog, by the way. No. Do you have any other questions for me? The answer to them is no too."

"How do you know about Nails?"

"He talked to me right before he died. Purely by accident—I came on him when he was napping. He talked in his sleep."

"Are you frightened?"

"Yes. Where are my pants?"

"You don't look frightened."

"If I stopped moving around now, I'd have a spastic attack. *Where are my fucking pants?*" I jumped up and moved madly around the room. I was scared to death, exhausted from fucking, curious as hell.

She grabbed my leg and pulled me toward her. "Do you want me to explain everything to you?"

"Explain *what*, Anna? Will you please let me go? What the hell is there to explain?"

"Galen. My father. Everything."

"You mean that none of what you've said so far is the truth? Well, that's wonderful. *Shit,* where is my goddamned shirt?"

"Please stop, Thomas. What you have gotten so far is true, but it's only part of it. Please stop pacing around. I want to tell you all of this, and it's important!"

I saw a corner of my shirt sticking out from beneath one of the pillows, but Anna's voice was so strong and insistent that I didn't go over to retrieve it. There was an old Mission morris chair near the bed, so I sat down on it. I didn't want her touching me while she said whatever she had to say. I looked at my bare feet and felt the cold wood floor coming up through my heels. I didn't want to look at Anna. I didn't even know if I could look at her then.

I heard a car horn honking outside. Maybe old Richard Lee was going to come over and join us. I wondered what Saxony was doing.

Anna padded over to a chifferobe that reminded me of an iron maiden whenever I saw it. She opened one of the doors and bent down into it. I didn't give a full look her way until I was sure she couldn't see me. Clothes and shoes were shuffled and pushed around. A sandal came flying out, followed closely by a thick wooden clothes hanger. After a while she reemerged with a large gray metal strongbox about the size of a portable typewriter. She opened it and took out a blue spiral notebook. She put the box on the floor and flipped through the first pages of the book.

"Yes, this is the one." She looked at it once more and then handed it to me. "The pages are numbered. Start reading at about page forty."

I did, and there it was again—the funny, long-stroked italic handwriting in faded brown fountain-pen ink. There were no dates on the pages. One continuous flow. No drawings, no doodles. Only descriptions of Galen, Missouri. Galen from the east, Galen from the west, everywhere. Every store, every street, people's names and what they did for a living, whom they were related to, the names of their children. I knew so many of them.

An individual description would sometimes go on for ten or twelve pages. The line of a man's eyebrow, the color of the faint mustache shadowing a woman's lip.

I skimmed through and saw that the whole book was like that. France had done an inventory of a whole town, if that was possible. Suspiciously, I turned to the last page of the book. At the very bottom it said, "Book Two." I looked up to find Anna. She was staring out the window with her back to me.

"How many of these books are there?"

"Forty-three."

"All like this one? Lists and things?"

"Yes, in the First Series there are only lists and details."

"What do you mean, the First Series?"

"The Galen First Series. That's what he called them. He knew that the only way he could even attempt the Second Series was to begin by making up a kind of Galen encyclopedia. The town and everything in it as he perceived it. It took him over two years to finish."

I put the notebook down in my lap. The room was colder than before, so I got my shirt from under the pillow and put it on.

"But what's the Second Series, then?"

She spoke as if she hadn't heard a word I'd said. "He stopped writing *The Night Races into Anna* so that he could devote all of his time to that. David Louis wanted him to rewrite whole sections, but by then that book didn't mean anything to him. The only important thing that had come out of it was discovering the cats."

"Wait a minute, Anna, stop. I think that I've missed something. What about cats? Where do they plug into all of this?" I picked up the notebook and fiddled around with the silver metal spiral.

"Have you read *The Night Races*? The version that the people here in Galen have?"

"Yes, it's longer."

"Eighty-three pages. Do you remember what happens on the last pages of our edition?"

Embarrassed, I said no.

"The old woman, Mrs. Little, dies. But before she does, she tells her three cats to go and stay with her best friend after she's gone."

I began to remember. "That's right. And then when she does die, the cats leave her house and walk across town to her friend's house. They understand everything that's happened."

Rain was pattering on the roof. A streetlight blinked on outside, and I could see the rain slicing down through it.

"Father wrote that scene the day that Dorothy Lee died." She stopped and looked at me. "In the book, he changed Dorothy's last name to Mrs. *Little*. Dorothy Little." She stopped again. I waited for more, but only the rain filled the silence.

"He wrote that scene the day she died? Christ, that's a hell of a coincidence."

"No, Thomas. My father wrote her death."

My hands were freezing. The rain came across the streetlight in diagonals.

"He wrote her death, and then an hour later Dorothy's cats came over to tell us, just as he had written. That's how he discovered it. I heard them and opened the door. They stood on the bottom step of the porch and their eyes caught the hall light so that they looked like molten gold. I knew that Father hated cats, so I tried to shoo them away, but they wouldn't go. Then they started to cry and whine, and he finally came down from his workroom to find out where all of the noise was coming from. He saw them down there, crying and eyes glowing, and he understood everything in an instant. He sat down on one of the steps and started to cry, because he knew that he had killed her. He sat there, and the cats climbed up into his lap."

I sat on the edge of the chair and rubbed my arms. A wind

blew around outside, whipping the trees and the rain. It died as suddenly as it came. I didn't want to understand, but I did. Marshall France had discovered that when he wrote something, it happened: it was: it came into being. Just like that.

I didn't wait for her to say anything. "That's ridiculous, Anna! Come on! That's bullshit!"

She sat down on the windowsill and put her hands underneath her sweatshirt to warm them. A picture of her bare breasts skipped blithely, incongruously across my mind. She started bumping her knees together. She continued to do it while she spoke.

"Father knew that something had changed in him after he finished *The Land of Laughs*. My mother told me that he was very close to having a nervous breakdown because he was so wrought up. He didn't write anything for almost two years after he finished that book. Then she died, and that almost drove him crazy. When the book was published, it became so famous that he could easily have become a big celebrity, but he didn't want that. Instead, he worked down at the supermarket for the previous owner and took his little trips to St. Louis and Lake of the Ozarks."

I wanted to tell her to cut the shit and answer my questions, but I realized that she would, sooner or later.

"I was in college by then. I wanted to be a concert pianist. I don't know if I was good enough, but I had the drive and dedication. That was right after Mother died, and sometimes I felt guilty about his being here alone in Galen, but whenever I brought the subject up with him, he would laugh and tell me not to be silly."

She pushed off from the sill and turned around to look out at the rainy night. I was trying to stop my teeth from chattering. When she spoke again, her voice, reflected off the windowpanes, sounded slightly different.

"I was seeing a boy named Peter Mexico at the time. Isn't that a funny name? He was a pianist, too, but he was great, and all of us there knew it. We could never figure out why he was still in America—he should have been in Paris studying with Boulanger or in Vienna with Weber. We were inseparable from the minute we met. We had only known each other for a week before we started living together. You've got to remember too that that was back in the early sixties, when you didn't do that sort of thing yet.

"We were totally gone on each other. We had these grand visions of living in an atelier somewhere with skylights and twin Bösendorfer pianos in the living room." She turned from the window and came over to my chair. She sat on the wooden arm and put her hand on my shoulder. She spoke to the darkness.

"We had this terrible little apartment that we could barely afford. We both had rooms in the dormitory, but this was our secret sanctuary. We would go there after classes or at night, whenever we weren't practicing. We would sign out for the weekend and fly over there as fast as we could. And the place was so absolutely barren. We had bought two army-surplus cots and had tied the legs together to make it into a sort of double bed.

"One morning I woke up and Peter was dead."

Do you know the tone of voice of the announcer in an airport or a train station? That absolute monotone? "Train leaving on Track Seven." That was Anna's.

"The police came and did their stupid little tests and said that it was due to a heart attack.

"As soon as the funeral was over, Father came to get me and I came home to live with him. I didn't want to do anything. I didn't care about anything. I sat in my room and read heavy tomes—*The Trial* and *Heart of Darkness*, Raskolnikov. . . ." She laughed and squeezed my shoulder. "I was so very existential in those days. I read *The Stranger* ten times. Poor Father. He was just recuperating from his breakdown, and I came home with my own in hand.

"But he was an angel. Father was always an angel when it came to things like that."

"What did he do?"

"What didn't he do? All of the cooking and cleaning, listening to me while I endlessly whined about how cruel and unfair life was. He even gave me the money to buy a wardrobe of black dresses. Do you know Edward Gorey's work?"

"*The Unstrung Harp?*"

"Yes. Well, I was like one of Gorey's dark women who stand

out in the middle of a field at dusk and look off toward the horizon. I was quite a case, believe me.

"Nothing really worked to bring me out of it, so Father started *The Night Races,* out of desperation. It was going to be a complete departure from anything he had ever done. I was the main character, but it was going to be a mixture of truth and fantasy. He told me that when I was a little girl he would tell me stories when I woke up howling from a nightmare. He thought that maybe if he wrote a story for me now it would somehow have the same effect. He was such a wonderful man.

"That ass David Louis had been harping on him to get something new done. When he heard that Father had started this book, he wrote and told him that he wanted to come out to Galen and read what he had written.

"It just so happened that he arrived two days after Dorothy Lee died. You can imagine what it was like having him around here then!"

"Anna, these are all incredible things. You're telling me that your father was *God*! Or Dr. Frankenstein!"

"Do you believe me?"

"Come on, what am I supposed to say to that, huh?"

"I don't know, Thomas. I don't know what I would say if I were you. It's quite a story, isn't it?"

"Uh, yeah. Yeah. I guess you'd say that."

"Do you want more proof? Wait a minute. Petals! Petals, come in here."

5

When I left the France house that night, I was convinced. I had seen books, papers, journal entries. Petals even came in and talked about her "former life" as the human being Wilma Inkler.

Can you imagine that? You're sitting there in a chair and a dog is at your feet staring you right in the eye. It starts talking about being a dog in this high gravelly voice that sounds like something out of Munchkinland. And you're sitting there nodding your head like it happens to you all the time.

Dr. Dolittle in Galen. Dr. Dolittle in Cloud-Cuckooland. It was the same goddamned thing.

I taught a creative-writing course once at my school. The kids were mad for writing brutal, horrible stories about beheadings and rapes and drug overdoses. At the end of them, the only way the "authors" could get out of the blood-soaked morasses they'd created was to say, "Keith rolled over in bed and touched Diana's silky blond hair. Thank God it had all just been a dream."

Talking dogs, a modern Prometheus who used an orange fountain pen instead of clay, a sexy daughter who gave you a hard-on just brushing her teeth, who slept with you and Elmer Fudds in baseball caps, and who may or may not have given past boyfriends heart attacks. "Thomas rolled over in bed and touched the bull terrier. 'You were only having a dream, dear,' it said."

But what was I supposed to do? Go on with the research for the book? Go on writing it? I got halfway home in the car before all of it started to drive me out of my mind.

"What the hell am I going to do now?" I slammed the still-cold black steering wheel with the flat of my hand and pulled over at a gas station that had a public telephone out front.

"Anna?"

"Thomas? Hi."

I wondered if Richard was there. That would have been perfect. "Anna, what am I supposed to do now? Now that I know everything. What do you want me to do?"

"Why, write the book, of course!"

"But why? You don't want anyone to know about this. Look, even if my book turns out to be good enough to publish, the whole world will freak out when they read about it. Your Galen will become like . . . I don't know . . . Like some kind of mecca for weirdos. Your father will be a joke, because no one is ever going to believe any of it. And those who do will be the scum of the earth."

"Thomas?" Her voice floated into the telephone booth from another planet. The heat from my body started to fog the windows around me, and the illuminated face of the Pepsi-Cola clock in the gas station office had stopped at ten after four.

"Yes?"

"Thomas, there is much more that I have got to tell you about this."

I put my hand on my temple. *"More?* What more could there be, Anna?"

"There is. The most important part. I will tell you about it tomorrow. You're very late now, so go home and we'll talk about it then. Have a good night, my friend. And, Thomas? Everything will be all right. You know the most shocking parts now. The other things are just P.S.'s. I'll see you tomorrow morning."

The fog was just creeping up the windows. A carload of kids went by just as I was hanging up. One of them held a bottle out the window and waved at me with it. A ribbon of foamy liquid came out and hung in the air like a frozen pennant before it fell and broke on the ground.

"Thomas, I know what's going on with you and Anna."

I was working on a mouthful of acorn squash that had been topped with brown sugar and burned black in the oven. Saxony and Julia Child. I pretended to chew until I remembered that you don't really chew acorn squash—you gum it once or twice and then swallow it. I put my fork down on the edge of the yellow plate, careful to make as little noise as possible.

Sax took a roll from the bread basket and tore it in half. She picked up her knife and daintily buttered one puffy piece. The silence held. You wanted to squint your eyes and stick your fingers deep into your ears. It was coming. Something loud and explosive. She picked up the other half of her roll and wiped it around her plate, very cool.

"Did you think I didn't know?"

My heart pounded.

"No, I don't know, Saxony. I'm not good at being a secret agent."

"I'm not good either, but you know, I think I knew what was going on almost as soon as it happened. Really. Do you believe that? I'm not just saying it."

"No, I know that. I can believe you. My mother always knew when my father was . . . up to something. I guess when you get to know a person well, then it's not hard to see when they're acting oddly."

"Exactly." She took a short sip of 7-Up. I was able to look at her for the first time since she dropped the bomb. Her face was slightly flushed, but perhaps it was just the stuffy room. I'm sure my face looked like Chief Thunderthud's.

"Do you love her?" She kept her glass in her hand. She put it against one of her cheeks and I saw the bubbles fizzing up the side.

"Oh, Sax, I don't know. Everything is so crazy now. I'm not saying that as an excuse, please understand. Sometimes I feel like I've just been born and am having menopause at the same time."

She put the glass down and pushed it away from her. "Is that why you went to her?"

"No, no, I went with her because I wanted her. I'm not blaming that on anybody but me."

"That's very nice of you." A little venom spilled over into her voice, and I was damned glad of it. Until then she had been deadly calm and objective. I listened to the last fight my parents had before my mother walked out and took me back to Connecticut. Everything there too was so cool and calm . . . they could just as easily have been discussing the stock market.

"What do you want me to do, Sax? Do you want me to go?"

She blinked and fingered the tablecloth. "You can do whatever you want, Thomas. I don't own you."

"No, please, come on. What do *you* want?"

"What do I want? Why are you asking me that kind of question now? I wanted you, Thomas. I still *do* want you. But does that make any difference at this point?"

"Do you want me to stay here with you?" I balled up my napkin and looked at it in my fist. Saxony loved using real linen napkins at every meal. She hand-washed and ironed them once a week. She had bought two green, two powder-blue, two brick-colored ones that she rotated constantly. I felt like a piece of shit.

I looked up and she was staring at me. Her eyes were full. A tear spilled up over the edge and moved down her pink cheek. She held her napkin to her face and looked at me again. I couldn't meet her eyes.

"I have no right to hold you to anything, Thomas." She was breathing deeply, irregularly. She began a sentence, stopped, and didn't try again. She looked at her lap and shook her head. She brought the napkin to her eyes and said, "Oh, *shit!*"

I unballed my napkin and tried to fold it very carefully along its original crease mark.

6

A woman met me at the door. She was smiling, and grabbing my hand, squeezed it tightly.

"Uh, hi, uh, how are you?"

"You don't know who I am, do you?" Her smile was a little crazy. I wondered where Anna was.

"No, I'm sorry, but I don't." I tried a winning smile and lost.

"Arf-arf. Bowwow." She grabbed my shoulders and hugged me. *"Petals?"*

"Yes indeed, Petals! But a little different now, wouldn't you say?"

"My *God!* You mean you really . . ."

"Yes, Thomas, I told you that it was over. I'm back from that life and I'm me again. Me. Me. Me." She patted herself on her full chest. She couldn't stop beaming.

"I don't know . . . Jesus. I don't know what to say. I mean, uh, congratulations, I'm really happy for you. I just, uh . . ."

"I know, I know. Come on in. Anna is in the living room. She wanted me to meet you as a surprise."

I swallowed and tried to clear my throat. My voice sounded like chalk squeaking on a blackboard. "It's . . . it's, uh, some surprise."

Anna was sitting on the couch drinking coffee from a thick porcelain mug. She asked me if I wanted some, and when I said yes, she looked at Petals, or rather at Wilma, who danced out of the room to get another cup.

"Are you still upset about what I told you?"

"Saxony knows about us, Anna." I sat down in a chair facing her.

She picked up the cup again, and holding it in two hands, brought it to her mouth. She peeked at me over the rim. "How did she react?"

"I don't know. As you'd expect. Half-good, half-lousy. She started crying after a while, but it wasn't anything big and weepy. She's pretty tough, I guess."

"And how do you feel?" She sipped her coffee but kept her eyes on me. Thin smoke from the cup moved quickly out from beneath her breath.

"How do I feel? Shitty. How do you think I feel?"

"You're not married to her."

I grimaced and drummed my fingers on the arm of the chair. "Yes, I know—I'm not married to her, I've got no obligation to her, everybody around here is a free agent . . . I've gone through that whole spiel in my head a thousand times, but I still feel shitty."

She shrugged and licked the rim of her cup. "All right. I just wanted—"

"Look, Anna, don't worry about it, okay? It's my thing, and I've got to work it out."

"It is partly mine, Thomas."

"Yes, okay, fine, it's all of ours. But let's just sit on it and see what happens, okay? I just spent the whole night fighting, and I don't feel like talking any more about it this morning. Okay?"

"Okay."

Neither of us said anything until my coffee came. Then I remembered that the woman serving it to me had supposedly been a dog the night before. As she passed it to me, I secretly sniffed to see if she smelled like a dog.

Anna said something that I didn't catch. I stopped sniffing and looked at her. "Excuse me?"

She looked at the other woman. "Let us talk alone for a while, all right, Wilma?"

"Of course, Anna. I've got to get that casserole ready for dinner. I can't tell you how much fun it is to cook again. I never thought that I'd say that!" She left, but the click of her high heels going away made me think of dog's toenails skittering across wooden floors.

"Is it really true, Anna? About Wilma?"

"Yes. Father got mad at the Inklers years ago for mistreating their children. He couldn't stand any kind of child abuse. When he found out that they were beating their son, he changed them into dogs. Don't look so skeptical, Thomas. He created them—he could do whatever he wanted with them."

"So he turned them into bull terriers?"

"Yes, and they would stay that way until Gert Inkler died. Then Wilma would be changed back into a woman. Father didn't want them around together again as a human couple. If they stayed together as dogs, that didn't bother him. He hated dogs." She snickered and stretched her arms out luxuriantly to the sides.

"Then are all of the animals in Galen people?"

"Many of them. But Nails and Petals were the only ones who could speak. Father made them that way on purpose. Remember, dogs can go places and do things that people can't. That's one of the reasons why Nails was living at Goosey Fletcher's house when you came. Normally the two of them stayed here with me. You didn't know it, but Nails spent a lot of time spying on you two."

I remembered all of the times he had come in in the morning, or slept on the bed with us at night, been in the room when we had made love. . . .

"All of the bull terriers in town are people. Father thought that they were the least offensive because they are so comical-looking. He said that they might as well be interesting to look at if we had to have them around."

I put my hand on my forehead. I was surprised to find it so cool. There were things that I wanted to say, but I had no way to say them then. I drank some coffee and it gave me back some voice.

"All right, if he didn't like them, then how come he didn't just erase them? Get out the old ink eradicator and finish them off? Christ, I don't know what the hell I'm saying here anymore. Why the *fuck* did you have a dog spying on me?" I wrenched up out of my chair and without looking at her walked over to the window.

A little girl in a yellow rain slicker rode by on a wobbly and battered bicycle. I wondered what she had been—a canary? A carburetor? Or always just a kid?

"Thomas?"

The bicycle disappeared around a corner. I didn't feel like talking to her. I felt like taking a nap at the bottom of the ocean.

"Thomas, are you listening to me? Do you know why I'm letting you do this? Why I am letting you write this biography? Why I'm giving you all of this information on my father?"

I turned around and looked at her. The phone rang and brought its shrill curtain down between us. She didn't answer it. We waited five-six-seven rings for it to stop: it finally did. I wondered if it might have been Saxony.

"Over there on my desk is a black notebook. Pick it up and look at page 342."

The notebook was unlike the one I had seen the night before. It was gigantic. It must have been fourteen inches long and had five or six hundred pages in it. I leafed through from the very back, and all of the pages were filled with the France scribble. The pages under my left thumb leaped from page 363 to 302, so I had to stop and flip back.

The ink color changed throughout the book; 342 was written in a kind of violent green: "The great problem here is that whatever I have created in Galen may only be a figment of my imagination.

If I die, is it then possible that they will die along with me because they have come from my imagination? An intriguing and horrible thought. I must look into this possibility and make provision for it. What an incredible waste that would be!"

I closed the book on my index finger and looked at Anna. "He was afraid that Galen would disappear after he died?"

"No, not the physical Galen—only the people and the animals that were his. He didn't create the town—only the people."

"I guess he was wrong then, huh? I mean, everybody is still here, aren't they?" Way off in the outside distance a train hooted.

"Yes, but not completely. Before Father died, he had written the history of the town up until the year three thousand—"

"Three *thousand?*"

"Yes, three thousand and fourteen. He was still working on it when he died. Absolutely unexpectedly. He lay down for a nap one afternoon and died. It was horrible. Everyone here was terrified that they all would disappear the moment he passed away, so when it actually did happen and things remained the same, we were jubilant."

"Anna, do you know the story by Borges, 'The Circular Ruins'?"

"No."

"A guy wants to create a man in his dreams, but not just a little dream man—a real flesh-and-blood man. The real thing."

"Does he do it?" She smoothed her hand across the top of the couch.

"Yes."

There's a point where even a sponge can't absorb any more water but reaches a saturation point. Too much stimulus, too many things happening all at once, all of them incredible, but taken together, they made my brain play five-dimensional chess.

She patted the cushion beside her. "Come on, Thomas, come here and sit down next to me."

"I don't think I want to right now."

"Thomas, I want you to know everything. I want to try to be totally honest with you. I want you to know about me, Galen, Father, everything.

"Do you know why?" She shifted completely around so that she faced me over the back of the sofa. Her damned breasts rested on that soft shelf. "A couple of years ago everything that Father had written was still happening. If someone was supposed to give birth to a boy on Friday, the ninth of January, it happened. Everything went as he had written it down in his *Galen Journals*. It was Utopian—"

"Utopian? Really? Well, then, what about dying? Aren't people here a little afraid of dying?"

She closed her eyes and shook her head. The dumb student was asking a dumb question again. "Not at all, because death is nothingness."

"Oh, come on, Anna. Don't get heavy and religious with me now, all right? Just answer the question."

"No, Thomas, you misunderstand me. Remember that when one of *them* dies, it isn't the same thing as when a normal person dies. When we go, there is a chance that there's a heaven or a hell. For the people in Galen, Father didn't create an afterlife for them, so there is no question in their minds. They just disappear. Poof!" She flung her unclenched hands up as if releasing fireflies.

"An existentialist's delight, eh?"

"Yes, and since they know that nothing comes afterward for them, they don't worry about it. Nobody is going to judge them or throw them into a fiery pit. They live and they die. As a result, most of them spend their lives trying to be as happy as possible."

"But doesn't anyone rebel? Don't at least some of them want to live longer?"

"Of course, but that isn't possible. They have to get used to it."

"And nobody complains? Nobody runs away?"

"Any Galener who tries to leave, dies."

"Uh-oh, now, look—"

She laughed and fluttered a hand at me. "No, no, I don't mean it that way. This was part of Father's security system. As long as the people live here, everything will be fine for them. But if they try to leave and they're gone for more than one week, then they die of heart attacks or cerebral hemorrhages, fulminating hepatitis. . . ." The hand fluttered again and floated, weightless, back down to the couch. "It's silly to talk about, because no one ever tries to leave, because it hasn't been written—"

"Written! Written! So all right, so where is this great almightly oracle of his?"

"You will see it in a little while, but I want you to know the story of it first, so that when you do see it, you will understand everything better."

"Ha! Fat chance of that. I'm not understanding things now!"

Anna's story was fantastic and involved, and she made a hundred detours along the way. I ended up sitting next to her on the couch, but only after I'd spent an hour perched uncomfortably on the hot radiator beneath the windowsill.

Marshall France began *The Night Races into Anna* to make his daughter feel better. One of the main characters in the book was his good friend Dorothy Lee, only he changed her name to Dorothy Little. After he accidentally "killed" her and the cats came to tell him, he realized what he was capable of doing. He stopped writing *The Night Races* and began *The Galen Journals*. For months he researched, wrote, and rewrote. Since he was a perfectionist, he would sometimes do twenty drafts of a book before he felt that it was right, so it isn't hard to imagine how long he worked and "prepared" for Galen.

The first person he created after Dorothy Lee was a man named Karl Tremmel. An innocuous plumber from Pine Island, New York, who brought his wife and two little girls out to Galen in a silver Airstream trailer. There hadn't been a plumber in Galen in years.

Then came a barber named Sillman, a mortician named Lucente (I tried to smile at the in joke, but I didn't have it in me) . . . and the parade of Marshall France characters was on.

They lived quiet, uneventful lives except for a post-office clerk named Bernard Stackhouse, who got drunk one night and accidentally blew his head off with a shotgun.

Et cetera, et cetera. A small factory outside of town that employed five hundred people caught fire mysteriously in the middle of the night, and after the insurance claims were settled, the owners decided to relocate a hundred miles closer to St. Louis.

"In a few years the only ones left here were Father and I, Richard, and 'Father's people.' "

"Why did he let Richard stay?"

"Oh, because we needed to have at least a couple of normal people in case some kind of emergency ever came up and one of us would have to leave here for a while. Remember, the others will die if they leave for more than a week."

"How did he get the rest of the 'normal' people to go? The ones who didn't work at the factory?"

"Father wrote it so that some of them—some of the normal Galeners—wanted to move on. One person was convinced that his house was haunted, another man's natural-gas tank exploded when he was away on vacation and he decided to move to Illinois . . . Do you want me to go on?"

"And none of them suspected anything?"

"No, of course not. Father wrote it so that everything would look totally natural and acceptable. He didn't want anyone to come around asking questions."

"Did he ever . . . ?" One of my fear-yawns took over. "Did he ever use, uh, violence?"

"No. No one was hurt when the factory burned down. But it depends on what you would call violence. He did cause the fire and he did make that man's gas tank explode. But he never hurt anyone. He didn't need to, Thomas. He could *write* anything he wanted."

France went on creating, but he didn't know how long it would last. That's why Anna had had me read that one notebook entry. In the end, he decided that the only thing he could do was to get down as much about each character as he could and then take it as far into the future as he could go. Then hope for the best to happen after he died.

"It will probably be explained in the notebooks, Anna, but just how much of people's lives did he control? I mean, does it say things like, 'Eight-twelve Joe Smith woke up and yawned for three seconds. Then he—' "

She shook her head. "No, no. He found that he could leave most of their lives up to them. Later on, he decided only about the big things in their lives, the big events—who they were to marry, how many children each of them would have, when they died and how. . . . He wanted them to have—"

"Don't you *dare* say free will!"

"No, no, I won't. But in a way it was. Look at what happened to Gert and Wilma Inkler: he let them go and do what they wanted with their son. When it got to be too much, he changed them into dogs."

"Our God is a jealous God, eh?"

"Don't say that, Thomas." Two nasty matches lit up in her eyes.

"Don't say *what*, that he played with them? Look, I don't want to piss you off, Anna, but if all this is true, then your father was the most . . ." I tried to think of appropriate words that would encompass what he had done, but there weren't any. "I don't know—he was the most amazing human being that ever lived. I'm not even talking about him as an artist either. The man put a pen to paper and actually made people come *alive?*" I realized that I was talking more to myself than to Anna, but I didn't care. "No, it's impossible." All at once it flooded over me thick and heavy and impossibly gluey. What the hell kind of idiot was I, believing this crap? But then again there was Nails, who had talked to me. And Petals, who had talked to me. And what little I'd read in the notebooks that coincided with what had happened. And Anna knowing that the little boy would die after he got hit by the truck. . . .

"Why was it so important for people to know if the little Hayden boy was laughing, Anna? How does that all fit in?"

"Because he was supposed to be killed that day. He was supposed to be laughing and happy right up to the moment when he got hit by the truck. The problem was that the wrong person was driving the truck. That's what Joe Jordan and all of the others were so upset about. He wasn't laughing, and he was killed by the wrong man."

As long as things went according to France's plans, Anna and the Galeners had little contact with the outside world. Once in a while one of them went shopping or to a movie in a nearby town, and the Galen stores were constantly being replenished by trucks from St. Louis and Kansas City, but that was about all. For appearance's sake, there was a real-estate office in town, but the only things for sale there were in other towns. What wasn't privately owned belonged to the town of Galen, and nothing was ever for sale. Nothing for rent either.

"But what about Mrs. Fletcher's? What about—?"

"You and Saxony are the first new people to live in Galen since my father died."

"So *that's* why she didn't mind our not being married that first day that we rented it! She must have told us ten times that she didn't care about that kind of thing. You set us up, didn't you, Anna? It was all a big plan!"

She nodded. "The moment I heard that you were coming out here from David Louis, I called Goosey Fletcher and told her to move upstairs in that big house. Then I sent Nails over to live with her."

"And I thought that she did it for the money."

"Goosey is a very good actress."

"Was she really in the insane asylum?"

"No."

"Just no? Nothing more?"

"How could she be in an insane asylum, Thomas, if she was one of Father's people? You can learn everything, Thomas, as soon as you start reading the journals."

I was right about the biographer from Princeton when I said that he came to the wrong place at the wrong time. Because of its secret, Galen was shut up tight then and nobody was about to tell the guy nuthin' about nuthin'. According to Anna, he stayed a few weeks and then fumed off toward California, where he said that he was going to write the definitive biography of R. Crumb.

But then it started happening. In the last two years, things started going wrong in Galen. A man who was supposed to live to be ninety and die peacefully in his sleep was electrocuted by a high-tension wire that broke and fell on him as he was passing. He was forty-seven. A child who was supposed to adore corn couldn't look at it without throwing up. A woman who had been changed into a bull terrier suddenly bore a litter of nine puppies. None of the dogs had ever done that before: none of them were supposed to.

I put my hands under my armpits to warm them. I yawned for the umpteenth time. "So what went wrong?"

Anna held her empty cup in her hand and tinked a fingernail against it. "Father's powers started to fade. They started to wear off. In one of the journals he wrote about the possibility. You can read it, but I'll just tell you the essence of it now. He said that two things might happen after he died. One was that everything he had created would disappear immediately."

"I read that part." I still had his journal in my hand and held it up for her to see.

"Yes. The second possibility was that everything would be all right afterward because he had filled them with such . . ." She tightened her lips and hesitated a moment. "He had filled them with such *life* spirit that they would continue to function even after he was dead."

"And they did. They have, haven't they?"

"Yes, Thomas, they have until two years ago. Until then everything had gone perfectly. But suddenly things were wrong— I told you about some of them. But Father saw this as a possibility too. He wrote about it in the same notebook that you have there."

"Just tell me about it, Anna. I'm really not in the mood to read right now."

"All right." She looked at the cup as if she didn't know how it had gotten into her hands. She put it down on the coffee table and shoved it brusquely away. "He was convinced that since he had been able to create the people in Galen, then if he died, someone somewhere would be able to recreate him."

"*What?*" Little freezing lizards ran up and down my back.

"Yes, he believed that his biographer"—she stopped and raised her eyebrows at me, *his biographer*—"if his biographer was good enough, then he could bring Father back to life if he wrote the story of Father's life the right way."

"Anna, Jesus Christ, you're saying that that's me? You're comparing pigs to swine! I mean *pearls* to swine! Your father was . . . was . . . I don't know, *God.* Who the hell am I?"

"Do you know why I've let you go this far, Thomas?"

"I don't know if I want to know. All right, all right, how come?"

"Because you have the first quality that Father said was necessary: you are obsessed with him. All you ever do is talk about how important his books are to you. His work is almost as important to you as it is to all of us."

"Oh, come on, Anna, it isn't the same thing!"

"Thomas, stop." She held her hand up like a traffic cop. "You don't know this, but since you wrote that first chapter, everything has gone right again in Galen. Things that he wrote to happen in the journals *have* happened, just as before. Everything—Nails's death was just the latest."

I looked at her and opened my mouth to speak, but there wasn't anything to say. I had just been paid the most outrageous compliment of my life. My mind was stuck in an elevator halfway between green-bile fear and total, life-hugging elation. For God's sake, what if she was right?

7

We continued working, only now Saxony wouldn't have anything to do with the biography. She carved three marionettes, and when she wasn't doing that, she read Eddison's *The Worm Ouroboros.*

I still went to Anna's, but only during the day and no later than five-thirty. Then I packed my little brown briefcase and toddled home.

One of my great problems was in deciding whether or not to tell Saxony the truth about France and Galen. At times I couldn't stand it, holding it in like that, keeping it from her. But then I knew that people had been committed to the insane asylum for less nutty views than mine, so I reasoned that it was best to wait and see what happened before I let the cat out of the bag.

A snowstorm whipped through town and painted everything thick white. I went out for a walk one afternoon and came across three cats romping it up in someone's open field. They were having so much fun that I stopped and watched. They went on leaping after each other for a couple of minutes, until one of them spotted me and stopped dead in his tracks. All of them looked my way, and unconsciously I raised my hand to wave. Very faintly, very whispery across the snow, I heard them mewing. It took several seconds for it to dawn on me that it was their way of saying hello.

But then everyone in town had begun to open up to me now. What they told me would have made me run the other way a few months before, but now all I did was nod and shake my head and have another of Debby's (or Gretchen's or Mary Ann's . . .) oatmeal-raisin cookies.

They inevitably went on in one of two directions: accusatory or beseeching. I'd goddamned better get the book written or else a lot of people were going to be in trouble, or, thank God I had happened along when I did, and would it be long before I was done? Depending on the day and the person, I felt either like the messiah or the telephone repairman. As to whether or not my finished book would bring Marshall France back, the thought went around and around in my brain like a kid's marble in a clothes dryer. Sometimes I stopped and laughed at everything because it was all so crazy and absurd. At other times, my fear lizards went walking on my skin and I tried to push it all out of my head.

"Uh, Larry, what does it feel like to be . . . uh, created?"

Larry farted and smiled at me. "Created? What d'ya mean, created? Look, man, you shot out of your old man, right?" I nodded and shrugged. "Well, I just shot out of someplace else. You want another beer?"

Catherine petted her gray rabbit as gently as if it were made of glass. "Created? Hmm. That's a funny word to use. Created." She rolled it around her tongue and smiled down at the rabbit. "I don't really think about it, Thomas. There's always so much else on my mind."

If I was expecting answers from the Inner Sanctum, I didn't get them. Galen was a lower-middle-class town in the heart of Missouri, made up of hardworking people who went bowling on Wednesday night, loved *The Bionic Woman,* ate ham sandwiches, and were saving up to buy new Roto-tillers or a vacation cottage out on Lake Tekawitha.

The most interesting anecdote I heard was from a guy who accidentally shot his brother in the face with a police revolver. The trigger pulled, the gun exploded, smoke, lots of noise . . . but nothing happened to the brother, Nothing.

But people talked and talked. Now that I was "one of them," they told me all kinds of things—about their lumbago, their sex lives, recipes for catfish. Not much of it had to do with my research, but they had talked to each other for so long about the same things that it was nice to have a fresh ear to tell it to again.

"Do you know what I don't like about what's going on now, Abbey? Not knowin' nothing. I used to be able to walk down the street and not worry about no fuckin' aeroplanes falling on my head. You understand what I'm talking about? When you know, you know. You don't have to worry about nothin' happening to you. Look at this goddamned what's-his-name—Joe Jordan. He goes out to pick up a fucking pack of cigarettes, and the next thing he knows, he's run over a little kid. No sir, thank you, I want to *know* when my time's coming. That way, I don't have to worry a bit about it until the time comes."

"But what will you do then? When your time comes."

"Piss in my fuckin' pants!" The old man laughed and laughed at his own joke.

The more people I asked, the more it seemed that the vast majority were content with France's "way," and horrified that suddenly, cruelly, they had been turned over to the clumsy hands of fate.

But there were a few who didn't want to know what would happen to them. That was all right. The way it had been arranged, years ago, was that the oldest member of each family was responsible for a detailed copy of the history and future history of his family that had been given to him by France. Anyone over eighteen who wanted to know what was going to happen could go to the "elder" and ask any question.

A man who worked in the supermarket looked at me as if I were crazy when I asked him if he wouldn't like to live more than the fifty-one years France had given him.

"Why? I can do everything I want now. What can't a man accomplish in fifty years?"

"But it's so . . . it's so locked in. I don't know, it's claustrophobic."

His arthritic hands pulled a black Ace comb out of an overall pocket and slid it through equally black hair.

"No, look, Tom, I'm thirty-nine now, right? I know for sure that I've got twelve more years to go. I never worry about any of that stuff—about dying and all. But you do, don't you? Sometimes you probably get up in the morning and say to yourself, 'Today might be the day I *die*,' or 'Today I might get crippled or busted up for life.' Things like that. But we never think two seconds about it, you know? I got some arthritis in my hands and I'll die of cancer when I'm fifty-one. So who's better off now, you or me? Be honest."

"Can I ask you one more question?"

"Sure, fire away."

"Let's say that I'm a Galener and I find out that I'm supposed to die tomorrow, that you're going to run me over in your truck. What if I go home and I never come out of the house tomorrow. What if I hide in my closet all day and I make it impossible for you to run me over?"

"You'll die in the closet at the same time you were supposed to be run over by me."

In my father's film *Café de la Paix,* there is a scene that I've always liked and which kept ringing in my head when I made my rounds in Galen.

Richard Eliot, aka "Shakespeare," who just happens to be England's most effective secret agent in Nazi-occupied France, has been found out. He sends his wife away via the underground, and then goes to the Café de la Paix to wait for the Krauts to come and get him. He orders a *café crème*, takes a small book out of his pocket, and starts reading. Cool as a cucumber. The coffee comes, but the waiter serves it as fast as he can and gets the hell out of there because he knows what is about to happen. The street is empty and some dead leaves move ever so slowly by the table legs. The director of the film was ingenious, because he didn't let anything happen for three minutes. By the time the black Mercedes comes screeching up, you've been pulling your hair out and are *glad* that they've arrived. Doors slam, and the camera follows two highly shined pairs of jackboots across the street.

"Herr Eliot?" The German officer is one of those good/bad guys (I think Curt Jurgens played it) who's been clever enough to track down Shakespeare, but along the way has grown to respect the man he's about to arrest.

My father looks up from his book and smiles. "Hello, Fuchs."

The other Nazi moves to get him, but Fuchs grabs the guy by the arm and orders him back to the car.

Father pays the bill and the two men walk slowly across the street.

"If it had been successful, Eliot, what would you have done when you returned home?"

"Done?" Father laughs and looks at the sky for a long time. "I don't know, Fuchs. Sometimes that possibility scared me more than being caught. Isn't that funny? Maybe in the back of my mind I have hoped all along that this would happen so that I would never have to worry about my future. Have you ever thought about what you'll do when Germany loses the war?"

How many bull sessions had I been in in my life where at three o'clock in the morning I was desperately trying to explain what life was about to a sleepy college roommate or lover? I got so caught up in all of the conflicting answers and possibilities that finally I'd end up either going to sleep or making love or being totally depressed because I realized that I didn't know anything at all.

The Galeners didn't have that problem. Theirs was the purest kind of Calvinism, except that they didn't have to worry about what happened to them on the other side of death. They couldn't change who they were or what would happen to them, but knowing that they would definitely get a B or a C on their final exam made all the difference in the world as far as their moment-to-moment living was concerned.

Saxony finally got the cast off, and although she limped around for a while because her leg was thin and weak, her spirits rose greatly.

The leaves had all parachuted from the trees and were slicked to the roads now. The days were short and either wet or gray or both. Galen went inside. The basketball team began playing on Friday nights and the gym was always packed. The movie theater, the stores—all the inside things were once again popular. You could smell the heavy winter dinners cooking in the houses, the damp wool of coats, the dusty closeness of gloves and socks and stocking caps left on a radiator to dry.

I thought of all the other little Galens everywhere else that were getting ready for winter. Chains for the car, oil for the heater, new sleds, bird food for the outdoor feeder, storm windows, rock salt for the driveway . . .

All of the little Galens were making the same preparations, only "out there," a man was getting into his car to go to the store. He didn't know that halfway there he would skid off the road and crash and die. His wife wouldn't think anything was wrong for hours. Then maybe one of his friends would discover the wreck, a gray plume of exhaust smoke still puttering out of the back end, melting the dirt-specked snow beneath it.

Or an old man in Maine would put on his L. L. Bean cardigan sweater and green corduroy pants and not know that in two hours he would have a heart attack while clipping the leash onto his pet dachshund's collar.

Mrs. Fletcher found out about my birthday and made me a huge, inedible carrot cake. I got a lot of presents too. Whenever I walked into people's houses they either had a cake or a present for me. I got a stuffed badger, ten hand-tied fishing flies, and a first edition of *None Dare Call It Treason*. When I came home from interviewing, Saxony stood at the door smiling and shaking her head long before I had even brought out my newest treasure to show and tell.

"You're a real hit here, aren't you?" She held the stereopticon from Barney and Thelma up to her eyes and looked at Dobbs Ferry, New York.

"Hey, look, that thing is worth a lot of money, Sax. Those people were really nice to have given it to me."

"Don't be so sensitive, Thomas. I was just saying that it must be very nice to be so wanted."

I didn't know whether she was being honest or facetious, but if I had had to answer her then, I would have agreed—it *was* nice. Sure, I knew why a lot of the Galeners did it—I wasn't that naïve— but I got to know what it was like to be respected and liked and held in awe: it was damned pleasant. It was a small taste of what both my father and Marshall France had known for most of their lives.

France had taken the cargo ship *Arthur Bellingham* from Liverpool to New York. On board he made friends with a Jewish couple and had a small romance with their nineteen-year-old daughter. He later dated the girl in New York, but nothing ever came of their relationship. He got the job with Lucente and rented a room in a transients' hotel a block away from the funeral home.

"Anna, how come you lied to me before when I asked you how long your father worked for Lucente?"

She was eating a bowl of Rice Krispies at the dining-room table, and I could hear the little snapping sounds inside her bowl.

"I don't want to get into a big discussion with you on it—it's just that I'd like to know why you lied."

She chewed up the mouthful she had taken and wiped her lips with a paper napkin.

"I wanted to see how good a writer you were before I really let you get going. That makes sense, doesn't it? That's why I gave you everything up until his immigration to the United States. That way, if you were good, then it would show in whatever first chapter you wrote. If you were bad, then I would just send you away and you would never have known anything. She plowed her spoon back into the cereal and went back to the magazine she had been reading.

"Anna? One more question: how come you never talk about your mother?"

"My mother was a lovely, quiet, Midwestern girl who made me join the Brownies when I was little and the Girl Scouts when I was big. She was a wonderful cook and she made my father's life very pleasant. I think he loved her and was happy with her because she was just the opposite of him—everything about her was down-to-earth. She admired people with great imaginations or artistic drive, but I think she was secretly pleased that she didn't have either. She once told me, secretly, that she thought Father's books were goofy. Isn't that a great word for them? Goofy?"

France's uncle, Otto Frank, was never very successful as a printer. He had moved to Galen from Hermann, Missouri, because he liked the location and because there was a printing shop for sale there cheap. He printed wedding invitations, business brochures, posters for church fairs and farm auctions. At one time he had had high hopes for starting a county newspaper (that's why he had written his brother in Austria and told him to send over one of the boys), but he had no money and found no one interested in staking him to his dream.

Martin arrived (having by then changed his name to Marshall France, much to Otto's dismay), and his uncle put him to work in the shop as an apprentice. Apparently France liked the work, and he stayed there until Otto died in 1945, the year *A Pool of Stars* was published.

The book didn't do very well when it came out, but the publisher liked it enough to offer France a thousand-dollar advance for his next work, which turned out to be the equally unsuccessful *Peach Shadows*. However, a critic named Charles White wrote a long back-of-the-magazine article about France in the *Atlantic Monthly*. He compared the author to both Lewis Carroll and Lord Dunsany, and it was one of the things that turned the corner for France's reputation. Anna had almost all of the letters he had ever gotten in Galen, as well as carbons of his replies to them; he had had no idea that White had written the article until months after it came out. He wrote the critic and thanked him. They corresponded for years, until White died.

Two years after *Peach Shadows, The Green Dog's Sorrow* appeared and almost immediately made the best-seller lists. White began a funny letter to France: "Dear Mr. France, sir: I never knew a famous author before. Are you one now? If so, can I borrow a hundred dollars? If not, thank God . . . " Suddenly the first two books were back in print, he was asked to do an anthology of favorite children's stories, Walt Disney had an idea for how to make *Peach Shadows* into a movie . . . Marshall France was a big shot.

But he wrote a nice letter to Disney and told him to buzz off. The same to the publisher of the children's anthology. He said no to just about everything, and after a while he didn't even write back; he had a card printed up that said Marshall France thanks you, but regrets . . . It looked like a form rejection slip from a magazine. Anna gave me a framed one for my birthday with a picture of a bull terrier on it that he had doodled.

Over the years literally hundreds of proposals came in. They wanted to do a series of rubber dolls depicting the characters in *The Land of Laughs*, *Green Dog* pencils, a radio patterned after the Cloud Radio in *Peach Shadows*. According to Anna and based on what I later saw, many of these companies went ahead with their products even after her father had rejected them. She said that he lost hundreds of thousands of dollars because he refused to get involved in any kind of lawsuit. David Louis had legal experts ready to pounce on these manufacturers, but France said no every time. He didn't want the trouble, he didn't want to be bothered, he didn't want the notoriety, he didn't want to leave Galen. Finally, even Louis gave up pestering him, but retaliated by sending him, over the years, example after example of these pirated dolls, flashlights, and whatnot, just to show him how much he was losing. We spent an afternoon in the basement pulling them out of musty, collapsing cardboard boxes that had been stowed away in corners years ago.

"If David Louis only knew, he would have been furious." Anna took a *Green Dog* coloring book out of the box. "These were half of my toys when I was growing up." She opened the book and turned it to me. There was a picture of Krang and the Green Dog walking down a windy road together, Krang's string tied to the dog's collar in a bow. The picture had been half colored-in. The dog was blue, Krang completely gold, the road wavy red.

"What would your father have said if he saw that you had colored the dog blue?"

"Oh, but that was all his fault! I remember it very clearly. I asked him if the Green Dog had ever been another color. He said that before the book was written he had been blue, but that I mustn't ever tell anyone because it was a big secret." She rubbed her hand lovingly over the blue body as if she was trying to pet either the dog or her father's memory.

I looked at her and tried to figure out what was going to happen with us. She was thirty-six (I had finally gotten up the nerve one day to ask, and she told me without batting an eye), and I was thirty-one, not that that made any difference. If I wanted her, then I would have to spend the rest of my life in Galen. But was that so bad? I could write books—maybe my father's book next—teach English at Galen High School, travel once in a while. We would always have to come back here, but that wasn't such a terrible thought. Live in my hero's house, make love to his daughter, be someone to the Galeners because in a funny way I might end up being their savior.

"You know that Saxony will have to leave soon, Thomas."

I came up out of my thought-fog and coughed. The cellar was

damp and cold, and I had left my heavy sweater upstairs in the bedroom.

"What? What are you talking about?"

"I said that she will have to leave soon. Now that you know everything about us here in Galen, you'll stay and write the book, but she has nothing to do with it anymore. She has to go."

Her voice was so calm and indifferent. She said all this while she flipped through the pages of the coloring book.

"Why, Anna?" I whined. What the hell was I whining for? I snatched it back and replaced it with some good, strong indignation. "What are you talking about?" I tossed the doll that I was holding back into the box.

"I told you before, Thomas: no one lives here but Father's people. It's all right now for you to stay, but not Saxony. She doesn't belong here anymore."

I gave my head a dramatic slap and tried to laugh it off. "Come on, Anna, you're beginning to sound like Bette Davis in *Hush, Hush, Sweet Charlotte*." I slipped into a stupid Southern belle accent. " 'I'm sorry, Gilbert, but it's time now for Jeanette to go.' " I laughed again and made a face like a nut. Anna smiled back sweetly.

"Come on, Anna! What are you talking about? You're just kidding me, right? Huh? Well, come on, why? What the hell difference does it make if she's here or not? I haven't told her anything. You know that."

She put the coloring book in the box and stood up. She closed the top and sealed it with some brown tape she had brought down with her. She started to shove the box back into the corner with her foot, but I grabbed her wrist and made her look at me.

"Why?"

"You know why, Thomas. Don't waste my time asking." The same anger flashed at me that I'd seen that day in the woods with Richard Lee.

She iced the cake ten minutes later by telling me that I had to leave because she had to go see Richard.

As soon as I got home that night Saxony and I had a huge fight. It centered around an idiotic errand that I had forgotten to do for her. Naturally the crazy anger that reared up out of both of us stemmed from everything that we had been suppressing all along. A few minutes into it she had turned poppy-red, and I caught myself clenching and unclenching my fists like an exasperated husband in a situation comedy.

"I keep saying this to you, Thomas, but if it's so bad around here, then why don't you just go?"

"Saxony, will you please take it easy? I didn't say—"

"Yes you did. If everything is so great over there, then go! Do you think I love your little soft-shoe back and forth from her to me?"

I tried to stare her down, but at the moment I didn't have the guts to go one-on-one with her for very long. I looked away and then back. She was still smoldering.

"What do you want me to do, Sax?"

"Stop asking me that question! You sound so helpless. You want me to answer it for you, and I refuse to. You want me to order you out or to tell you to leave her and come back to me. But I won't, Thomas. You're the one who has caused all of this. You're the one who wanted it, so now you can decide how you're going to handle it. I love you, and you know that very well. But, I'm not going to be able to put up with it for much longer. I think that you had better decide something fast." Her voice was almost a whisper when she finished, and I had to lean forward to catch the last words. The next ones came out in a blast, and I jumped back. "I can't get over how damned stupid you are, Thomas! You make me want to strangle you. How dumb can you be? Don't you know what a great time we would have together? Once you finish this book, we could go off somewhere and live a hundred different, wonderful lives. Can't you see what Anna is doing to you? She's pulling you down to worship in front of her horrible little altar to her father—"

"Hey, look, Saxony, what about your interest in Fr—"

"I know, I know, me too. But I don't want Marshall France

anymore, Thomas. I don't want to be lovers with a book or a puppet now. I want to be lovers with you. All of those other things, we can do in our spare time, but the rest is for us. Wait! Wait a minute!" She got up from her chair and limped off to the kitchen. She was back in two seconds with a few marionettes in her hand. "Do you see these? Do you know why I carved them? To take my mind off everything. That's right, it's the truth. It's so pathetic the way I dig-dig-dig at the wood all afternoon, trying not to think too hard about where you are or what you're doing. When we were driving out here in the car, that was the first time in my life that I haven't worked every single day. And I loved it! I didn't care about these things. There was too much to do with you. I know how important your book is to you, Thomas. I know how important it is that you finish it. . . ."

"I don't know what you're saying, Sax."

"Okay, all right. Look, do you remember that first day that we got here? The barbecue that they were having downtown?"

I bit my top lip in and nodded.

"Do you remember that the first thing I did when I started talking to Goosey was to tell her about the book?"

"You're damn right I remember! I wanted to kill you. Why did you do that after all we'd talked about?"

She put the puppets down on the couch and ran both hands through her hair. I realized from the gesture how much longer it had grown. I had never told her how nice it looked. "Do you know about women's intuition? Don't start making faces, Thomas, because it's true. There is something there a lot of the time. Another sense or something. Remember I told you that I knew when you and Anna started sleeping together? Anyway, whether you believe me or not, I was sure almost from the moment that we got here that somehow things between us were going to go wrong if you started to do that book. I was trying to get them to throw us out of here that day. I'm sorry, but I was. I thought that if I told them what we wanted to do, they wouldn't let us get within three feet of Anna France."

"Sabotage."

"Yes, that's right. I was trying to sabotage this whole thing. I didn't want it to happen after how strong we'd become in just those few days together. I knew that once you got involved here, everything would go bad. And I was right, wasn't I?" She picked up her puppets and walked out of the room. We didn't talk any more that night.

Two days later I bumped into Mrs. Fletcher outside the market. Her metal cart was filled with a fifty-pound bag of potatoes and about ten quart bottles of prune juice.

"Well, hello there, stranger. I haven't seen much of you lately. Working hard?"

"Hi, Mrs. Fletcher. Yes, pretty hard."

"Anna tells me that the book is going along fine now."

"Yes, it's good." My mind was on a million things, and I had no desire to shoot the breeze with her.

"You've got to get Saxony out of here soon, Tom. You know that?"

A dog barked, and I heard a car start up. The cold air filled with exhaust smoke.

A chunk of anger and despair moved up through me and stopped in my chest. "What the hell difference does it make if she stays or goes? Christ almighty, I'm getting goddamned *tired* of being told what to do. What the hell difference does it make if Saxony stays?"

Her smile fell. "Anna didn't tell you?" She put her hand on my shoulder. "She really didn't tell you anything?"

Her tone of voice scared me. "No, nothing. What is it? Come on, what are you talking about?" Cars and people moved around us like fish in an aquarium.

"Did you see . . . ? No, you couldn't have. Look, Tom, if I really say anything to you about this, I could get into some real trouble. I'm not kidding. All of this is very dangerous. I'll tell you this much, though . . ." She pretended to straighten some things in her cart while she spoke. "I'll tell you this—if you don't get your Saxony out of here, she'll get sick. She'll get so sick that she dies.

That was part of the journals. That was how Marshall kept Galen away from everything else."

"But what about me? Why won't I get sick too? I'm from the outside."

"You're the biographer. You're protected. That's the way Marshall wrote it. There's no way to change it."

"But, Mrs. Fletcher, what about the journals? The things in them haven't been happening for a long time. Everything is out of whack here."

"No, you're wrong, Tom. Ever since you started writing, everything's gone right again, that's the point." She rubbed her mouth with the back of her hand. "You have to get her out, Tom. You listen to me. Even if the journals are screwed up and she doesn't get sick, Anna don't want her around. That's what you've got to worry about most of all. Anna is a strong woman, Tom. You don't ever want to play games with her." She hurried away, and I heard the shivering rattle of her metal cart as it moved away across the parking lot.

"Do you have a minute?"

She was chopping celery on a small wooden butcher-block square I'd bought her.

"You look like you're sick, Thomas. Are you feeling all right?"

"Yeah, sure, I'm fine, Sax. Look, I don't want to lie to you anymore, okay? I want to tell you exactly how I feel about all of this and then let you decide."

She put her knife down and walked to the sink to wash her hands. She came back to the table drying them on a yellow dish towel I had never seen before.

"All right. Go ahead."

"Sax, you are incredibly important to me. You're the only person that I've ever been with who sees the world almost exactly the same way that I do. I've never experienced that before."

"What about Anna? Doesn't she see things your way?"

"No, she's totally different. My relationship with her is totally different. I think I pretty much know what would happen if you and I stayed together."

She dried her hands slowly, carefully. "And is that what you want?"

"That's what I don't know, Sax. I think I do, but I don't know yet. What I am sure of is that I want to finish this book. It's amazing that at the same time of my life I've come across two things that are so important to me. I wish that it could have happened a different way, but it hasn't. So now I've got to try to do it the right way, even though it will probably end up stupid and wrong.

"Anyway, what I've been thinking of is this, if it's all right with you. If I could have it my way right now, I'd have you go away for a while. Until I finish this draft and get through whatever is going on between Anna and me."

She smirked and dropped the dish towel on the table. "And what happens if you don't 'get through' with Anna? Huh? What then, Thomas?"

"You're right, Sax. I honestly don't know what then. The only thing that I'm sure of is that this way stinks. Nobody likes what's going on now, and all of the hurt and worry and confusion is totally fucking everybody up. I know that it's my fault. I know it, but it's something that has to happen, or else . . ." I picked up the towel and wrapped it around my fist. It was still damp.

"Or else what? *What* has to happen—writing your book or going to bed with Anna?"

"Yes, all right, both. Both have to happen if—"

She stood up. She picked up a small block of celery and popped it into her mouth. "You want me to go away so that you can finish your draft and supposedly get through your 'thing' with Anna. That's what you want, right? Okay. I'll go, Thomas. I'll go up to St. Louis and I'll wait there for three months. You'll have to give me some money, because I don't have any left. But after those three months, I'm going to leave. Whether you're there or not, I'll be leaving." She started out of the room. "I owe you that much, but you've been a shit about all of this, Thomas. I'm just glad that you could finally make up your mind about something."

The day she left, it snowed. I woke up about seven and groggily looked out the window. The sun hadn't risen yet, but it had grown light enough to paint everything outside blue-gray. When I realized what was going on, I didn't know if I was happy or sad that we might be snowed in and Saxony wouldn't be able to leave. I stumbled over to the window for a better look and saw how high it had drifted up on the porch. It was still falling, but the flakes were big and slow and falling vertically, and I remembered somewhere that that meant it would stop soon. The house hadn't betrayed the snow's secret yet—the floors were warm under my bare feet, and although I wore only a pajama top and underpants, I wasn't cold.

Snow. My father hated it. He once had to make a movie in Switzerland in the winter, and he never got over the shock. He liked warm tropical places. The swimming pool in our backyard was heated to about three hundred degrees for him. His idea of heaven was heat stroke in the Amazon jungle.

Saxony was only taking one suitcase this time; all of her other things—the notes, the marionettes, and her books—were being left with me in Galen. She wouldn't tell me what she planned on doing in St. Louis, but I was worried because she hadn't packed any of her puppets or her tools. Her bag was on the floor near the window. I went over and pushed it a couple of inches with my bare foot. What would be happening in three months? Where would I be? The book? Everything? No, not everything—the Galeners would be in Galen, and so would Anna.

Saxony was still sleeping when I sneaked my clothes off a chair and tiptoed into the bathroom to get dressed. I wanted to make a really nice going-away breakfast for her, so I'd gotten a fat Florida grapefruit for the occasion.

Sausage, scrambled eggs with sour cream, fresh whole-wheat bread, and a grapefruit. I got them all out of the refrigerator and

lined them up like soldiers on the Formica counter. Sax's breakfast.
By noon she would probably be gone. No more hairs in the sink,
no more fights about Anna, no more Rocky and Bullwinkle on
television at four in the afternoon. Christ, enough of that. I started
to work on the meal like the mad chef, because I was already starting
to miss her and she wasn't even out of bed. When she came into
the kitchen, she was wearing the same clothes that she'd worn the
first day we met. I ended up burning three sausages.

She asked if I would call the bus station and find out if the bus
to St. Louis was still running in the snow. I called on the phone in
the downstairs hall. I gazed at the snow through the half-window
in the front door. The flakes had stopped.

"The snow's stopped!"

"I see from here. Aren't you delighted?"

I grimaced and tapped my foot.

"Galen Bus."

"Hi, yes, uh, I'd like to know if your nine-twenty-eight to St.
Louis will still be going today?"

"Why wouldn't it?" Whoever it was sounded like a cigar-store
Indian.

"Well, you know, the snow and everything."

"He's got chains on it. That bus don't stop running for nothin',
friend. Sometimes he's late, but he doesn't stop running."

Saxony came out into the hall with half a grapefruit in one hand
and a spoon in the other. I put my hand over the mouthpiece and
told her that it was going. She walked to the front door and looked
at the snow.

I hung up and couldn't decide whether to go back into the
kitchen or go to her and see what she would do. I chickened out
and went back to the kitchen.

My eggs were still warm, so I scooped some sour cream onto
the side of my plate and ate quickly.

"Sax, aren't you going to finish your breakfast? That's a long
bus ride to St. Louis."

When she didn't answer, I thought it best just to leave her alone. While I ate, I envisioned her eating her grapefruit at the front door, watching the snow end.

I had finished my second cup of coffee when I started to get a little nervous about her. Her plate was filled with food and her teacup was up to the top.

"Sax?"

I threw my napkin on the table and got up. She wasn't in the hall, and neither was her coat or her suitcase. She had left the hollowed-out grapefruit rind and spoon on the radiator near the door. I unhooked my coat from the rack and moved toward the door. The phone rang. I cursed and snatched it up.

"Yeah? What?"

"Thomas?" It was Anna.

"Look, Anna, I can't talk to you now, okay? Saxony just left, and I've got to catch her before she's gone."

"What? Don't be ridiculous, Thomas. Obviously if she left without telling you, she doesn't want you with her. Leave her alone. She doesn't want to say good-bye to you. You can understand that."

That made me mad. I had had enough of Anna's gems of wisdom, and there were things that I wanted to say to Saxony before she took off. I told Anna that I would call her later and hung up.

The cold sucked away all the heat from my body before I had left the porch, and my teeth were chattering as I went through the front gate. A car went slowly by, its chains ka-chunking and throwing snow out from beneath the wheel wells. I knew that the bus didn't leave for another hour, but I started running anyway. I had on heavy insulated work boots that the man in the shoe store had guaranteed against frostbite down to thirty degrees below zero. But running in them was a slow-motion jog. I didn't have my gloves, either, so I ran with my hands stuffed into my pockets; I didn't have my wool hat, so my ears and even my cheeks began to ache.

When I finally saw her, I stopped running. I didn't know

what I wanted to say, but I had to say something to her before she left.

She must have heard me coming, because she turned and faced me just as I was about to catch up with her. "I wish you hadn't, Thomas."

I was out of breath, and my eyes were watering from the cold. "But why did you just go off like that, Sax? Why didn't you wait for me?"

"Am I allowed to do something my own way for a change? Is it okay if I leave this place the way I want to?"

"Come on, Sax . . ."

The anger fell away from her eyes and she closed them for several seconds. She began speaking while they were still closed. "This is all hard enough for me, Thomas. Please don't make it any harder. Go back to the house and go to work. I'll be all right. I've got my book with me and I can sit in the station and read until the bus comes. Okay? I'll call you at the end of the week. Okay?"

She gave me a quick smile and reached down for her bag. I didn't even try to take my hands out of my pockets. She took a couple of crunching steps and then hefted the suitcase for a better grip.

But she didn't call at the end of the week. I made a point of staying home from Wednesday night on, but she didn't call. I didn't know if that was good or bad, nasty or forgetful or what. Since she wasn't the kind of person who normally forgets to do things like that, I was nervous. In my fantasies I saw her tiredly trudging up the stairs of a dingy building that had a curling brown sign in a downstairs window advertising rooms for rent. She knocked on the door and the mad rapist or butcher-knife murderer welcomed her and invited her in for a cup of tea.

Or else, what was worse was a shiny new building where the landlord was six foot two, ash blond, and sexy as hell. I was hopeless. If I spent the night in our apartment, the bed felt as big and as cold as the ocean. If I spent the night at Anna's, then I thought about Saxony all the time. Naturally I knew that if Sax was there, my desire for her would have been less and we'd be fighting again, but she wasn't there and I missed her. I missed her very much.

She called on Tuesday night. She sounded ebullient and excited and was full of news. She knew an old friend from college who used to live in St. Louis. It turned out that he still lived there. She had even found a job working part-time at a children's day-care center. She had gone to the movies twice and seen the new Robert Altman. Her friend's name was Geoff Wiggins.

I tried not to swallow my tongue too fast. I smiled sickly at the receiver, half-thinking that it was Saxony. I asked her who this Geoff was. A professor of architecture at Washington University. Was she living . . . uh . . . staying with him until she found a place? No, no, that was what was so great—she didn't have to look now because Geoff had invited her to stay there with himmmm. . . .

I got the address and telephone number of old Geoff from her and then tried to finish our conversation with as much cool as possible, but I know that I came across sounding like a cross between Hal the Computer and Woody Woodpecker. When I hung up I felt totally miserable.

I got a letter from one of my students. Seeing the kid's name on the return address was a shock in itself, but the contents of the damned thing knocked me for a loop.

Dear Mr. Abbey,

How are you? I guess you're pretty glad to be away from here this year. I don't know what that feeling is like yet, but I will in June, when, believe it or not, I'll be graduating. I got into Hobart early decision, so I'm pretty much taking it easy these days. I go over to the Senior House a lot to watch television, and I've even been reading some of the books on that list that you gave us last year that you said we'd like.

My favorite so far has been *The Young Lions* (by Irwin Shaw), but I really also liked *The Metamorphosis* (Franz Kafka) and *Look Homeward, Angel* (Thomas Wolfe). I guess talking about books is the best way to tell you why I'm writing this letter. I've been here for almost six years now (and you can believe me when I say that they've been six long ones!) and I've had every teacher in the school at one time or another (or just about). Anyway, I was thinking about it the other day, and I realized that you were the best one. I wasn't any big "A" student in your class and I know that I fooled around a lot in your class with Romero, but believe it or not, I got more out of that English class last year than any other course I took. Whenever we had a discussion they were always interesting, and I know that more than once I'd read something you had assigned and not really liked it, but after you had finished talking about it in class, I either did like it or at least I understood what the writer was trying to say. You always asked us for examples on our essays to support what we said, so the one I'm thinking about here is when we read *Walden* and most of us thought it was bad, no offense. After you had gone through it, though, I could see what Thoreau was trying to say even though I never did end up liking the whole book.

I have Stevenson this year for Senior English (we're right in the middle of *King Lear*), and since you're not here, I guess I'm allowed to say that compared to you, he's bad news. Half of the time we fall asleep in his class and the other half I spend doodling in my notebook. I know that I doodled in your class too, but I want you to know that I was always listening and that even though I only got C's from you, it was the best class that I've had here, bar none.

I hope that everything is going well for you out there. Maybe you'll be back in time for graduation and you can laugh when I go up to get my diploma. Ha Ha!

Tom
Rankin

Tom Rankin was one of those boys who look like something out of a jar of eels. Thin and hunched, greasy long hair, rumpled clothes, big thick smudged glasses. I had always known that he wasn't any dummy, just totally unmotivated. One of those students who are able to skim a book the night before a test and still squeeze out some kind of C or C−.

Another dream-vision of "Abbey's Future" floated up through my mind: finish the biography and then go back East with Saxony. Teach part-time at some school (maybe even at the old one, after Rankin's letter!) and write the rest of the time. Buy an old house with bay windows and brass door plates, with room enough for each of us to have separate studies. I don't know if it was Geoff Wiggins' doing, but after that phone call, I thought about Saxony a hell of a lot.

8

"Mrs. Fletcher, has anyone ever left Galen? Any of Marshall's people?"

She had asked me up to her apartment one night for a cup of organic cocoa, whatever that was. It tasted all right.

"Left? How far have you read in the journals?"

"I'm up to January of nineteen sixty-four."

"Nineteen sixty-four? Well, there was one girl, Susy Dagenais, but you'll be reading about her in the nineteen sixty-five book. I can tell you about her anyway if you'd like."

"Please."

"Susy Dagenais was a real pistol. She was one of those people that you were asking about before—one of the ones who didn't want to know her fate? The whole time she lived here she hated being one of us. She said it made her feel like a freak in the circus and that one day she would leave because she didn't believe where she'd come from. You know all about that, don't you, Tom? As soon as a child can understand things, their parents tell them who they are and why they're so special. They don't tell them anything else until the kid's eighteen, but some things got to be explained early so that they don't go do something foolish like run away from home."

"Yes, I know about that, but what was Susy like?"

"Oh, she was a great gal—pretty, real smart. We all loved her around here, but there wasn't anything we could do to stop her. She packed a bag, got on the bus to New York, and was gone. Poor thing—she'd just been in New York a couple of days when she died."

"But Marshall was alive then. Why didn't he stop her? He could have done it if he wanted to."

"Tom, Tom, you're not thinkin'. Yes, Marshall was alive, and sure he could have stopped her."

"But he didn't!"

"No, he didn't. Think, Tom. Why do you think he didn't?"

"The only thing I can imagine was to show people that he meant what he said. He used her as a kind of hideous example."

"Right. You hit it on the head. But I wouldn't use the word 'hideous.' "

"Of course it's hideous! He wrote this poor character so that from the beginning she didn't want to know, then he wrote that she would leave Galen and die in a week? That's not hideous?"

"Nobody else has ever tried to leave since then, Tom. And she was happy—she thought she was getting away. She did get away."

"But he wrote it that way! She had no choice!"

"She died doing what she wanted, Tom."

Phil Moon and Larry Stone worked together in the Galen post office. They were friends long before they married the Chandler sisters, but the marriages brought them closer.

Their passion was bowling. Both of them owned expensive custom Brunswick balls and matching bags, and if they had been a little better, they might have been pro material. As it was, they bowled every Wednesday and Friday night at Scappy's Harmony Lanes in

Frederick, the next town over. They alternated cars and split the cost of gasoline. Once in a while their wives went with them, but the girls knew how much their husbands appreciated their Boys' Night Out, so they often splurged on their own Wednesdays and Fridays and went to the movies or dinner and shopping afterward at the Frederick Town Mall.

There were two ways to get over there. You could hop onto the Interstate and then get off at the next exit, or you could take Garah's Mill Road that more or less paralleled the Interstate until it came to the Frederick traffic circle that spun you off in any direction you wanted. Most of the time they took the Mill Road because they timed it once and it was four minutes faster from door to door, although you could really blow your car out for a mile or two on the Interstate.

I knew all of this because I had gone bowling with them once, and on the way over, the four of them discussed the ins and outs of Wednesday and Friday nights.

On the night of their accident, they took the Interstate. Larry came down the exit ramp too fast in his lavender 442. He hit a long patch of ice, and fishtailing from side to side, took out the stop sign at the bottom of the hill. A Stix, Baer and Fuller trailer truck broadsided them and pushed the car almost two hundred feet up the road.

Larry's whole side was crushed, and it was a wonder that he wasn't killed. His wife, sitting directly behind him, broke both legs and her right hand. Phil got a severe concussion, and his wife broke her collarbone.

None of it was supposed to happen, according to the journals.

I heard about it from Anna, who called me from the county hospital. She told me straightaway what had happened. Her voice was thin and frightening. I totally misunderstood why until she reminded me.

"I don't know what any of this means now, Thomas." I could hear things bustling, people talking, someone being paged over the loudspeaker in the background.

"What *what* means?"

"This is the first thing that has gone wrong again since you started writing the biography. I don't understand what's going on."

"Look, Anna, it doesn't *mean* anything. You just got your hopes up too high before. How can things start to go right until the book is written?" As I spoke, I realized how convinced and confident I sounded. Like it was all a snap now: I would just finish writing this book, and bango, there would be Marshall France, back from the dead.

A Dr. Bradshaw was paged while I waited for her to speak.

"Anna? Is there anyone there with you?"

"Richard." She hung up.

I started working like a man possessed. Two, three, four pages a morning, research in the afternoons, three or four more pages at night.

I had never gotten over the initial shock of "discovering" Galen, but being there every minute of the day forced me to accept it. I was the moth and the town was the flame, and the damned place had me going in such circles that I didn't know what to do much of the time except to keep writing.

I was living in the middle of the greatest artistic creation in the history of the world. In my own tiny way, I was chronicling the life of the man who had done it. Whether that chronicle would bring him back to life . . . No, no, that's not true. I was going to say that it made no difference to me whether that chronicle brought him back to life, but that's a bunch of bullshit. He had said that it was possible, and then his daughter had chosen me to do it. That's partly why I sent Saxony away. The other "part" was of course Anna, but after the car accident we didn't make love much. I assumed that old Richard was still socking it to her, but even that didn't really bother me that much, because all of my energy—*all* of it— was going into the work. I would like to have known, though, why she slept with him, but I had a sneaking suspicion now. Suppose Richard had gotten bored with living in Galen. Since Anna and he were the only two "normals" in the town, how could she keep him there? Simple: go to bed with him. Never in his wildest imaginings would a guy like him have thought (or hoped!) of having someone like Anna France. So, so long as she kept him hot and bothered and interested, he was hers. And Galen's. I wondered if his wife knew what was going on between them.

I went out very rarely. Mrs. Fletcher started cooking for me, and Anna came over once in a while to see how things were progressing. Saxony called a couple of times, but our conversations were short, dry, and stale. I didn't ask about Geoff Wiggins and she didn't ask about Anna. I was too tired by then to want to play games, but I did realize that it would be better not to tell her how celibate I had become. Nevertheless, she got so fed up with our conversation one time that she called me a sourpuss and hung up.

Joanne Collins gave birth to a bouncing baby boy who was supposed to be a bouncing baby girl according to the journals.

Anna came over and demanded to see my manuscript. I astonished myself by holding fast and not letting her. She went away but was not at all happy.

Saxony called and asked if I was aware of the fact that she had already been gone a month.

I wrote Tom Rankin back and told him that I would try very hard to get back for his graduation in June.

My mother wrote, and feeling guilty for having been out of touch since September, I called her and chatted on about how wonderful things were for me these days.

Joanne Collins went in to take care of her new baby one morning and found a three-week-old bull terrier fast asleep in the crib.

I had had enough work for one day and decided to go over to the Green Tavern for a drink. It was nine at night and the town was dead quiet. The snow was slushy in the streets, but up on the sidewalk it was still white and crunchy under your feet. A silent, nasty wind drilled through the dark. Once in a while it stopped, waited for you to come up out of your shell, and then shot back, sniggering. The telephone wires were glazed over, but when the wind gusted it shook them and the ice fell into the street in short straight pieces. By the time I got to the bar I knew I either should have stayed at home or else taken the damned car. It was that cold.

The place had a thick oak front door that you really had to get your shoulder behind to open. A warm blast of stale heat, cigarette smoke, and George Jones's voice from the jukebox. The bar dog—really a dog, as far as I knew—whose name was Fanny, came over wagging her tail. The official greeter. I took off a glove and patted her head. It was warm and wet.

Because of the dark outside it didn't take long to get accustomed to the dark fog light in the bar.

I knew most of the people in there: Jan Phend, John Esperian, Neil Bull, Vince Flynn, Dave Marty.

"How are you doin', Tom?"

I turned around and squinted into the darkness. Richard Lee got up from a table and came over.

"What're you having, Tom?"

I sniffed back my runny nose. "I guess a beer and a shot."

"A beer and a shot. That sounds good to me. Johnny, two beers and two shots."

Richard smiled and came closer. He slapped me on the arm and kept his hand there. "Come on over and sit down at the table with me, Tom. Fuck these up-your-ass bar stools."

I took off my coat and hung it on a wooden peg by the door. There were other smells in the room now: perfume, potato chips, wet leather.

"So, kid, how're you doing over there at Goosey's? Here's the drinks. Thanks, Johnny."

I took a sip of beer and a taste of whiskey. One bitterer than the other, the whiskey thick and fiery in my stomach. But it felt good after being outside so long.

"I bet I know one thing for sure, buddy. Ever since Phil Moon's accident, I bet Anna ain't so happy with you, is she?"

"You've got a point there." I drank some more whiskey.

"Yep, that's what I figured. Did you hear about the Collins baby?"

"Yes. Is it still . . . a dog?"

Lee smiled and drank off the rest of his beer. "I guess so. The last I heard it was. Things are changing around here so fast lately, you never know." He drank some of the whiskey and stopped smiling. "I'll tell you one thing, buddy, it scares the hell out of me."

I hunched in close to the table and tried to talk as quietly as possible. "But why you, Richard? I can see it for the others—the worrying, I mean—but you're normal." I lowered my head toward him and said the word in a whisper.

"Normal, shit! Sure *I* am, but my wife isn't, and neither are my kids. You know what's been happening to my Sharon lately? I rolled over in the bed one morning last week, and there was fucking *Krang* on the pillow next to me! Can you believe that?"

I didn't say anything, but I believed it. I had seen it happen the night we went over there for dinner.

"I'm not shitting you, Tom. All of a sudden all of Marshall's characters are beginning to run together. Not only aren't things going like they're supposed to in the journals, but now they're mixing up all together, changing back and forth. Look at the Collins kid. One minute it's a kid and the next it's a fucking *dog*!" He snatched up my glass of whiskey and drank it off with one flick of the wrist. "What the hell is a man supposed to do, huh? I can't even turn around nowadays without being afraid that my wife or one of my little girls is going to be different. And then what'll happen if one day one of them stays that way?"

"How are they reacting to it?"

"How the hell do you expect? They're scared shit!"

"How many people has it happened to so far?"

He shook his head and turned the shot glass upside down on

the table. "I don't know. Not that many yet, but everybody's scared that they'll be next. What I want to know is when you're going to finish that goddamned book."

The jukebox was still playing, but the talking had stopped all around us.

I fought down a yawn and wanted very badly to be out of there. "I've done a lot. But there's still so much more to go. I have to tell you that. I don't want to lie about it."

"That don't answer his question, Abbey."

"What can I say? What do you want me to say? That it will be done in ten minutes? No, it won't be done in ten minutes. You all want this thing to be good and right, but then you all want it done now. Argh, there's a contradiction there, don't you see?"

"Fuck your contradiction, asshole!"

"All right, fuck it! Fuck it! You say that because you're not writing it. If it stinks in the end, then nothing is going to happen here. That's why France was so great, don't you understand? That's why you're all *here*. He could write like no one else in the world. For God's sake, why don't you understand that? Whoever writes this book has got to try to write it as well . . . I don't know, *better* than he wrote his books. . . . The journals, everything, everything that he wrote. It's got to be better. It's got to be."

Another voice climbed out of the swampy gloom at the bar. "Fuck that noise, Abbey. You just get that book done soon or we'll fuck you up like we did that other biographer."

The door opened and a fat man and woman came in, beaming. I had never seen them before and assumed that they were from out of town. Normals. The man was slapping his hat against his leg. "I don't know what the hell the name of this town is, Dolly, but so long as they got a drink for me, then it's friendly territory. How are you doin' there, friend? Colder than the dogcatcher's heart out there, huh?"

They sat down on bar stools in front of me and I was so glad that they had arrived, I could have kissed them. I got up to go. Richard had an empty whiskey glass in his hand and was slowly turning it round and round on his fingertips. He watched me get up but didn't say anything more. I went over to get my coat. I glanced at the bar and saw the fat couple talking animatedly with the bartender.

When I got outside, the wind ate me alive, but this time it felt like ambrosia. A Ford Econoline van pulled into the parking lot. The Priest of Spiders from *The Land of Laughs* got out and turned up the collar of his red mackinaw. He saw me and gave a half-wave. "How are you doing, Tom? How's your book going?"

He loped over to the big oak door and went through it, still the Priest of Spiders.

I stopped where I was and waited to see what was going to happen. If the fat couple hadn't been in there, it would have been all right, but they *were* there, and who the hell was going to explain what they were seeing?

The door flew open and three men came racing out, the Priest of Spiders held fast in the middle. The door bammed shut, and the only sound was feet moving through the slush. They were almost to the van when Mel Dugan saw me and stopped.

"You finish that fucking book, Abbey! You finish it or I'll cut off your fucking balls!"

I checked the *TV Guide* for late movies. *Café de la Paix* was on at 11:30. It was 11:25, so I got a Coke from the icebox and some green-pepper cheese that I had bought at the market.

The television was an old wooden Philco black-and-white with a huge screen. It also made a great foot warmer on cold nights. I pulled my rocking chair up, arranged the TV table with the Coke and cheese, and put my stocking feet on the side of the set. The music stomped on—a combination of "The Marseillaise," "Rule Britannia," and "My Country, 'Tis of Thee." You've got to remember that the film was made in 1942.

A shot of the Eiffel Tower. A slow pan down the Champs-Elysées. It's plastered everywhere with Nazi flags. Cut to a *tabac* where a little fat guy in a beret is selling newspapers to a kid, cigarettes to an old man, then a bunch of magazines from under the counter to a hand which takes them but doesn't pay. Shot of the fat guy's face as he hands them over. Pure adoration. *He* says *"Merci"* as the sound comes up. The camera moves slowly up—the hand, the arm, the face. *His* face. He winks and walks out of the *tabac*, the magazines up under his arm. A morning's read at the corner café.

I had a slice of cheese in my hand and was about to eat it when I started crying.

He walks slowly down the street—this guy is in no hurry. Tanks rumble past him. Motorcycles with sidecars full of important-looking men in German uniforms.

I got up out of my seat and turned off the sound. I just wanted to watch him. I didn't want to think about the movie, the plot, or the action. I wanted to watch my father. The lights were off in the room. Only the castoff glow from the set onto the living-room floor.

"Pop?" I knew it was crazy, but suddenly I was talking to the screen, to him. "Oh, Pop, what am I going to do?" He walked into a corner bakery and pointed to three pastries that he wanted inside the display case.

"Pop, what the hell am I going to *do?*" I closed my eyes as tightly as I could. The tears cut wet lines in my face that I felt when I put my hands up to cover it. "Jesus *God.*" I squeezed the heels of my palms into my eyes and watched the perfect colored patterns explode outward. When the pressure began to hurt I took my hands away and watched him through the last of the receding colors. He was in the back of the bakery now, climbing down the steps of a trapdoor ladder. Right before his head disappeared, he stopped and took off his hat. The sound was off but I knew what he said. "Watch my hat, Robert. I just got it for my birthday and she'll boil me in oil if I get it dirty!"

"Fuck you! Fuck you, Father! Everything's always so good for you! Your fucking new hats and everybody loves you. You even get to die the right way. Fuck you! Fuck you! Fuck you!" I turned off the set and sat in the darkness watching the screen grow gray, brown, black.

My eyes opened and I was wide-awake. I looked at the green glow of my watch and saw that it was three-thirty in the morning. When I click awake like that I can't get back to sleep for a long time. I put my arms behind my head and looked into the darkness above me. The only sound was the frantic ticking of my watch and the wind blowing outside. Then there was something else. Outside. Outside in the wind and the blue-black night. I turned my head to the window. It was right there, its face and paws pressed up and squashed against the glass. Its body glowed like an unlit white candle.

The moment I heard Mrs. Fletcher drive away, I pulled my suitcase out of the closet and started yanking sweaters, shirts, and pants off hangers. One bag. What the hell did I need? One of Saxony's skirts fell on my head. I tore at it and threw it on the floor. I told myself to be calm, be cool, you have at least an hour before she'll be back. You can be packed and out of here in fifteen minutes if you don't flip your lid, I stopped and tried to breathe regularly. I sounded like a dog in heat.

What do you take when you're running away? When you know that every nightmare you've ever had is breathing down your neck? Things. You throw a lot of things in a bag and slam it closed and you don't even try to think, because that takes time and you don't have any time.

The phone rang. I was going to ignore it, but people knew that I was at home, Anna knew I was home, and I wanted everything to appear normal right up to the moment I jumped into my car. I got it on the fifth ring. That in itself was bad, because by now people knew that I was a one- or two-ring answerer.

I cleared my throat a couple of times before speaking. "Hello?"

"Oh, Thomas, you *are* there. It's me, Saxony. I'm down at the bus station. I'm here. I'm in Galen."

"Oh, Christ!"

"Well, thanks a lot! I'm sorry if—"

"Shut up, Sax, shut up. Look, uh, look—I'll be down there in ten minutes. Just *wait* for me. Be out there in front and wait for me. Don't move."

"What is the matter with you? What—?"

"Look, do what I say. Stay where you are."

She must have sensed the fear in my voice because she only said, "All right. I'll be in front," and hung up.

I wrapped a green blanket completely around my suitcase and carried it outside, held in front of me. If anyone was watching, I wanted them to think that it was only a package or some dry cleaning to be done. I pushed a half-smile onto my lips and walked jauntily to the car. I skidded on a patch of ice and almost fell down. When I regained my balance, I was sure that hundreds of eyes were boring into me from everywhere. I stared straight ahead.

"Abbey just came out."

"What's he doing?"

"He's got some kind of package or something in his arms."

"It isn't a suitcase, is it?"

"I don't think so. It looks like . . . No, I don't know what it looks like. Maybe you should have a look for yourself."

"Or maybe we should call Anna."

By the time I had the keys out and was fumbling by the car door, I knew any moment I would hear a shout and a stampede of feet. I got the door unlocked and oh-so-casually leaned in and placed the blanket-wrapped suitcase on the backseat.

Key in the ignition. *Vroom.* I had to wait two minutes to let it warm up because I always warmed the car in the morning. No Le Mans start today, much as I wanted to. Nothing suspicious. My eyes flicked from the windshield to the rearview mirror looking for Anna's gold-and-white Dodge or Mrs. Fletcher's black Rambler.

The wheels spun when I pulled out onto the street, but then they caught and moved forward. That was the first of a dozen heart attacks I had on the way to the bus station. Once I thought I saw the Dodge. Once my car started to fishtail in the middle of the street. Then a freight train went by with 768 cars, all crawling along at a snail's pace.

While I waited there, some smart ass kid threw a snowball at the car. It hit a side window and I pulled a muscle in my neck wrenching around to see what was about to eat me. The only thing I saw was his little measly body running away.

The last car of the train passed and the crossing gates went up. The bus station was two blocks away. My plan was to pick up Saxony, take the road right out to the Interstate, and drive for at least two hours before I stopped again to breathe.

She was talking to Mrs. Fletcher. The two of them were standing in front of the blue bus station. I could see the vapor of their breath puff out in cold smoke signals.

"Well, what do you think of this, Tom? I was coming back from shopping, and there she was, standing out in the cold. She came in on the morning bus."

Saxony tried to smile but gave up.

"Now, I won't hold you up any longer. I'm on my way home. I'll see you two later." She touched Saxony's arm, gave me a dirty look, and disappeared around the corner of a building.

"Come on." I picked up her suitcase and started back across the street. I heard her behind me. She coughed. It was a thick, wet, racking cough that went on and on. She barely managed to get out a "Wait!" I turned around and she was bent over, one hand on her stomach, the other over her mouth.

"Are you all right?"

She kept coughing but shook her head at the same time.

I put my arm around her and pulled her to me. Panting, wheezing, she leaned into me and gave me her full weight. I led her around to the other side of the car and opened the door for her. She sat down and let her head fall back on the headrest. The coughing stopped but her eyes were teary from exhaustion.

"I'm really sick, Thomas. I've been sick ever since I left you. But it's gotten much worse recently." She rolled her head on the headrest and looked at me. "Camille, huh?" Her eyes tightened and she started coughing again.

"Nothing. There's nothing that can be done."

"Anna, for God's sake, come on! You can't be that horrible!"

I got Saxony home and put her into bed. Luckily she went right to sleep. As soon as I could, I shot out of the house and over to Anna's.

"It has nothing to do with me, Thomas. It was in the journals. It was written. It is done."

"But everything else in the journals is screwed up. Why can't you screw this up too? She went away, didn't she? She did what you wanted."

"She shouldn't have come back." Her voice was very cold.

"She didn't know anything, Anna. I never said a word to her about anything. She's scared to death. For Christ's sake, have a little compassion for once in your life!"

"Thomas, the journals say that if unnecessary people stay here for a long time then they will get sick and eventually die. If they go away, they'll get better. Saxony wasn't sick when she left, was she? You said yourself that she wasn't. So the journals are screwed up now anyway. She went *away* and got sick. It was supposed to happen the other way around. I have no control over any of this anymore." She spread her hands and even looked a little sorry for the first time.

I knew long before anyone else that it was either Saxony's presence, or her proofreading the manuscript, or our *combined* presence that normalized Galen.

As soon as she was rested, she read over everything that I had written since she'd left—and cut it to pieces. This was wrong. Why didn't I talk about this here instead of this? This had no bearing whatsoever, this was just silly to include. . . . She told me to keep perhaps a third of what I had done.

Mrs. Collins went into the kitchen to feed the bull terrier four days after I started rewriting with Saxony's suggestions in front of me. The woman found a baby girl asleep on the freshly torn newspaper in the box beside the stove.

Sharon Lee, who had taken to staying inside the house all the time (along with a number of other people, including the Priest of Spiders), was seen in town shopping again, smiling as if she had won the Irish Sweepstakes.

And Saxony stopped coughing. I told her that Anna and I weren't sleeping together anymore, but I still didn't tell her anything else.

When I understood how necessary it was for her to be there for the success of the book, I spent a morning with Anna explaining what I knew now was the truth. She listened but said that she would have to see for herself. After the Collins baby, she agreed with me. We would tell Saxony nothing, but she was allowed to stay.

Nothing more unexpected happened in Galen.

9

I heard her flip-flopping into the room in the fuzzy slippers I had bought for her at Lazy Larry's.

She never bothered me when I worked, so I put the pen down and turned to face her. She looked so much better now. Her cheeks had gotten some color and her appetite had returned. In fact she was holding a chocolate-chip cookie in her hand with a half-moon bit out of it. Yours Truly had baked them that morning.

"How far are you now?"

"The same. I'm just copying some stuff over. France is getting on the train to come here. Why?"

She threw the cookie in the wastebasket and looked at me. I looked at my cookie in the wastebasket.

"I have a couple of things to tell you, Thomas. They're two of the reasons why I came back here. But when I arrived I didn't know if I should or not. Then I was sick. . . . But I've got to tell them to you." She came over and sat down in my lap. She never did that. "Have you ever heard of Sidney Swire?"

"Sidney who? Sounds like an English actor."

"Sidney Swire was the man from Princeton who came out to do the biography of France."

"Really? How did you dig that up?" Saxony was the absolute queen of research. I had been convinced of that months ago, but I was inevitably astonished when she dug up some other totally un-discoverable gem.

"That was one of the reasons why I went to St. Louis. It's not important how I found out."

"Wiggins?" I leaned as far back in the chair as I could.

"Oh, come on, Thomas, please. This is important! Sidney Swire came to Galen for two weeks. When he left, he was supposedly going to California, where he had a brother living in Santa Clara." She licked her lips and cleared her throat. "But he never got there. He got off the bus in Rolla, Missouri, at a rest stop and disappeared off the face of the earth. No one has seen him since, including his brother."

"What do you mean?" The lizard walked halfway up my spine and waited for her to speak before he moved again.

"He disappeared. Nothing. No trace. Nothing."

"Well, what about his brother? What did he do?" I pushed her off my lap and stood up.

"The Swire family had the police out, and then, when they didn't find anything, a private-detective agency spent six months looking around. Nothing, Thomas."

"Well, that's intriguing." I looked at her, and she wasn't smiling.

"There's a second thing I want to tell you that I found out when I was there. Please don't get mad at me. Did Anna ever tell you about a man named Peter Mexico?"

I sat forward in my chair. "Yes, he was her lover when she was in college. He died of a heart attack."

"No, Thomas, it wasn't a heart attack. Anna and Peter Mexico were in a subway station in London and he fell in front of a train."

"What?"

"Yes. There was an investigation, and some things were never cleared up. Besides a drunk who was there, they were the only two people on the platform."

"Anna? What happened to Sidney Swire?"

"Sidney Swire?" She smiled at me and blinked her eyes fast a couple of times. Very flirty and cute. "Sidney Swire left here and, thank God, no one ever saw him again."

"What is that supposed to mean?" I tried to sound curious rather than scared.

"He disappeared. Poof. He left here, took a bus over to Rolla, and disappeared. The police were here for days and days looking around and asking questions. Thank God he wasn't living in town when he vanished. That would have been big trouble for us."

"Didn't it bother you?"

"No, not at all. He was a pompous ass, and good riddance."

"That's a pretty rough thing to say about a guy who's probably dead by now."

"So what? Am I supposed to say I'm sorry? I'm not. One look at him and you could tell that he would never have been able to write Father's book."

As a surprise, I had decided to give her a copy of what I had written. The rough draft of the first section of the book was done, and I thought that it would be a perfect idea to let her see how far along Saxony and I had gotten. Sort of as added insurance for letting Sax stay.

There was so much more to do on the manuscript before it

was done that I hadn't, until then, thought about what would happen to us after we had finished. I knew that there were a lot of dangerous possibilities, but it was all in a distant, cloudy future that was both tantalizing and ominous.

Of course I knew that the biography could never be published if it succeeded. Stir up new interest in Marshall France so that people would come gaping and poking at Galen to see where the great man had lived? No, the book was the means to one end. We all knew that. Except Saxony.

But what would happen if I didn't succeed? What did Anna have in mind for us if we failed? Make us live in Galen? Make us vanish like Sidney Swire? Kill us? (How well I remembered now what the guy in the bar had said that night about what they did to the other biographer.) I considered all that, but it was all a long, long way off. Months and months. One thing at a time. Saxony was well again and the book flowed out of me like Niagara Falls, and there were no more Krangs in town or things looking in my window. . . .

Anna handed me a piece of pound cake. Austrian *gugelhupf,* to be exact. It was the one thing that she made well.

"Thomas, how long will it take you to write the scene of Father's arrival here?"

"How long? It's almost done now. I already wrote it once, but Sax said that it should be more drawn out and dramatic. She said that there wasn't enough importance in it."

"Yes, but then how long?"

I nibbled on my cake. "I don't know. Today's what? Tuesday? I guess by Friday."

"Could you . . . ?" She smiled and looked at the floor shame-facedly, like she had been about to ask an impossible favor.

"What? Could I what?" Seeing Anna embarrassed and shy was a rare thing.

"Do you think you could finish it before five-thirty in the after-noon?"

"Sure. Why?"

"Superstition. You see, he arrived on a five-thirty train and . . . I don't know." She shrugged and smiled. "Superstition."

"No, no, I can understand that, Anna. Especially around here I can understand it!"

"All right, well, I wasn't going to tell you this, but I'm going to have a party for the two of you to celebrate Father's arrival."

"Then you'd better wait about six months and keep your fingers crossed."

"No, I mean symbolically. As soon as I saw how far you had gotten, I got this idea to give you a party on the day he arrives in town in your book. It was going to be a surprise, but just pretend that it is one when everyone comes running up to you."

"You're planning on inviting the whole town?"

I was kidding, but her face lit up and she took both of my arms and pulled me down next to her on the couch. "Well! I guess I have to tell you the whole thing now to let you see what I have in mind. This is the way I want it, Thomas: you write the section on his arriving, all right? But you have to tell me on exactly what day you will finish it, okay? Then *on* the day, all of us from town will go down to the station at five-thirty and pretend that he is coming in on a train."

"But no passenger trains stop in Galen anymore, do they?"

"No, no, it's pretend! Wouldn't it be great? It will be like a Midwinter Festival! Five or ten minutes later we'll march back up to your house and have a big potluck dinner."

"At my place?"

"Yes! You and Saxony are the ones who will be bringing him back, so we'll bring you offerings. Offerings to the Gods of the Typewriter!" She pulled me over and kissed me on the cheek. I realized how long it had been since we had made love. "Won't it be wonderful? It will be like an old torchlight parade. You and Saxony will be in your house, and then all of a sudden you'll hear this big bunch of us coming down the street. You'll both look out your window and see these hundreds of people carrying food and torches, and they'll come right up to your doorstep. It's marvelous!"

"It sounds like a Ku Klux Klan meeting to me."

"Oh, Thomas, don't be cynical and horrible for once."

"I'm sorry, you're right. But can't we come to the train station too? I mean, if we're the bringer-backers and all?"

She bit her lip and looked at the floor. I knew that she was going to say no. "Do you want me to tell you the truth? We've already talked all of this over, and everybody would appreciate it if you would just let us be there. Is that a terrible thing for me to say? Have I really hurt your feelings?"

Yes, she had, but I understood why she said it. No matter how important we were in bringing Marshall France back, we would never be part of Galen. Never.

"It's fine, Anna. I completely understand."

"Really? Are you sure? I'd hate to think that I—"

"No, look, don't say anything more. I totally understand. We'll stay home and wait for your procession to arrive." I smiled at her and twinked her cheek. "And I promise to be done before five-thirty on Friday."

Saxony liked everything about what she called "The Phantom Homecoming" party except for the fact that Anna would be there. She didn't want to see Anna. Not even in a crowd. So far, they had successfully avoided each other, but that was only because Sax had been in the house for so long.

In the end I was able to convince her that even if the old girl was there that night, there would be so many other people around that she could easily avoid any kind of confrontation.

I spent an afternoon just studying the Galen railroad station so that I was able to go into detail about what it looked like inside and out. It had been built in 1907, but time had laid a light hand on it. I walked out on the platform and looked up and down the track. Nothing. Not even a boxcar on a siding. There were still patches of snow on the ground, sparse and dirty.

But Marshall France had arrived here. That was one of the reasons why he was so fascinated with train stations. Arrivals and departures. Beginnings and endings and in-betweens. That's from his journals, not me.

While I stood there looking at the dull silver rails, I wondered how I would end up changing the biography so that at the end of his life, instead of dying of a heart attack, he would . . . Have an attack but somehow survive it? Go off someplace and then later return to the town? I didn't know. That was all such a long way off. I shook my head and walked back to the car.

For the rest of the week Galen was jumping. The stores were jammed with people, everyone who passed you on the street looked like he was running from one important job to another, even the voluntary fire department brought the trucks out onto the street and washed them, preparing for the parade. There was a kind of pre-Christmas excitement in the air, and it was fun just walking around and soaking it in and knowing that I was the cause of it. Me.

"Hiya, Tom! All set for Friday? We're going to have some party!"

"Tommy, you just finish up that part that you're doing and leave the rest up to us!"

I got a free drink at the Green Tavern and all in all spent the whole time feeling like the conquering hero.

Once in a while someone would do something strange like run for his car and slam down an open trunk lid when he saw me coming toward him on the street, but I assumed that they were making special foods or little presents for us and wanted it all to be a surprise on the big day. I was all for that.

I finished the scene at ten o'clock Friday morning. It was eleven and a half pages long. I brought it in to Saxony and stood in a corner of the room while she read through it. She looked up at me and gave a professional nod.

"It's just right, Thomas. I really like it now."

I called Anna and told her. She sounded delighted and told me that my timing was perfect because she had just come back with hundreds of bags of flour and after calling everybody, would get right to work on the *gugelhupfs*. She reminded me to tell Saxony not to even go near the stove—they would do everything.

Before lunch I went out for a walk, but the streets were almost completely deserted. All of this anticipation was floating around in the air—you could feel it—but the streets were as empty as a ghost town, with the exception of a car zipping by now and then on a secret mission. I gave up and went home.

The scent of some delicious meat sneaked down from Mrs. Fletcher's all the rest of the day. In spite of my vast hatred of parties and social gatherings, I was tremendously excited about the evening to come.

Around four o'clock Saxony stopped work on her newest marionette head—a bull terrier, no less—and barricaded herself in the bathroom behind her bubble bath and shampoo.

I tried to read Bettelheim's *The Uses of Enchantment,* but it was no use. I wondered if Saxony had slept with Geoff Wiggins. Then I tried to figure out what was cooking upstairs.

At 4:45 Mrs. Fletcher went to the door without saying goodbye or leaving instructions about her roast upstairs. I watched her walk down the street, and as soon as she was out of sight I knew that I wanted more than anything to be at that train station at 5:30 to see what they were going to do. I told myself that I had every right to be there. They should have invited us in the first place, dammit!

I got up and went over to the bathroom door. I hesitated for a second or two, then went in. It was steamy gray, and the dampness made me feel hot and sweaty.

"Sax?"

"Yes?" She poked her head out between the shower curtains and squinted at me. Her head was turbaned in white lather.

"Sax, I'm going to sneak down to the station and watch what they do anyway. I just have to see what they're going to do."

"Oh, Thomas, don't, really. If anyone sees you over there they'll get really angry and—"

"No, no, no one will ever see me. I'll sneak over at a quarter after five and easily be back here in time for the parade. Come on, Sax, this is great."

She curled her finger for me to come over. "I love you, Thomas. I thought about you all the time that I was away. Please don't let anyone see you out there. They'll be so mad!" She took hold of the back of my neck, and dripping water down my back, pulled me over for a hard wet kiss.

It had been full dark for almost half an hour before I left the house and tiptoed down the stairs like one of Ali Baba's thieves. The first feel of night made me think that it would snow again. It wasn't as cold as it had been. It was very still, and the sky was that milk-chocolate brown it gets just before the flakes start to fall.

10

It has taken me over three years to figure out why I didn't throw Saxony in the car at that moment and get the hell out of Galen while all of them were still down at the station preparing for the "arrival."

He asked me one day when we were in Grindlwald, looking up at the Eiger from a sunny terrace restaurant in the middle of town. I glanced at him, but the morning sun was right on his shoulder, so I turned back to the mountain.

"God knows, I should have. Jesus, it would have been so damned easy! But you've got to look at what was going on: I had never thought in a million years that I had an ounce of the artist in me. Suddenly I was on the verge of . . . of . . . I don't know, being *Prometheus* or something. Stealing fire from the gods! Through my art, or through *our* art rather, we were going to recreate a human being. And the person that I would be doing it with was my lover! The person I knew I wanted to be with for the rest of my life. There were all kinds of other things too. There always are at times like that. The Galeners loved me again, and naturally that was a total ego trip. Anna was even doing what I told her. . . . When

Saxony came back, things stopped screwing up in that town immediately. I felt invulnerable. As long as we were there together,
nothing could happen to us. How could it? We were the new Marshall Frances, you know? We had his power. We controlled the
whole fucking town."

"And you never once thought . . ." He looked at his coffee cup
so as not to embarrass me.

"Not in a million years." I picked up my espresso spoon and
placed it inside my cup.

The houses on both sides of the street were lit up and cheery, but
there was no sign of life in them. All of the people were at the
Galen station, all happy to be out of their houses for a while, together, anticipating the moment in the future when Marshall France
would really come back and take over the direction of their lives
forever.

The smell of pine and car exhaust stayed with me all the way
down to the railroad crossing that I had passed hundreds of times.
I looked at my watch. It was 5:21. It would take five to eight
minutes to walk the street parallel to the railroad tracks all the
way to the station. That would be cutting it thin, but it was exciting, and already I could feel my heart thumping hard in my
chest.

I took a right and went east on Hammond Street, breaking into
a little run every once in a while. There was some snow on the
sidewalks and I felt it up under the soles of my shoes—like walking
over sharp stones.

I was breathing hard and my arms pumped back and forth at
my sides, pushing me forward. What would they do down there?
How would they all look right at 5:30? What would . . . ? And then
I heard it off in the distance. I stopped and my eyes blurred. There
were two short hoots and then a long one. A long one that rose
and stayed in the air like an eerie animal calling out to someone.

I leaped off the sidewalk and into the street. The whistle blew again and I knew that it was closer, almost there, the train almost in Galen station. *But passenger trains didn't stop at Galen station anymore.* . . . The street ended in a small circle, but I vaulted the low stone wall there and kept running. I saw the station for the first time. It was so brightly lit that you would have thought that they were filming a movie. Where had the lights come from? There were hundreds of people milling around out on the platform. I was still too far away to distinguish between any of them, but there was so much noise, voices all talking at once. Then someone yelled, "There! There!" and the voices fell away. From the blackness on the side of the station away from me, from the East, from New York and the Atlantic Ocean and Austria, a pale yellow light appeared, and when I stopped running, I saw the engine pulling into the station. I stood there and my whole body shook. The engine was so old and black, and it was puffing sparks and steam out of its stack. It lumbered in and pulled out again, hauling its gleaming silver passenger cars up parallel to the platform.

It stopped. It was quiet except for the hissing and the clanking of the engine.

I just barely saw a conductor descend the steps and the crowd push up tight to one of the cars.

Then a wave of incredible heat moved out over everything. I could actually see it coming, and when it passed over me it felt like a strong hot summer breeze. Not stronger. Pleasant. I remember thinking that it was very nice.

People down there started to jam even closer to the train. Their noise returned.

And then from behind me the explosion came. This huge sound ripped through the sky, and without thinking, I turned around to see what it was. An oleo-yellow cloud of flame blossomed up and fell halfway back down to just above the tops of the houses and trees. Separate flames kept swimming up and away.

I turned back to the station and saw them mobbed around something on the platform. No one had turned toward the explosion. The train hooted twice and began to chug forward.

I was running up Hammond Street again, running for my house. I heard the train whistle, I saw the flames in the sky in front of me.

The train was picking up speed and was right behind me when I reached the crossing and turned left again up my street. I saw the flames, and now I knew the house. I wanted to stop and look for a moment and take in what was happening. The right of any person whose house is burning down, wife is shot, child is run over. The right of the already doomed to see what their future is about to be. But I didn't stop. I heard the train pass behind me, and I kept running. The house was a kid's sparkler in the middle of the street.

"AN-NA! AN-NA! YOU ARE SO FUCKING SMART! YOU WERE SO FUCK-ING SMAAAAART!"

That's all that was really necessary, wasn't it. Have us write a first draft that was so good that it didn't need to be fixed or redone. Write it right up to the moment that Marshall France arrives in Galen. Go down to the train station then and see if it works, see if it comes in at 5:30 . . . if *he* comes in at 5:30. If he doesn't, then you've lost nothing. If he does, all you've got to do is get rid of your writers, get rid of your evidence. They're unnecessary now. Father's home.

I watched the house burn from the other side of the street. I couldn't get any closer. There was debris strewn everywhere, some of it still burning: a pillow, an upside-down chair, books. And there was part of a body near the front gate. It wore the shredded remains of the bright red mackinaw that I'd bought at Lazy Larry's.

I didn't know how much time I had, but I needed every bit of it. My car was parked a few feet away. The fire owned everything. I was in the car, the yellow light flickering across the dashboard. I remember thinking that I wouldn't have to turn on the headlights for a while because it was so bright. I put it into gear and slowly drove away. There was another explosion while I was still driving down the street. The oil heater? Another stick of dynamite? Looking in the rearview mirror, I saw things flying high in the air over the house, high and in slow motion.

Epilogue

I saw a bull terrier the other day. It isn't the first one I've seen since then, but it is the first time that I haven't either cringed or run away. It was white with black spots and reminded me of Pete the Dog in the *Our Gang* comedies. I was sitting at a little round cast-iron table out in front of a café. I had been drinking *pastis* and writing a couple of things down in my diary.

The car had thrown a rod, but luckily there was a Citroën repair place in town: one guy in a blue beret smoking one of those yellow Gitanes cigarettes. It wasn't so bad to stop for a couple of days anyway. The trip from Strasbourg had been done in thunderstorms and I had done most of the driving. But as soon as we got to Brittany the skies cleared and the sun threw out the welcome mat.

The dog's name was Bobo and he belonged to the owner of the café. After looking at him for a while I went back to my diary. Since Galen, I've been pretty good about keeping a record of what has been happening to me.

I bought the book in Burke, Michigan. The first entry went on for pages and pages. Half-coherent, messy, paranoid. A lot of "They're coming to get me!" sort of thing. Naturally I still have that paranoia, but you get used to living with anything after three years, even that. I don't know how long it took them to figure out that I wasn't killed in the explosion, but from the very first I assumed that as soon as they knew for sure, they would come for me.

So I ran like hell, I stopped to pick up a passport in Detroit and then went right over the river to Canada. I worked in Toronto at a paperback bookstore for a while; then I got in touch with my bank in America and had them transfer all of my money up there. When it arrived I quit my job and got on a plane to Frankfurt, Germany. My itinerary since then? Frankfurt, Munich (in time for the Oktoberfest), Salzburg, Milan, Stresa, Zermatt, Grindlwald, Zurich, Strasbourg, Dinard . . .

My mother still doesn't know what the hell is going on, but good Joe that she is, she's never asked questions. When out of the blue she got a wire from me asking for every bit of biographical material on my father that she could find, two weeks later a nicely wrapped package arrived special delivery at the funny post office in Altensteig. It was full of books and articles and yellowed studio handouts that she must have kept over the years.

I started the book in Germany in the winter and worked constantly on it in small mountain towns that had few tourists. Writing was the only time in the day when Saxony wasn't on my mind. I've cried, I've loathed myself for not having saved her, and I miss her more than anything else. In fact I think I might miss her more now than I ever loved her. If that phrase sounds strange, I'm sorry, but it's the best I can do now.

I also began it because I needed something solid to work on while I tried to figure out what I was going to do. The only thing I knew for sure was that someday I would turn around in Holland or Greece or someplace and see a familiar Galen face smiling evilly at me. But how long would they pursue me? Forever? Or only until they were sure that I wasn't going to get them back for Saxony's death? I started the biography of my father to take my mind off my moment-to-moment fears, and because Sax had said that it would be good for me, and because I wanted to.

There were very few long entries in my diary that year. Just brief words of excitement and depression that I would jot down when I could pull myself away from the life of Stephen Abbey, movie star.

I had just gotten him from North Carolina to New York to try out for Broadway when I went to the post office one day and happened to see a package addressed to one Richard Lee, in care of Gasthaus Steinbauer, on a table behind the window clerk. Thank God for small European post offices. Bags and notes were in my brand-new Deux Chevaux in three seconds, and I was on my way down the mountain as fast as that frogmobile would go.

I stayed in Stresa for almost three months because it was lovely and empty, and Lieutenant Henry and his Catherine had rested there before they rowed across Lake Maggiore to Switzerland.

It was so stupid to send Lee after me, but maybe it had a purpose. Maybe now that *he's* back, they're trying to purify Galen completely—no more real people, no more normals in Marshall France Town. At least then Anna wouldn't have to fuck Lee anymore. Yes, and maybe even Anna will be next, who knows? Her father could re-create her, better than ever, the new Anna model. She would never age, never get sick. Maybe that's why they sent Richard—if anything happened to him, the master would just make another.

It doesn't make any difference. We waited for him in Zermatt and killed him on a small side street in the middle of the night.

"Hey there, Richard!"

"Tom, Tom Abbey! What do you say!"

He had a long corrugated knife that he was trying to hold close to his side. He smiled and looked around as he walked toward me, just in case any friends of mine happened to be nearby.

When Richard was five or six feet away, Pop stepped out of the pitch dark behind me and said lightly over my shoulder, "Want me to hold your hat for you, kiddo?"

I screamed with laughter and shot right into the middle of Richard's sad, astonished face.